UNDAUNTED

BLOOD BOND SAGA: VOLUME THREE
PARTS 7 - 8 - 9

HELEN HARDT

UNDAUNTED

BLOOD BOND SAGA: VOLUME THREE
PARTS 7 - 8 - 9

HELEN HARDT

WATERHOUSE PRESS

TABLE OF CONTENTS

*For everyone who loves all things
that go bump in the night...*

BLOOD BOND SAGA

PART 7

PROLOGUE

DANTE

Shovels, check.

Gloves, check.

Garbage bags, check.

River donned a black leather duster and handed another to me. "This is my old one," he said. "Should fit you fine. It's supposed to get cool tonight."

"Vampires wearing dusters. So cliché."

"They're warm. And they're black. They'll help us stay invisible in the dark." I didn't own a pair of black jeans, so I was wearing dark-blue denim. River's jeans were black.

He handed me a black ski mask. "We'll need these too."

My father stood quietly in the corner as we prepared for the evening's event. How did he feel about all this? About seeing his body? I had to mentally prepare myself as well. He hadn't been gone very long, so flesh wouldn't be falling off his bones yet. Still, it would show signs of decomposition.

Humans often defecated upon death. Did vampires? We'd find out. Whether my father had or not, there would still be an unbearable stench. The body would have started to digest the intestines upon death, eating outward, helping the decomposition process.

Rigor mortis would have ended by now. Since he was underground, his body might have been spared the infestation of larvae. But probably not. I'd read that maggots could digest sixty percent of a body within a week. My father had been dead for several.

His skin, what was left of it, would be turning purple, and his body would be cold.

Yes, I'd had to mentally prepare myself.

But had my father?

Didn't matter. It was time.

I looked to River.

"Let's roll," he said.

ONE

Erin

Before I could stop myself, I spilled the whole story about Dante and River breaking into the graveyard tonight. I conveniently left out the part about Julian being a ghost and glamouring anyone who crossed their paths. Oh, and I also left out the part that all three of them were vampires.

"Oh my God," Lucy said.

"I know. But what can I do? I can't call the cops. I don't want to get them in trouble. And River *is* a cop."

"We could call Jay," Lucy suggested. "Maybe he can talk them out of it."

"That wouldn't do any good."

"Why not?"

Because they would glamour him. I couldn't say that to Lucy. She would think I was more of a nutcase than the nutcase I was currently channeling.

Lucy picked up her cell phone from the bottom of her locker. "Oh!"

"What is it?"

She bit her lip. "Family issue," she said after glancing at her phone. "It's a good thing I have a few personal days available. I'm going to need to take some days off."

"Is everything okay?" I wanted to sound more concerned. I wanted to *be* more concerned. I just couldn't get my mind off Dante and River desecrating a cemetery.

"Yes, everything's fine. Don't worry."

She fumbled in her locker and pulled out an envelope, handing it to me. "This is for you."

"What is it?"

"It's personal. Please, just trust me. If baby Bianca comes back into the emergency room, open it. Do what it says."

"Luce..."

"Don't open it unless she comes back."

"But—"

"Trust me. Everything is okay. Trust me." Her tone was almost hypnotic.

The white envelope burned like a heated coal against my palm.

I opened my mouth to speak, but Lucy raced out, disappearing in a flash.

My fingers itched to rip the paper.

But I'd made a promise to Lucy, and no matter where my mind had gone during the last couple of days, she was still my best friend and had been there for me when I needed her.

I snatched my purse out of my locker and buried the envelope in the bottom of it, determined to forget it.

I was on duty, and now, with Lucy gone at the last minute, we would be shorthanded.

I changed into my scrubs and hurried out of the locker

room. I still had a few minutes before I needed to clock in, so I decided to visit the blood bank to make sure the B positive had been restocked. As I walked down the corridor, a strange sound resonated off to my right. A supply closet, and the door was cracked.

Another sound, like a squeak.

"Hey, anybody in there?"

I pushed the door slightly. Another squeak.

My skin chilled as I opened the door farther.

Then—

"Oh my God! Logan? Is that you?"

I removed the black blindfold. Yes, it was Logan, sans his tortoiseshell glasses and still in his green scrubs. His hair was greasy and matted down, and he struggled against the ropes binding him and the duct tape over his lips. The skin around both of his eyes was a mass of purple and yellow bruising. The yellow meant he was healing. He'd been beaten days ago. Maybe as much as a week.

When had he disappeared? My mind raced, but I couldn't quite remember. With all that had gone on in my life since then, time had gotten fuzzy. Days had morphed into weeks.

"Are you okay?" I fingered his cheeks gently. "I'm so sorry. Who did this to you?"

"Mmm!" he mumbled.

"Oh, yeah. Let me get that." I knelt down and ripped the tape from his mouth.

"Ow!"

"Sorry. You know as well as I do that it's better to rip off a bandage."

"Still. Jesus, Erin."

"You remember my name. That's a good sign. Where have you been, Logan?"

"I honestly have no idea."

"I have to tell you. The doctors are furious. Especially Bonneville. You're lucky she just went on a three-week vacation."

"That's one small silver lining. Could you get these ropes untied, please?"

"Who took you? Where have you been?" I asked again.

"Do I look like I know?" He struggled as I worked on the ropes binding him.

"All right. Tell me what you can, then."

"I don't need to tell you anything. I'll be talking to the cops."

"My brother is a cop." *And so is my vampire boyfriend's cousin, and they're off desecrating a graveyard tonight.*

My skin numbed. Couldn't think about that now. I tried to be gentle, but Logan's wrists were chafed from the coarse rope. He grumbled as I worked the knot.

"Could you maybe go a little faster?" He tugged against the bindings.

"I'm doing the best I can. These aren't knots I'm familiar with, and they're tight. Quit resisting. It's making it more difficult. Whoever tied these must have had superhuman strength."

Superhuman strength.

Vampire strength?

No. I was done thinking Dante could possibly have anything to do with these hospital disappearances.

Wasn't I?

The first woman disappeared the night he showed up, Erin.

No. No. No.

You love him. He loves you. You are bonded.

He had nothing to do with any of this.

I worked furiously at the knot binding Logan's wrists. Finally, it loosened, and I was able to untie the rope.

Logan rubbed at his wrists. They were red, but no skin had been broken that I could see.

"My feet, please," he said.

"Yeah. Of course." *Though you might be a little nicer about it.* I began again on an equally secure knot. "Can you tell me anything? Do you remember anything? What about the girl who disappeared with you, the one who had open-heart surgery?"

"She disappeared too?"

"Yeah. We all just assumed you disappeared around the same time. The cops are on it. Someone reported you missing just recently."

"Who?"

"The cops wouldn't tell us. Said whoever it was wanted to remain anonymous. Don't you know who it might have been?"

"How would I know? I don't have any family here in New Orleans. I'm an only child, and my parents are both gone. There's no one I keep in contact with on a regular basis. The only people who see me regularly are the hospital staff. Didn't someone here report it?"

"Well...no. We all just figured you had a good reason for being gone."

"Let me get this straight. I've been gone for—how long have I been gone, anyway?—and no one fucking reported it? No one fucking cared?" He continued rubbing at his wrists.

"It's not that we didn't care, Logan. It just wasn't—"

"Unbelievable." He shook his head.

"Let me finish. It wasn't our business. Dr. Bonneville told us—"

"Screw that bitch."

"You're a grown man. You could have gone home."

"I'm a doctor, Erin. A resident. Who the hell will hire a physician who bails on his residency? You really think I would just up and leave?"

No, I didn't. Truth be told, I'd been too involved in what was going on in my own life to think of filing a missing persons report on Logan or anyone else. "I'm sorry," I said, and I meant it.

"The bitch told you all to mind your own business, huh?"

"Pretty much. But I should have made more of an effort. We all should have."

"Yeah, you should have." He sighed. "But the ER is a busy place."

"Busier since you've been gone."

"I'm back now. I'll be talking to the cops, though, before I go back to work. If they *let* me go back to work."

"Why wouldn't they? None of this is your fault. Do you remember anything about what happened?"

"Not really. Just bits and pieces. I struggled at first, but got the shit kicked out of me, as you can see."

"Nothing else?"

He rubbed the back of his head. "I'm pretty sure I did some surgeries."

"You're *pretty* sure?" No doctor should be performing surgeries when he's not in the right state of mind. Plus, Logan was an ER resident, not a surgical resident.

"Shit, Erin, I just don't know. It's bits and pieces. Maybe I dreamed it."

I hoped so, for his sake. Performing surgeries he wasn't qualified to do could cost Logan his medical license.

"Come on. I'll help you up. I think we need to take you up to the ER to be looked at. What else did they do to you?"

"I don't want to talk about it." His lips formed a thin line.

"I can help, and it's probably nothing I haven't heard before. I'm a nurse, Logan."

"And I'm a doctor. I outrank you."

I kept my lips shut. I had no idea what else had been done to him, so I'd cut him some slack. Not like I could do anything about it anyway. He *did* outrank me. Again, I wished I'd been able to afford med school, but no time to mourn that now.

Right now, I had to help Logan. I was a nurse, and that was my job, no matter how big an asshole the patient wanted to be.

I'd make him pay for it later.

TWO

DANTE

Sneaking into St. Louis Cemetery One hadn't been as daunting as I'd imagined. My father easily glamoured the guards into submission, and River and I, our flashlights on the dimmest setting possible, sneaked through the graveyard, looking for sod that had been recently disturbed.

Supernatural energy vibrated around us. Nothing was visible, but ghosts were here. The chills on the back of my neck were not from the cool temperature this night. The pathways were narrow, as crypts were large and ornate throughout. Most of the vaults dated from the eighteenth and nineteenth centuries.

"Let's head toward the Protestant section," River whispered.

"Why? And why are you whispering?"

"I don't know. Seems the thing to do among the dead. There are larger grassy areas in that part. More likely your dad would be there."

We passed the vault where the self-styled voodoo queen,

Marie Laveau, reputedly lay. It had been painted and repainted time and time again, and even now, triple Xs had been carved into the concrete, and flowers, candles, coins, Mardi Gras beads, and other small items—including several beer cans—graced the ground around the grave. I stopped for a moment.

"What?" River whispered.

"What's all this about?"

"Some belief. Apparently if you break off a piece of brick from another gravesite, spin around three times, and carve three Xs on this one, the voodoo queen will grant you a wish. You leave an offering as well. That's what all this is." He gestured to the gifts left on the ground and shook his head. "Tourists."

"A beer can is an offering?"

"Apparently. Or someone decided this was a wastebasket. Shitheads. The city spends a ton of money cleaning up after the tour groups that come through here. Makes me kind of sick, to be honest."

The air was thick around the white vault. Something held me there, wanted me to stay.

But River grabbed my arm. "Stop it. Let's get this done as quickly as we can. I'm getting creeped out."

"You? The detective?"

"Shut up. I work nights in New Orleans. I've seen some shit you wouldn't believe."

I chuckled under my breath.

We continued walking through the cemetery, the subtle rays from our flashlights helping our acute vision. I was supposed to be concentrating on the grassy areas, but the markings on the vaults kept drawing me away.

Something was pushing me toward something, but I had no idea what it was.

"Come on," River urged.

I summoned my strength and trudged forward, trying to ignore the pull of the vaults. My father stayed outside the graveyard, taking care of anyone who might get in the way of our progress. But would he be more help to us in here? Could he feel where his body might be located?

No. The word came to me quickly. He knew it was here, but that was all he knew.

The body—the shell—was no longer him. He had no connection to it now. Did I? I was still a live body. A body that had come from his. Could that be what was pulling me?

"Damn," River said. "I haven't seen any areas where the grass is disturbed so far. We're looking for a needle in a haystack here, man."

"Seems that way," I replied.

"Let's split up. We'll cover more ground. Text me if you find anything. Keep your phone only on vibrate."

"Got you." I turned off my ringer and set off down another part of the cemetery.

More vaults, some kept up nicely, others in need of major repairs. Some with ornate designs topped with statues, others plain and dull.

Dante.

No. Not now. Not *her*. I should have stayed with River.

Follow me.

Like hell I will.

Then, like a bolt of lightning, a wave of peace swept over me. A calmness I'd known only when—

An unseen force drew my gaze upward. On top of a silvery-gray vault sat a woman I hadn't seen since I was three years old. Her dark hair flowed over her shoulders, and she wore a white gown that came to her knees.

A hospital gown.

"Mom?"

She had died in the hospital, giving birth to Emilia.

The image smiled but said nothing. Why was she here? My father had said she was no longer able to come to this plane.

"Mom?" I said again in a whisper. "I...see you. Can you help me? Can you show us where Dad's body is?"

Chills swept over me, but they were good chills this time. I felt only peace from them.

My mother wasn't buried in this cemetery. She'd been laid to rest in a smaller graveyard outside the city along with my grandmother and aunt. So why was she here? And why could I see her?

My thoughts raced to my father. Would he be able to communicate with her if he were here?

"Don't go away!" I whispered urgently to my mother's ghost. I turned and hurried back to the entrance. "Dad? Dad? Where are you?"

Nothing.

The guard sat, mesmerized, still at his post. Still under my father's glamour.

But where was my father?

"Dad?" I whispered again. "I need you."

He appeared before me instantly, making me jerk backward and nearly lose my footing.

"What is it?"

"Mom. She's here. Inside the cemetery."

"That's impossible."

"Apparently not. She's here, but she won't talk to me. Come on. I'll show you."

He shook his head. "I'm sorry. I can't leave the perimeter. If I do, we risk someone coming along and disturbing you and River while you work. Get this done, Dante."

"We haven't found you—er...your body, yet."

"Move along then. It's here somewhere."

"But I—"

"Dante! This is important. Take care of it."

"But Mom—"

"I can't help you with that. I'm sorry. I'm going back out to check the perimeter."

I sighed. Perhaps I hadn't seen anything. Perhaps it was only my imagination playing tricks on me.

No. She'd been real. Well, as real as a ghost could be.

I retraced my steps back to where I'd seen my mother.

Yes, she was still there, sitting atop the vault, but this time she was pointing.

"Mom?"

No reply, so I followed where she was pointing. The vaults were high, so it was impossible to see what she might be gesturing to, but I turned and followed the direction she was giving me.

I had to zigzag around, but I was determined to make it where she wanted me to go.

On my way, I found River. "This way," I said.

"I've been over that way."

"Trust me."

He shrugged. "Okay. We've covered a lot of ground and haven't found shit. Maybe you're on to something."

I didn't try to explain that my mother's ghost was leading me. He wouldn't believe me anyway. Or maybe he would, but I was too anxious to find what my mother was pointing me toward. As we ducked around a stately pyramid tomb, I lifted my eyebrows.

A large white dog sat on top of a small grassy area.

I nudged River. "What's that dog doing in here?"

River walked forward a few steps and then stopped abruptly.

"That's no dog, Dante. That's a wolf."

THREE

Erin

A couple of blues were talking to Logan. Detectives hadn't been called in yet, and Jay was off tonight anyway.

So was River, who, at this very moment, was most likely digging up a body in St. Louis Cemetery along with Dante.

I had to trust that Dante knew what he was doing. With a body, he could file a death certificate and begin the probate of his father's estate. I understood the necessity of what he was doing. Didn't mean I liked it.

I hated it.

Totally hated it.

I itched to be there with him to look after him, but realistically I knew I'd be more of a handicap, especially with a gang of vampires trying to find me. Vampires were nocturnal, and though I had nothing to base my assumption on other than old myth, I figured they might be hanging around a graveyard.

Chills speared through me.

A gang of vampires was after me.

So unreal.

Dante would protect me with his life. I was sure of it. But he was only one vampire—one who'd been held against his will long enough that he never finished high school.

I closed my eyes.

Still so much I didn't know about this man I adored, this man I needed, ached for.

I needed him so badly, and at the moment, fear for him raced through me like a combat plane twisting and turning to avoid being shot down.

"Erin!"

I opened my eyes. Dale and Renee, two of the other nurses, stood in front of me.

"Are you all right?" Dale asked. "You seemed almost catatonic."

"I'm sorry. No. I'm fine."

"Are you sure? We heard you're the one who found Dr. Crown tied up in that supply closet."

"Guilty," I said.

"The poor thing," Dale said. "He looks like someone messed him up pretty badly. Did he tell you where he'd been?"

"No. He doesn't remember much. My guess is he was drugged with something."

"This is all too scary," Renee said. "I've been talking to my boyfriend, and we agree I should find another job. I was ready to walk out of here a few nights ago."

"No, please," I said. "We need you. Lucy has taken a few nights off, so we're going to be really shorthanded."

Renee sighed. "All right. Until Lucy gets back. Where did she go, anyway?"

I shrugged. "I don't know. She said something about a family emergency."

"She didn't tell you what it was? I thought you two didn't have any secrets." Dale giggled.

Yeah, I'd thought that too.

I'd been wrong.

Either she'd had sex with River in his car and didn't tell me, or she was a—

Stop it, Erin!

"Lucy doesn't tell me everything."

"Did she tell you she fucked Dr. Crown?"

My eyebrows flew up. "No. She told me she absolutely did not."

"Oh." Dale giggled again. "That's not what *I* heard."

I opened my mouth to speak, when the sirens wailed. I had more important things to do than worry whether Lucy had lied to me yet again. Dale was a bigger hospital gossip than Steve was, so I had to factor that in as well.

I assisted with a heart attack and then with a drug overdose. Both of them pulled through, thank goodness. I wasn't sure I could handle losing a patient tonight.

Dante was never far from my mind, even when I was working. I compartmentalized as well as I could because my patients deserved my very best. Still, the unstoppable worry nagged at me.

Because we were so shorthanded, Logan had scrubbed up and was assisting. Dr. Thomas must have been desperate, because in my opinion, Logan wasn't in any condition to practice medicine.

He worked swiftly, though, despite his injuries, and didn't make any mistakes that I could ascertain. Somehow his glasses had returned as well. What happened hadn't taken away any of his skills as a physician. Whatever personal things had occurred between us, or between him and Lucy, he was still a very good doctor, and we needed him.

When we finally got a break, he joined me at one of the sinks to wash up.

"You doing okay?" I asked.

"Like riding a bike," he said.

"How did you find your glasses?"

"I keep an extra pair in my locker."

"Oh." I wiped my hands dry with a paper towel. "What do the police think? Can they figure out who did this to you?"

He shrugged. "They still haven't found the two girls who disappeared. The one with the supposed ruptured appendix and the one with the heart transplant. I figured they'd turn up again, like Cynthia North and that other woman from the free clinic did."

"I think we all did," I agreed. "They still might."

He shook his head soberly. "I don't remember a lot about what happened to me, but one thing I feel certain about. Those girls won't be returned."

"Were they with you?"

"I'm not sure."

"Then how can you— Never mind." Now wasn't the time to interrogate him, but I'd certainly tell Jay and the other detectives about his cryptic comments. "Did you have a doctor look at you, to make sure you weren't...violated in any way?"

"Erin, I wasn't violated. Other than getting the shit kicked out of me, which is a violation, yes, but probably not what you're talking about."

"Still, don't you think..."

"When I get around to it." He walked off in a huff.

For a nerd, Logan was acting awfully macho. I didn't

particularly like this new arrogant side of him. But how would I know what it was like to be held captive against my will for several days?

And Dante...

Dante had been held for years.

So much I didn't know.

I couldn't ponder much longer though. I still had a few hours on the clock, and another ambulance was arriving.

FOUR

DANTE

"No way," I said. "What would a wolf be doing here in the city? That's a—" I was about to say "white German shepherd," but something was off. The animal *was* white, but the snout wasn't quite right. It *was* a wolf.

"I don't know why it's here, but that's definitely a wolf." He approached with caution. "Here, boy. Come here."

The wolf stood and turned toward River, giving me a side view.

"Riv, that's not a boy. It's a girl."

"Quiet, Dante. Don't freak her out." He held out his hand tentatively. "Hey, girl. We won't hurt you."

"My mother was pointing to her," I said.

River twisted his neck to meet my gaze. "What?"

"No time to explain. I saw my mother's ghost sitting on top of one of the vaults."

"You've got to be kidding me."

"I wish I were. But I saw her, man. She acted differently than my dad. She didn't talk or anything. Just pointed over here, to where the...wolf is sitting."

"Hmm. Maybe this is where Uncle Jules is. But we have to get her to move first." He slanted slightly forward. "Come on, girl. We're not going to hurt you."

"I don't think she's worried about us hurting *her*."

"She's no bigger than a large dog," River replied.

"But she's not a dog. She's a wolf. A wild animal."

River turned on his flashlight.

"You might spook her," I said.

"How else are we supposed to know if this is where your dad is? We have to see if the sod has been disturbed."

"It has to be. Why would my mother point to a wolf? She had to be pointing to my dad's body."

"Not necessarily. She could have been warning us about the wolf."

"In which case," I said, "you shouldn't be freaking her out with the flashlight."

"Good point." His light disappeared. "Don't need it anyway, with all the ambient light reflecting in. I think she's fine, though. She hasn't attacked us yet, has she?"

"True." The wolf didn't appear at all vicious. If she'd fed recently, she'd have no reason why she'd attack us...unless she perceived us as a threat.

"If she was going to attack us, she'd have done it by now."

"Yeah, you're probably right." I eyed her. She was a beautiful animal. Nearly snow white. "Wait."

"What?"

"She's white."

"Yeah? So what?"

"She's an arctic wolf."

"Yeah? So what?" River said again.

"An arctic wolf is a subspecies of the gray wolf, and it's native to the Queen Elizabeth Islands up north. How the hell did she get here?"

"I don't know. And why do you know that, anyway?"

"I paid attention in high school. I used to want to be a doctor, remember? I needed good grades to get into college and med school."

"Yeah. Right. You still can, you know."

"No, I can't. Not now."

"Dante—"

"Now's not the time, Riv." The last thing I needed was to get emotional and have River feeling sorry for me. Not anytime, and especially not in the middle of the night while we were trespassing in a graveyard. "What I want to know is, what is an arctic wolf doing in a cemetery in New Orleans?"

River shook his head. "You got me."

The wolf still appeared docile. "Hey, girl," I said, approaching.

"You stopped me when I tried that."

"I know. But this is *my* father we're looking for, and I need to see if he's here." I tentatively eyed the perimeter of the ground where the wolf stood.

The grassy area looked the same as all the other areas we'd seen. If it had been disturbed recently, I sure couldn't tell. I walked slowly forward. I needed to get behind the wolf so I could examine the rest of the area. "Easy, girl," I said softly.

No reaction from the animal.

"That's a good girl. We're not here to bother you. We just need— Ow!" An icy sword speared the back of my neck. "Shit, Dad. What is it?"

"He's not here," River said, his voice a low whisper, "but I felt that too."

A low snarl percolated from the wolf's throat.

"So did she, apparently," I said.

She didn't move from her place on the grass, but she turned her head slightly to the right. I followed the wolf's gaze, but nothing seemed out of place. I took advantage of her distraction and moved forward to check the rest of the area.

Again, nothing seemed out of place. Just to make sure, I fired up my flashlight and shined it over the entire area, edge to edge. If this sod had been disturbed, it wasn't giving anything away.

"Damn!" I whispered urgently. The ice pick had lanced into my neck again. "What is that?"

The wolf cocked her ears, tilting her head slightly, and then she jumped seemingly into thin air.

Away from us.

"Quick, Riv," I said. "Let's check this area out better." The rays from our flashlights dueled like lightsabers as we quickly looked at the entire grassy area where the wolf had been.

"Nothing," I said. "Do you see anything?"

"Nope. Looks like a dead end. If we couldn't see it with vamp night vision, I don't know why we thought flashlights would help." He looked around. "Where do you think she went?"

"I have no idea. I'm just as glad she's gone, though."

"She seemed friendly enough."

"That just means she wasn't hungry. I paid attention in school, remember? Wolves will attack if they need to eat, just like any carnivorous wild animal."

A faint growl drifted across the air.

"Did you hear that?" River asked.

"Yeah. She's still around. It boggles my mind. How did a

white wolf get here?"

"Maybe she escaped from the zoo," River said.

"Yeah, maybe. Are there wolves at Audubon Zoo?"

"I don't know. I haven't been to the zoo in ten years, at least."

"Ha! Neither have I."

"Oh. Sorry."

Another snarl made its way to my ears.

"Maybe she *is* hungry," River said. "Sounds like she's found a meal."

"As long as it wasn't us. We should probably get out of here before she decides she's hungrier than she realized."

River patted his ribs. "I'm packing. I'll take her out before she can do anything to us."

"Ah," I said. "No wonder you weren't frightened when you saw her."

"You really think I'd come to a cemetery at night unarmed?"

"You can't kill ghosts with a gun, Riv."

"Ghosts weren't my concern. I know Uncle Jules said he'd keep everyone out, but—"

Amidst the snarls, a low scream ripped through the air.

My stomach dropped. The wolf was not attacking another animal. She was mangling a person. Most likely a man.

"We should help, Riv," I whispered urgently.

"Yeah, let's go."

We hurried toward the sounds.

Growling. Gnashing of teeth. More screams. Shit! She was going to tear whomever it was apart.

Then a high-pitched yelp sailed across the air, followed by soft canine whimpers

River turned. "Sounds like she's hurt."

The whimper got progressively louder as we edged farther to the other end of the graveyard. The sound changed from whimper to...weeping?

River drew out his pistol while I shined the flashlight.

Then—

"What the fuck?"

FIVE

Erin

Exhaustion weighed on me as I washed up after my last case. One hour left. Logan was still working, though Dr. Thomas had told him to go home hours ago, after the rush. I rubbed at the beginning of a headache on my forehead.

Dante.

Had he found his father's body?

Or had he been arrested for trespassing?

The latter probably wouldn't happen. River or Dante's father could glamour anyone who crossed their path.

Correction—any *human* who crossed their path.

God, I so couldn't go there right now.

Before I could find a couple of ibuprofen to pop—

"Erin! We need you!"

Renee's voice. Another emergency. This was the ER, after all.

I raced back out to the ER, and—

"Dante!"

River was next to him, holding a bundle wrapped in black leather. "Thank God," he said when he saw me. "Help her. Please."

An orderly came running with a stretcher. "Get her on here. The doctor is coming."

A lump lodged in my throat when I saw the patient's face. Lucy.

"What happened?" I said to River.

"She's been stabbed. I don't know how or why. Just help her. Please!"

"But you were—"

Dante grabbed my arm. "Shh," he said under his breath.

Right. I couldn't announce that they'd been in St. Louis Cemetery at night. But they had been, and apparently, so had Lucy.

Lucy was naked under River's leather coat. I didn't have time to ask the questions that burned in my mind.

Dr. Thomas ran toward us. "Erin?"

"Female, late twenties. Stab wound to the abdomen. Possible concussion. Doctor...it's Lucy."

"Get her into trauma one and page the on-call surgeon," Dr. Thomas said. "Erin, you're with me."

River tried to follow us, but I pushed him back. "I'm sorry. I'll let you know as soon as I know anything."

"Please, Erin..."

I looked to Dante, pleading with my eyes.

"Come on, Riv," he said.

I rushed into trauma one. Lucy was unconscious. I got two IVs started.

"Definitely concussed. She's lost a lot of blood. I need two units of O neg stat. They'll go with her to the OR."

An orderly nodded and ran out while I took a little more of her precious blood for a typing and complete blood count.

"She's B positive," I said. "She told me."

"You know we can't administer anything other than the universal donor before typing." Dr. Thomas examined the wound and began applying pressure. "We're out of B positive anyway."

Of course we were.

While another nurse sponged the wound and applied pressure, Dr. Thomas examined Lucy. "Looks good. No bile. No vital organs have been damaged that I can see."

Though we wouldn't know for sure until a surgeon had explored, a weight lifted off my shoulders.

Still, she wasn't out of the woods quite yet. She'd lost a ton of blood.

The orderly came back with the blood, and I gave him Lucy's sample to take to the lab.

Was it ethical to be working on my best friend?

No time to ponder that. Right now, Lucy needed me.

Dr. Thomas applied a dressing to Lucy's wound, which was off to the right side. She was lucky the weapon hadn't punctured her liver.

Who had done this to her? She'd been in the middle of a family emergency. I'd seen her at the beginning of my shift. Where in the world had she been where she could have gotten stabbed? And why was she naked?

"Doctor..." I said, gulping.

"Yes?"

"We should do a rape kit. She was naked when she came in."

"Do it quickly. The trauma surgeon on call will be here in minutes."

"Yes, Doctor. But she's my..."

Dr. Thomas nodded. "I understand. I've got her bleeding stabilized. Get the kit and I'll do it myself."

I sighed in relief. I'd done no less than a hundred rape exams in my career, but looking into my best friend's privates? I couldn't do it. Well, I could, and I would have, if no one else had been available.

Dr. Bonneville would have no doubt made me do it, thinking it beneath her to do such a menial task.

Again, I was thankful for her three-week vacation.

I grabbed a rape kit quickly from the row of white boxes. This wasn't unusual in the ER. We saw a lot of sexual assault. But *this* white box was for my best friend. I delivered the kit to Dr. Thomas and found Steve and Renee in with her.

"Go," Steve said to me. "We've got this covered."

I shot him a look of gratitude and mouthed, "I owe you one."

I walked out in a daze, removing my mask and gloves and throwing them away. I hurriedly washed my hands, and then walked out to the waiting area to talk to Dante and River.

River stood as soon as he saw me. "Lucy?"

I nodded. "It looks like she's going to be okay. We don't think any vital organs were damaged, and she'll probably be getting some blood. The trauma surgeon is on his way. He's likely here by now, and she's headed into the operating room. They'll get her patched up." I purposely didn't mention the rape kit.

"Thank God," River said.

"I'm sorry, but I have to ask, because these questions are going to come up. Where did you find her?"

"Where do you think?"

I sighed.

"You know where we were, Erin."

"What was Lucy doing there?"

"We have no idea," River said.

"You're going to have to tell the cops something," I said. "This is, at the very least, an assault and battery. At worst, it's attempted murder."

"The cops have already talked to us," River said. "I took care of it."

I sighed again. He'd glamoured them, of course.

"Look," I said. "I get that you have to protect yourself, but you also have to think of Lucy. Whoever attacked her left her in the cemetery. If you guys are going to find out who did this to her, you need to know where to look."

"It's covered," River said. "I'll be investigating this myself."

"What about Jay?"

"I'll take care of Jay."

"You will *not*—"

A warm hand covered mine.

Dante.

"No, Erin. He won't glamour Jay. We've had words about it already."

"The truth is..." River began.

"What?"

He let out a breathy sigh. "I've been thinking about telling Jay about Dante and me."

"You can't." I clenched my hands into fists. "Not now."

Dante rubbed my shoulders. "Maybe *you* should tell him. He might take it better coming from you."

"I've only just come to grips with it myself," I said. "I can't."

"But—" River began.

"It can wait a little while longer," Dante said soothingly.

River sat down with a plunk. "Whatever, man. But you *know* he has to be told at some point."

SIX

DANTE

I shot River a look that I hoped said "shut the fuck up."

I hated keeping the secret that my sister was carrying Jay's child, but that was Emilia's story to tell. Not mine. Erin was a woman, and she would understand that.

I hoped, anyway.

"Why?" she asked.

"It's okay, love. We won't keep you. Do you need to get back to work?" My fangs had already descended. It wasn't quite time to feed, but this night had taken a lot of my willpower. And here stood Erin, her scent permeating every part of me.

I needed her. Now.

She looked toward the large clock on the wall of the waiting area. "I'm off duty as of now, but I want to go check on Lucy. Though she's probably in surgery."

"I can meet you back home," I said.

She smiled. "I kind of like that."

"What?"

"You said 'back home.' As in our home."

"You said I could move in."

"Wait," River said. "What?"

"I'm moving in with Erin. It just makes sense, you know?"

"Yeah, I suppose so."

"All right. You want to wait and ride with me?" Erin turned to River. "I assume you want to stay here and see Lucy after surgery."

"Yeah. I do."

She nodded. "I need to change. I'll be right back."

Need.

Want.

Ache.

Yearning. A pounding yearning that had me grasping at the last shreds of control.

I'd had to look straight ahead as Erin drove us home. If I had glanced her way—

But I didn't.

And now we were home, unlocking her door—

I pushed her against the wall as soon as we were inside, slamming my lips onto hers.

She opened, our tongues danced, and my fangs nicked the inside of her mouth, giving me the slightest taste of her.

I ripped my mouth away and sank my sharp teeth into the creamy flesh of her neck.

Red nectar. The essence of life.

It flowed into me from her jugular, nourishing me, sustaining me.

Completing me.

She moaned as I sucked, letting me take what I needed from her.

I slid one hand down the contours of her sleek body and under her sweat pants, fingering her folds. She was already wet, so ready for me, and as I sucked her blood, I rubbed her clit.

Her moans lengthened, and when she began her climax, I inserted two fingers into her as I sucked the last drop of sustenance I could take from her. I released her, licking the puncture wounds.

Then, with one hand, I unsnapped my jeans and freed my aching cock. I brushed her sweats and underwear over her hips and pushed into her. The angle was weird as she couldn't spread her legs, but still the suction was sweet against me as I thrust.

But I needed more.

I pulled out and turned her around, placing her hands against the wall.

Her red pussy glistened from behind, and before I plunged back in, I fell to my knees and buried my face between her ass cheeks, inhaling her luscious fragrance. I slid my tongue into her folds and tasted her fruity nectar, so slick and sweet.

"God, Dante. Please."

"I'm coming, baby. I just wanted to taste you." I stood and shoved my cock back into her heat.

She gloved me in warmth, in love.

The angle was perfect, and as I pushed into her again and again, my only regret was that I couldn't kiss her perfect full lips.

Later.

Later I would make love to her slowly, with reverence.

Now? I'd fuck her until she couldn't stand.

I fucked her.

And I fucked her.

And when she began to contract around me, I shoved myself as deeply inside her as I could, flattening both our bodies against her wall.

My balls seized, and I filled her, gasping as I gave her everything I could.

Everything she'd already given me.

When our orgasms subsided, both of us panting, I stepped backward, holding on to her when she lost her footing a bit.

She turned to me, her eyes wide, her cheeks flushed. "Wow."

I smiled. "I wanted to fuck you until you couldn't stand."

"I'd say you met your goal. My legs are kind of like jelly."

"I'm sorry. I had to have you. Couldn't wait."

"It's okay. I understand."

"Last night. It got to me."

"Did you find your dad? His body, I mean."

Reality hit me like a lead pipe. We hadn't. We hadn't accomplished our goal.

Which meant we had to go back.

"No. But we *did* find Lucy. If we hadn't been there..."

She nodded. "I know. I can't go there."

"I can't figure out what she was doing—" I held back a gasp.

The white wolf.

Erin had been worried that—

I shoved my fingers through my hair.

"What is it?" she asked.

"Nothing. It's crazy, really."

Erin cleared her throat. "I didn't want to say this in front of River, but we did a rape kit on Lucy. Just in case."

"But she wasn't—" I stopped. A rape kit was a good call, of course. And Lucy and the wolf were not one and the same. They couldn't have been.

Could they?

"You need to tell me, Dante. Where did you find her? And how?"

I wasn't about to lie to Erin. She already had questions about Lucy, and I'd basically told her she was making things up. Now I was thinking she might be right.

"We heard a—" He rubbed at his temples. "It's crazy, Erin. It was a wolf. She was sitting in the cemetery."

"A wolf? At St. Louis Cemetery?"

"I know. It's nuts. She was sitting on top of a grassy area, and then her ears perked up and she ran away. We heard a... dog fight. Or a wolf fight. Whatever. There was definitely a person involved. Then a yelp and whimper in the cemetery. We followed it, and we found Lucy. She was naked, and she'd been stabbed."

She clamped her hand onto her mouth.

"She was unconscious. Did you check for a concussion?"

She nodded. "What could she have been doing in there?"

"Erin, baby, I think you were right."

"Oh my God..."

"I think Lucy might be a wolf shifter." I got Erin a glass of wine and sat down with her on her sofa, and then told her what River and I had experienced at the cemetery.

"A wolf. In the cemetery. And your mother. Another ghost."

"Yeah. I know how surreal it all sounds."

"This goes so far beyond surreal." She took a gulp of wine.

"I know."

"What about your dad? Where was he while this was going on?"

"He was guarding the perimeter. Making sure everyone was glamoured. And we haven't seen him since we found Lucy."

"You don't think he—"

"No, baby. He's a ghost. He's not corporeal. He can't stab anything. And my father wouldn't do that."

She nodded. "I know. I'm sorry. But who?"

"I wish I knew. Someone who couldn't be glamoured. That's all we know."

She dropped her mouth open.

"What?"

"The vampires. You can't glamour other vampires, can you?"

"No. Of course not."

"You can't smell each other, but can you smell the humans other vampires have been around?"

"Yeah. But only in an amorphous sense. The scent isn't exact." Except during pregnancy. No vamp could mistake the smell of Jay all over Emilia.

"What if it's a really compelling scent?"

"I don't know. Maybe. Probably."

"It's those vampires. The ones Abe said were after me. They smelled me on you."

SEVEN

Erin

This was all my fault. Lucy had been there, trying to protect River and Dante. And those vamps had come after Dante because of me.

"Erin..."

"You've been drinking my blood, Dante. My smell must be all over you." I stood and paced around the room, taking another gulp of wine. "Lucy left work as soon as I told her where you two were going tonight. She claimed she got a text, but I didn't hear her phone buzz."

"She could have had it on silent."

"It's never on silent. She made it up. She left because she was scared for you. She went to protect you. I can't believe I'm even saying all of this. But it makes perfect sense. No, it makes no sense at all. Yet it does."

"Baby, it's okay. You've learned to deal with what I am. You can deal with Lucy as well."

"The werewolf baby..." I rubbed my temples to ease the

hot thrumming between them.

"What?"

"She gave me some instructions in case the baby came back to the ER." I searched for my purse and found it on the floor by the door. I'd dropped it as soon as we got inside and Dante attacked me.

I opened it, turned it upside down, and let its contents fall on the floor.

The envelope sat among them, staring at me, its stark whiteness nearly blinding me and pulsing as if it had a heartbeat.

"She told me not to open it. Not unless the baby came back."

"What are you talking about, Erin?"

I picked up the envelope. It burned my skin. I held it for a moment and then walked back over to the sofa and sat beside Dante. "Lucy gave me this. Said to open it if the baby came back to the ER."

"You don't have to open it."

"I do. How else can we be sure that Lucy..." It had taken me so long to apply the word vampire to Dante. How long would it take to accept Lucy as...

I shook my head. "I can't."

"Then don't."

But I ripped open the envelope anyway and pulled out the piece of white paper inside. I unfolded it slowly.

Erin,

I can't tell you how I know this, but please take care of Bianca if she comes back in. Her fever is normal for who she is, but it does need to be brought down if it continues. Use an herbal tonic made of feverfew and borage leaves. You can find these herbs dried in any voodoo or magick shop. Take one ounce (no more!) of each and infuse in three cups of water that has been boiled but allowed to cool for five minutes. Give two fluid ounces of this herbal infusion with each bottle. It can be mixed with her formula. If the taste bothers her, add just a touch of sugar or stevia.

Please, Erin. Bianca needs this remedy if the fevers continue.

Do not give this to a human baby. Only a were or half-werewolf baby.

Love and Hugs,

Lucy

"Baby?"

I handed the note to Dante and then sank my head into my hands.

His hands were warm and soothing on my shoulders. "Has the child come back?"

I shook my head.

"I don't know much about shifters, but maybe this will help the baby."

I lifted my head up and met Dante's dark gaze. "She was transferred to pediatrics. I assumed they were taking good care of her there. I haven't heard otherwise."

"All right."

"Right now...what about Lucy? She's been attacked by rogue vampires."

"We don't know that for sure."

I said nothing. I knew.

I knew for sure.

"We can go talk to someone at a voodoo shop," he said. "Find out what these herbs are for."

"We already know what they're for," I said. "But there is someone I need to talk to. I need to go back to Claiborne Bridge."

"No way," Dante said, shaking his head vigorously. "You're not safe there."

"It's broad daylight— Oh!"

Julian Gabriel appeared in my living room.

"Dad, you can't just—"

"I'm sorry, Dante, but this is important. I suppose you're wondering where I was last night, why I didn't follow you when you took the girl to the hospital."

"It had crossed my mind."

"I found a way to waylay the vampires who were stalking you and River."

"Ha!" I said. "I told you it was the vampires."

"Yes. After they attacked the wolf—"

"Ha again!" I said.

"Then you know."

"We—Erin—suspected," Dante said.

"When the wolf went down, she shifted, but I was able to chase the vampires—"

"Vampires?" I nodded. "So there was definitely more than one."

"Yeah."

"That makes sense," Dante said. "I can't imagine a wolf would leave her flank exposed if she was fighting just one person."

"She wouldn't," Julian continued. "She had a vampire flat

on his back and was preparing to strike his neck, when another vampire appeared and stabbed her in the side. Anyway, I managed to chase the vampires away before they saw her shift."

"How?" Dante asked.

"I have a few ghostly tricks up my sleeve. Remember, most vampires think ghosts don't exist. I doubt they'll fall for it again, though, so we'll need to take special precautions next time."

"Next time?" The words sounded like they'd come from someone other than me. This whole story had numbed me.

"Well, yeah, Erin," Dante said. "We still have to find my dad's body."

"Your mother and the wolf found it for you," Julian said. "It's buried where the wolf was standing. Once I stood over the area, I knew."

"I thought you had no connection to the physical body." Dante scratched his forehead.

"I don't. But I still have a connection to your mother's energy, and I trust it. Her essence was strong over that area. And then the wolf—"

"Her name is Lucy," I said.

"Yes. I'm sorry. She's a friend of yours, Erin?"

"My best friend. Though I really don't know her at all, apparently."

"You *do* know her. Just as you know Dante. She was only keeping her true self from you because she had to."

"How do you know that?"

"He's right, baby. We have to hide in plain sight. It's just our way. We don't have a choice."

"But she's my—"

"She didn't have a choice," Dante said again in the commanding tone that made my knees weaken.

I sighed and nodded. "Still..."

"I know it hurts, baby. She didn't do it to hurt you. Not anymore than I did."

I nodded again. I *did* get it. Didn't stop it from hurting, just as it did when I found out what Dante was.

"If you can learn to accept me, you can learn to accept her."

Once more, I nodded. What else was there to do? "At least she's going to be okay."

"We're all glad about that," Julian said. "River seems to have quite strong feelings for her."

"They only went on one date," I said.

"Vampires tend to know quickly if a connection is there," Julian said. "Right, Dante?"

"Not that I have a lot of experience, but I'd say yes." Dante smiled.

"Can you call River?" I asked. "Get an update on Lucy?"

Dante nodded and pulled out his cell phone.

"And then we're going to Claiborne Bridge." I ran upstairs to change before he could argue.

Workout clothes and my best jogging shoes. If I had to run, I was going to be ready.

❧

"Ah, Mr. Vampire, and I see you've brought a ghost with you."

"I might have known," Dante said.

"Of course. I see all. What brings you under the bridge today?"

I stepped forward. "It was my idea. What can you tell me about"—I pulled Lucy's note out of my purse—"feverfew and borage leaves?"

HELEN HARDT

"What can you give me in return?"

I rummaged in my purse while Dante rolled his eyes. I pulled out a twenty. "It's yours after you tell me what you know."

"Feverfew is a part of the daisy family. Its flowers resemble daisies."

"I'm not looking to spruce up my garden, Bea," I said. "I want to know how it's used medicinally."

"Mostly for headaches. Sometimes for digestive problems."

"What about fever?"

"Oh? Well, yes. It's a common holistic treatment for fever." She laughed. "In dogs."

"What about wolves?"

"Of course. Dogs and wolves come from the same lineage."

I gulped. "And borage leaves?"

She cackled. "In humans or in wolves?"

I cleared my throat. "Wolves."

"Borage will also calm fevers. And it's used to help nursing mothers with their milk supply. Nursing bitches, that is."

I'm a horny little bitch.

Oh, Lucy. All this time, had she been trying to tell me something?

I shook my head to clear it. "Are these herbs safe for babies?"

"Babies? Or pups?" She cackled again.

"Well...er...both."

"Perfectly safe."

"What's the proper dosage?"

"I didn't treat a lot of wolves in my practice," she said. "But in humans, both are nontoxic in most dosages. Just don't give the feverfew if the patient is allergic to any flowers in the daisy family."

Did werewolves have allergies? Baby Bianca was half human, if her mother was to be believed. Lucy obviously believed her, or she wouldn't have left me this werewolf remedy.

Bea held out her hand.

I pushed the twenty-dollar bill into it. "Where can I find these herbs?"

"Any magick shop in the Quarter should stock them. Why do you need them?"

"No reason."

"Fine. Have it your way." She turned to Dante. "You've been to a graveyard."

"What business is that of yours?"

"The dark presence. I can feel it."

"Right now?" he asked.

"No. But you encountered it recently. In a graveyard."

Dante rubbed the back of his neck. "I don't know what you're talking about."

"You *do*."

"What can you tell us?" From Julian.

"What can you give me?"

"I'm a ghost. I don't have anything."

She nodded to Dante. "He does. So does she."

"How about you tell us, and I don't have my nephew arrest you for loitering?"

Bea cackled, rolling her eyes. "You're a funny ghost, eh? I'll tell you what I know out of respect for your kind. It's not a demon, as I already told these two. It's something new."

"Vampires?" I asked.

"No. Vampires are mortal creatures. This is an energy. A dark energy."

"The ice pick in the back of my neck last night?" Dante said.

"That's not the presence. That's something warning you away."

"Dad?"

"It wasn't me. I was outside guarding."

Dante rubbed his neck again. "Mom..."

"Possibly," Julian said, "though I don't understand how."

"His mother has been gone how long?" Bea asked.

"Twenty-five years," Julian said.

"Unlikely it was her," Bea agreed.

"But I saw her!" Dante said.

Bea's eyes widened. "You saw a twenty-five-year-old ghost?"

"In the cemetery. She guided me. She didn't communicate, though, other than pointing."

"Fascinating," Bea said. "And you recognized her?"

"Yes. It was my mother."

"This is worse than I feared," Bea said.

"What do you mean?" My skin chilled.

"For a ghost who left her body twenty-five years ago to appear, the situation is dire indeed. Be careful, all three of you. All is not what it seems."

"You're speaking strangely again," I said. "Like when you quoted Shakespeare the other day."

"Me? Quote Shakespeare?" She laughed.

I rolled my eyes. "Yeah. You did."

"So I did." She held out her hand.

"We're done here for now," Julian said. "She's no more help to us."

Bea's eyes took on an unnatural gaze, as if she were looking through us to something beyond. "'There are things known, and there are things unknown, and in between are the doors of perception.'"

I looked to Dante, who shook his head.

"Aldous Huxley," Julian said.

"Who?" Dante asked.

"He wrote *A Brave New World*, a dystopian novel. That's his quote."

"I read that in high school," I said. "I don't remember that line."

"It's not in that book. It's from a lesser-known book called *The Doors of Perception*."

"Very good," Bea said. "A well-read vampire. Perhaps, then, you've read the most important work of all."

EIGHT

DANTE

The ice pricked my neck once again.

"Dante," my father said, his voice low and urgent. "Take Erin and run!"

I didn't stop to think. I grabbed Erin. "We need to go. Now." I entwined my fingers through hers.

My heart thundered, and we ran toward the parking lot where her car was. She kept up well, even surging ahead of me a few times.

Once we were safe inside the car, she turned to me. "What was that about?"

"I'm not sure, but my father was serious. Start the car and get us out of here."

She didn't ask questions. She revved the engine, and soon we were on the road.

"Maybe the Claiborne vamps. Then again, he didn't sense them last night, so it was most likely something else." The dark presence. Just the thought of Bea's words sent shivers through me. "The vamps don't usually come out during the day, Riv says."

When we got to Erin's home, I ushered her out of the car and to the door as quickly as I could. When we were safe inside, I breathed a little easier.

"You need to sleep," I said. "You have work tonight."

"You were up all night too," she said. "You need to sleep as well."

She was right, but I wouldn't sleep at all until I'd talked to my father. "Go ahead up. I'll be there as soon as I can."

"Dante..."

"Please, baby. I need to speak to my dad and figure this out."

"Then I'll stay with you." Her face split with a giant yawn.

"Go to bed, love. I'll come get you if I find anything out."

She finally relented and headed upstairs.

"Dad?" I said.

Nothing.

"Dad?"

Then he appeared.

"What was that about?"

"Honestly? I'm not sure. But I felt something, the same thing I felt that day in the restaurant when I warned you to leave."

"Before I could see you?"

"Yes. Bea is right. There's something dark that has attached itself to you. No. Attached isn't the right word because it's not always around. But I can certainly feel it when it's here."

"It's gone now?"

"Yes."

"Was it at the graveyard last night?"

"I don't think so. Not that I could tell, anyway. I think Erin is right. It was the vampires last night. If it had been this dark thing, I would have known. I feel certain. And..."

"And what?"

"If your mother was truly there, she would have known too."

"Bea said something big was happening if a twenty-five-year-old ghost had come out."

"Yes, and though I'm not sure how much Bea truly knows, what she says seems to make a lot of sense."

"She seems pretty nuts sometimes."

"I'm wondering if she's a medium."

"Huh?"

"You and I both agree that she's not the type to go around quoting Shakespeare or Aldous Huxley. I'm wondering if she's channeling them in some way."

I lifted my brow.

"I know it's a lot to take, but she seems to be warning us of something. More important than finding out what this thing is that has targeted you, is finding out why."

"Okay."

"And to figure it out, Dante, we're going to need to be straight with each other."

"Meaning?" I didn't like where this was going. At. All.

"You need to tell me what happened while you were in captivity. And I will do the same."

I'd been electrocuted, clamped in unimaginable places, tortured with burning candles...

I lay limp, my wrists and ankles bound once more.

I'd kept my promise to myself. I hadn't screamed. Hadn't begged for mercy.

It had required the last of my strength.

My head had rolled to the side, saliva dripping from my lips.

If only death would come, free me from this madness, this pure hellacious existence.

But death never came.

I didn't truly wish it, didn't want my life to end, but sometimes, it seemed the only way.

The only way to conquer what had become of me.

A click of a key in the lock. A dreaded sound, but I was too weak, too used, to move. To even cringe.

Then she *entered.*

"Look at me, Dante."

I couldn't. Couldn't move my head.

"Look at me, or I'll bring them back."

No. No more torture. In painful agony, I turned my head until I was looking up into her masked face. Her evil blue eyes.

The light flickered above me, and I squinted.

"I'm going to show you something, Dante." She *held up a large square block of wood painted red. "What color is this?"*

I didn't answer. We'd played a variation of this game before.

"Answer me. What color is this?"

"Orange," I said, my voice hoarse.

She *laughed like a maniac. "Don't play games with me. Tell me the color."*

"Red," I rasped.

"What if I tell you it's blue?"

I said nothing, just attempted to swallow the dryness in my throat.

"Answer me, Dante. What if I tell you it's blue?"

"It's red. You know it as well as I do."

"No. I think it's blue."

I stayed silent. I knew what was coming, and though I wanted to mentally prepare myself, I was still recovering from the morning's torture.

She moved backward and opened the door, allowing one of her goons to reenter. He was masked, as always. Too much of a coward to let me see his face. I tried not to inhale. The acrid scent of garbage was too much to take.

In his hand was the cattle prod. More electricity.

No.

Just no.

He fired it up, a wicked gleam in his eyes.

"Tell me, Dante, what color is this?" She held up the red block once more.

I didn't answer.

"You will answer, or I'll have him prod you."

I drew in a breath.

Strength. Give me strength. I called on my father, my uncle, my grandfather, pleaded for their strength.

I said nothing.

The electricity surged through me, reducing every cell in my body to tiny careening pellets ricocheting off my organs.

But I'd promised myself.

Never would I cry out again.

Urine trickled from me onto the platform below. Humiliating, yes, but what could I do?

"Pissing yourself again?" The goon laughed. "All you need to do is tell her what color it is."

"It's fucking red," I said through clenched teeth.

She shook her head slowly.

And again, my body seized as the current traveled through me.

"Again, what color, Dante?"

"Red," I whispered, the word barely registering above the electric ringing in my ears.

Surge.

Surge.

Surge.

My eyes rolled upward, and saliva trickled from my lips once more. My body was burning, imploding upon itself in a molten mess.

Be strong. You're a Gabriel vampire. Be fucking strong, Dante!

"What color, Dante?"

"Red."

Surge.

"Red."

Surge.

"Red."

I lay listless, bound, hardly able to speak.

"What color, Dante?"

I opened my eyes, squinting.

The block was red.

No.

It had turned. It had metamorphosed.

Unreal. How had this happened?

"Answer me. What color?"

"Red." Though I truly didn't see red.

The last surge was so terrible, I thought for sure it had taken my life.

"Open your eyes!"

Her voice. Her shout.

I used my last shred of strength to obey her.

She *held up the blue block.*

"What color, Dante?"

"Blue," I whispered, *actually seeing blue, actually believing the hoarse word that fell from my dry lips.*

She *smiled with evil gleaming from her eyes. "Blue what?"*

"Blue...my queen."

NINE

Erin

The emergency room was empty when I got into work. I looked around.

"Hello?"

Something was wrong. I logged on to my computer to check on Lucy.

No Lucy. She wasn't registered at this hospital. Even if she'd been transferred, she'd still be in the computer from her initial admission to the ER the previous night.

I keyed in more patients frantically, my heart racing.

Nothing. No data.

No patients?

No one in this hospital?

Then—

I jumped when a faint tap landed on my shoulder.

I turned.

"Abe?"

Abe Lincoln stood behind me.

"What are you doing here? Are you all right?" I looked him over for injuries. He seemed to have recovered nicely from his beating a few nights ago. In fact, I saw no indication that he'd been injured at all.

"I see the transfusion helped. Why did you leave the hospital? You should have been monitored."

No response.

"At least you're okay. Next time, you need to wait until I or someone else tells you it's safe for you to leave. What if your body had rejected the blood?" Unlikely, but it could have happened.

He stayed silent.

I stood and reached toward him. "What's the matter?"

Redness rimmed his tired, sunken eyes. "I'm sorry, Erin."

"It's okay. Just don't do it again. If you come in here for treatment, stay until we're sure you're okay? Got it?" I smiled. Or tried to. Something about this night was definitely off.

I waited, but he didn't respond.

"I need to get back to work. Our system has crashed or something. We've lost all our patient records."

The silence in the ER hovered over me like a smothering cloak. I turned back toward my computer, ready to sit, when Abe touched my shoulder once more.

I turned to meet his gaze.

"I'm sorry, Erin."

"It's okay. Just remember that next—"

A chill swept the back of my neck.

"I'm sorry, Erin."

Another man entered the nurse's computer station. Tall and burly. A leather jacket. Dark hair and beard.

And fangs.

I gasped, my heart hurtling in my chest. "Wh-Who are you?"

The vampire closed his eyes and inhaled. "Finally, we will taste you."

I eased backward until the back of my legs hit the computer table.

Nowhere to go. The vampire was between me and the door.

"Abe...please..."

"I'm sorry, Erin." His eyes were shadowed, glazed over.

"Are you glamoured?" I whispered.

"I'm sorry, Erin."

The vampire took one step forward slowly and then another, inhaling deeply again.

"I'm hungry." Another breath in. "Really fucking hungry."

"Really fucking hungry," another voice echoed.

A second vampire had entered.

Then another behind him.

And another.

"I'm sorry, Erin."

"Abe!" I screamed, furiously glancing around. "Dante! Help me! Dante! Dante!"

"He's not coming for you," one of them said, his eyes dark and full of fury. "No one is coming for you."

"You belong to *us* now," said another.

"Us," they all echoed.

"I'm sorry, Erin." Abe moved away slowly, his lanky body shifting awkwardly, like an automaton.

"Help!" I cried with desperation. "Help me. Please!"

But no one was here. The ER was desolate. Where was everyone? Anyone?

Four vampires, their faces pale and their eyes smoking, stalked toward me slowly, their canines stark white.

Fangs. So many fangs. So many fangs that wanted to bite into my flesh. Suck my blood.

"I'm sorry, Erin."

"She's pretty, too," one said. "We can take more than her blood. Have fun with her hot body while we drain her."

I screamed once more, slinking against my computer table. Nothing I could do. Nowhere to run. They formed a wall between the door and me. I felt around for the knob to the drawer under my station and pulled it open slightly.

A few pens and a package of chocolate cupcakes. The pens could do a little damage, but I couldn't take on four of them.

The bearded one lunged toward me, his fangs dripping with saliva.

I closed my eyes and screamed once more.

I'm sorry, Erin. I'm sorry, Erin. I'm sorry, Erin.

I shot up in bed at the piercing shriek.

It had come from my own throat.

Within seconds, Dante raced into my bedroom. "Erin! What's the matter?"

I jumped out of bed and ran into his arms.

"Baby? What is it? What happened?"

"They came for me," I sobbed. "They came for me, and there was no one to help me."

"Shh." He pressed a kiss to the top of my head. "You're safe here with me." He led me back to the bed and pushed me gently into a sitting position. Then he sat next to me. "You had a dream."

I shook my head. "That was no dream. It was a nightmare."

"It's over now."

"It was so real, Dante. I went to work tonight, and no one was there. The ER was totally vacant. And then Abe Lincoln..."

"What about him?"

I poured out the guts of my dream to the vampire I loved. "They were going to drain me, Dante. Four huge vampires. They were nothing like you and River. They were mean and evil, and they wanted my blood. Not like you want it. They wanted it *all.*"

He rubbed my back, caressing me, trying to soothe me.

"Abe Lincoln brought them to me."

"He won't. He can't."

I nodded furiously, gulping. "He *can.* He was in the ER the other night. They beat him bad, Dante. They beat him because he wouldn't bring them to me."

"Shh," he said in a soothing voice. "It might not have happened that way."

"It did. He said it did."

"He lives on the street, Erin. He could have been beaten for any number of reasons."

"No. No. He had a hemoglobin of six point nine. He'd nearly been drained."

His eyes widened for a second, but he calmed down quickly. "That was a nightmare, baby. You're all right. I'm not going to let anyone have you. I promise."

I shivered against Dante's strong, hard body.

I believed him.

I just wasn't sure he was a match for four hungry vampires.

"Is everything okay up here?"

I looked up from Dante's chest, both of us rising from the bed. Julian stood in my doorway.

"She's okay," Dante said. "But I'm glad you're here, Dad. Maybe you can help us."

"Oh?"

"You want to tell him?" Dante asked me.

What could it hurt? I spilled it all out once more for Dante's father. He listened intently.

"Did you get a good look at these vampires?" he asked.

"I...don't know. Why?"

"Perhaps you'd be able to recognize them."

"It was a dream, Dad. How would she recognize them?"

Julian entered the bedroom, though he didn't sit. Had I ever seen him sit?

"You learn a lot when you pass out of this corporeal life," he said. "As you most likely know, we rarely remember our dreams unless we awaken quickly, which I assume happened to you after this one, Erin."

I nodded.

"Our brains keep our dreams from us for a reason," he continued. "Many times we're not ready or able to process the information in them. Some say dreams are answers to questions that we haven't learned to ask yet. Some say dreams signify past life regressions. I've found both to be true, relatively speaking, depending on the dream."

"I don't have any questions about being attacked by vampires," I said. "And I can't imagine that it's something I need to learn to ask."

"I agree," Julian said.

"Then you think she was attacked by vampires in a past life?" Dante asked.

Julian shook his head. "Once you leave the corporeal plane, you realize time has no meaning as you once believed it to. It's fluid, with all moments in time existing simultaneously."

My brain was apparently fried from the vampire dream. I didn't understand anything Julian was saying.

Apparently, neither did Dante.

"Okay. Exactly what does that mean, Dad?"

"When you leave the corporeal plane, which you do in your dreams, there's not much difference between a regression...and a premonition."

TEN

DANTE

Erin pulled away from me, her gaze resting on my father's ghost. "You think I had a premonition?"

"I do."

"But nothing else made sense in the dream. The ER would never be empty, and patient records would never be erased from our system. We have backups to our backups to our backups."

"A premonition is rarely literal," my father said. "But it can be a warning. In this case, it might be warning you to stay away from these particular vampires."

"I don't need a warning for that."

"That's not what I mean. It's showing you who they are. That's why I asked if you might be able to recognize them. Can you remember anything about them from the dream? Anything at all that would help us find them?"

She shook her head. "I don't think so. I was crazy scared All I was thinking about was finding a way to get out of there. There was no exit for me. I was trapped, and they were going to drain me. After they raped me."

I growled without meaning to, my fangs itching to descend.

"Relax, Dante," my father said. "It didn't happen. We won't let it ever happen."

My father meant well, but his words didn't relax me. Not even slightly.

"Try, Erin," my father continued. "Anything at all you can recall, even the tiniest thing."

"Dad, she's still shivering. Maybe we could do this later?"

"No, Dante. I understand you want to protect her, but her mind will forget the details quickly. She must remember *now*."

Erin cupped my cheek. "It's okay. I know I'm safe with you here. I'll try."

I smiled and pressed a kiss to the palm of her hand. "If you're sure."

"If your dad is right, maybe we can figure out who these vampires are and get to them before they get to me. I have to try."

"Erin, there's one more thing," my father said.

"What's that?" she asked.

"I can help you. I can take you back to your dream. But to do that, I have to glamour you."

She stiffened beside me.

"No," I said adamantly. "Absolutely not."

"Dante..."

"No, baby. It nearly killed me when I found out he'd glamoured you. And you weren't happy about it yourself, as I recall."

"I wasn't, but if we can figure out—"

"No!" My fangs descended, and I growled as a sharp pain shot through me—a new sensation I'd never felt before. I touched my lips.

"You're maturing, Dante," my father said. "Your teeth descended almost instantly. After a while, you won't notice the pain."

Another thing I didn't know.

"You and I need to spend some time together. I'm sorry we haven't had a chance for that yet. What you're dealing with is normal. Around the age of thirty, some changes occur in our physiology."

"I'm twenty-eight."

"Bodies are different. But we need to get back to Erin."

"I'll do it." She stood tall. "I'll let you glamour me."

"No—"

"Dante, it's not your call." She caressed my forearm, her touch a soothing presence.

"We have to do it now, son, before the specifics of her dream leave her mind."

"I can't be here for this." I moved away slightly.

"That's all right. Take a walk if you have to, Dante. I'll protect her."

I didn't move, though. My feet stayed glued to Erin's carpet. Leaving felt all wrong. My place was here with Erin. Beside her. No matter what.

"I'm not leaving. I can't."

"Dante..." Erin reached toward me again.

"You do what you have to do, Erin. I don't have to like it."

"But I don't want to make you unhappy."

"I will do whatever I need to do to protect you. If that means letting my father glamour you, so be it. My place is next to you, no matter what."

"Lie down on your bed, Erin," my father said. "Free your mind. I won't place you under a strong glamour. You'll remember everything. I'll just give you a short wave of energy, one that will filter through your thoughts and bring you where you need to be."

She lay down, her eyes pleading with me. "Dante, lie next to me? Please?"

I couldn't deny her. I took my place next to her, our bodies touching, her warmth soaking me with a nice feeling I hoped would morph into calmness.

"Close your eyes, Erin. You won't feel me in your mind. I can't extract your thoughts from you. I can only manipulate where they go."

I hoped Erin was more relaxed than I was. My father was about to poke into my lover's mind. I wasn't sure I wanted him to know her secrets.

"It's not like that, Dante," he said.

"How did you—"

"No, I'm not clairvoyant. Neither is my father. We're both just very intuitive where our children—and in his case, grandchildren—are concerned. I can tell what's bothering you by the way your body reacts. Right now you're as rigid as a wooden plank."

"I'd be happy to be *only* that rigid right now," I said with sarcasm.

"You know what glamouring is. It's manipulating thoughts, not extracting them. I can't see what's in Erin's mind. I can only manipulate what I know is there."

"Yeah, yeah. I know how glamouring works. I'm just not very good at it."

"I'll teach you. Once we have more time. For now, relax. You have a calming effect on her. You want to help her, don't you?"

"Of course I want to help her. I'd do anything for her."

"Then relax. Help *her* relax."

I drew in a breath and let it out slowly. Still my pulse raced. Another breath. In. Out. In. Out.

I entwined my fingers around Erin's. Perhaps my touch would help.

"That's it," my father said. "Relax. Both of you."

Beside me, Erin breathed softly. Slowly. She was relaxing. She was doing what she had to do.

I could do no less.

"You won't feel anything, Erin," he said. "You'll just start reliving your dream. But you'll know it's a dream. You'll know they can't hurt you. The only purpose of my manipulation is for you to take a good look at these vampires. Notice anything specific about each one of them. Remember if they call each other by name. Anything that can help us identify them."

"I understand," she said softly.

"Now tell me what you see," my father said, his voice oddly comforting.

"I'm at my computer station in the ER. Abe Lincoln is coming in. He keeps telling me he's sorry."

"Remember, it's just a dream," my father reiterated.

"I know. I'm standing. A vampire is there now. His teeth are out." She stiffened.

I caressed the palm of her hand.

"Just a dream," my father said.

"He has a beard. A bushy beard. Not a goatee. His eyes are brown, I think. Maybe dark blue. A really dark blue."

"Anything else?"

"No. All four of them are there now. I can't... I can't,, I can only see the first one. He seems to be their leader or something."

"Look around. Anything? Is he tall?"

"He's big. Burly. But...I don't think he's as tall as Dante."

"What is he wearing?"

"Black. They're all wearing black. Leather, I think. Black pants. No, they're jeans. Really dark blue jeans."

"What are they saying to you?"

"They want to taste me. God. Fangs. Their fangs are everywhere. They're all I see. Just the white, dripping fangs. Everywhere. They want—"

I jolted upward into a sitting position.

"Dante?" My father said.

"I saw them," I said, not even believing the words that tumbled out of my mouth.

"Saw the vampires?"

"Yeah. She was describing them, and I thought I was just picturing them in my mind, but I saw them, Dad. I actually saw them."

"Are you sure?"

"I know it sounds crazy, but I'm completely sure."

A vile rage permeated my gut.

The bearded one was their leader. Erin was right. His eyes were dark blue, not brown.

And he wore a gold pin on the lapel of his black leather jacket.

A symbol I couldn't see, no matter how hard I squinted.

A symbol that I knew—and I didn't know how I knew—was important.

"The others," I said, "are inconsequential. They need to feed, but they're nearly invisible next to their leader. The one with the beard."

"He's right," Erin said. "I can't make out their features. I thought it was because I was scared, but now that I'm looking straight at them, they're just...blurs."

"A dominant personality will sometimes cause that, especially in a dream," Julian said. "No matter. Find the leader, and we'll find the others."

ELEVEN

Erin

Dante and I left for the hospital a couple of hours before I was due on my shift. We wanted to check on Lucy.

She was lying in a hospital bed in the surgical unit, awake. "Shh," she said quietly when we walked in. She pointed to River asleep in a recliner.

"He's still here?" Dante said.

Lucy nodded.

I walked to her and sat down in the chair next to her bed. "Shouldn't *you* be sleeping?"

Lucy yawned. "Yeah. But I woke up a few minutes ago. I guess I knew you were coming."

I grabbed her hand. She was warm. I stood and leaned over and kissed her forehead. Also warm.

"Normal for me," she said.

Dante sighed. "So...that's who you are."

"And who *you* are," she said. "River told me. Imagine. Vampires exist. How many other species are out there, keeping themselves secret?"

I hoped her question was rhetorical. "I'm feeling like the odd person out here," I said, trying to sound nonchalant but failing miserably. "I can't believe you're a werewolf."

"The term werewolf is kind of antiquated," she said. "Only humans use it. We prefer the term 'wolf shifter.' And you're not the odd person out. We're no different than you are."

I rolled my eyes. "I think that's a crock."

"We're mortal, just like you. Born, just like you."

"And one of you turns into a wolf and the other two drink blood. Not a lot like me after all."

"Erin..." Dante's voice was commanding and a little patronizing.

But he was right. Lucy was recovering from an attack and emergency surgery. She didn't need any additional stress. As a nurse, I knew better.

"Do you remember who attacked you, Luce?" I asked.

She nodded. "I didn't realize it at the time, but looking back, I think he was a vampire."

"With a dark-brown beard?"

"I see only black and white in wolf form. But yes, it was dark. I got a good scent, though. I can help you find him."

"Vampires don't have scents," Dante said.

"Not to other vampires," Lucy said. "River told me. But I'm not a vampire. I smelled him just like I can smell anyone when I'm in wolf form. He doesn't have a 'vampire' scent. Just a unique scent like any other living being."

"Your sense of smell is only more acute when you shift?" Dante asked.

"It's slightly better than a human's when I'm not in wolf form, but it's very strong when I shift."

Again, reality was taking a big hit. I had tons more

questions, but they'd have to wait. Right now, Lucy needed her rest. But there was one question that couldn't wait. I had to know.

"The night of River's accident?"

She closed her eyes, sighed, and then opened them. "I shifted. Out of fear. I charged through the windshield and escaped before impact. I'm very fast in wolf form."

"You were the dog the witnesses saw at the scene," Dante said.

"Yup. And those tattered clothes in the car were mine."

"Why doesn't River remember you changing?" he asked.

"I don't know. He was probably using all his attention to try to avoid the accident, and the impact jarred him. He knows now, though. His fragmented memory was really freaking him out. I feel terrible about lying to him about retrograde amnesia, but I have to be very careful, just like the two of you do." She smiled. "Luckily, he has forgiven me."

I couldn't help a smile as well. "We both love vampires."

She pinked a little. "I don't know about love yet, but I'm interested to see where it goes."

River budged a little then, stretching his arms and opening his eyes. "Oh. Hey, guys."

"Not to bring up the elephant in the room," Dante said, "but we have to go back to the cemetery."

Chills erupted over my skin.

Lucy flinched. "No. Not until I can go with you."

She was clearly agitated. Maybe they'd put it off.

"We can't wait. We have to get my father's body as soon as possible, before it decomposes any further."

"Decomposition doesn't matter," I added. "You can always check his dental records."

"No." Dante shook his head. "We need to get a death certificate so Em and I can claim his estate. Plus..." He closed his eyes.

"Plus what?" I asked.

"I don't want to see my father any more decomposed than I have to. Erin, we have to do it now." He turned to River and nudged him. "When do you have to go into work tonight?"

"I don't." He cleared his throat. "I...made arrangements to have tonight off."

"I thought you didn't want to take any personal days because of the—" Dante stopped abruptly.

I knew the words he didn't say.

River had "made arrangements."

He'd glamoured his boss. But what about—

"Jay?"

"I'm sorry, Erin," River said. "I didn't have a choice."

Dante went rigid, and for a moment, I was afraid he would shout. But he backed off.

"He's right, Erin. We need to do this. Tonight."

"But the vampires..." Lucy began.

"We know what to expect this time, and we know where the body is. We'll be quick about it. My father will be with us, and my mother too."

"Aren't they both dead?" Lucy said.

Dante and I both looked to River.

"I didn't get around to telling her *everything*," he said. "But I guess you just did."

"What are you keeping from me?" Lucy asked, glaring at River.

River spouted out the truth about Dante's father in a rush of nearly incomprehensible babble.

"Seriously," she said. "You need to wait. I can scent this bastard out in wolf form. I can keep him away from you while—"

"No, sweetie," River said. "Not tonight. You stay here. We'll be in and out as quickly as we can. We know where we're going this time."

I turned to Dante. "Is there any way you can get my smell off of you? They'll have no reason to follow you if they don't smell me."

"Not that I know of. But don't worry, baby. Like Riv said, we'll be in and out in a flash."

In and out in a flash.

Why didn't I believe that?

TWELVE

DANTE

The moon shone above us as we stood outside St. Louis Cemetery once again.

"I'm coming into the cemetery with you tonight," my father said.

"You can't," River said. "It's more important that you hold the glamour on the guard and anyone else who comes along."

"I've taken care of that," he said.

"How?" My first thought went to Bill. He'd arranged for his father to be there to keep everyone glamoured. The idea gnawed at me. I didn't want Bill there. He couldn't know why we were doing this—to get the money to find out what was in the *Vampyre Texts*.

"Just leave it to me," he said.

"Please don't tell me that Bill—"

"I *said* leave it to me."

I'd learned long ago not to question my father when he used that tone. The tone that said "I'm in charge here and I don't owe you any explanation."

Except that I was a grown man now, and I deserved an explanation.

"Sorry, Dad. That's not going to fly with me anymore. You're still my father. I get that. But River and I need to know what we're dealing with here."

"All right." He sighed. "I had the voodoo priestess cast a protective shield around the cemetery. It will keep everyone out but us. No vampire is getting in, and no guard or other human either."

"Which voodoo priestess?" River frowned. "Oh, no. You don't mean that crazy lady from Claiborne Bridge."

"Really, Dad? I have to agree. Her hocus-pocus won't protect us. Riv and I can act quickly, but we can't take the chance of being stopped like last night."

"I did a little research. And by research, I mean I talked to a few ghosts still on this plane. They all know her. I was right. She *is* a medium, and a powerful one. I'm not sure she even knows this, but her power comes from the ghosts who speak to her and inhabit her. That extra energy amplifies her own, and her spells rarely fail."

"Extra energy?"

"Ghosts are pure energy," he said. "We no longer have a body to keep alive, so all of our energy can be used for other purposes."

"You can't be serious," River said. "What did she charge you for this service?"

"Not much. Just a romp in the hay with both of you."

A burp of acid lodged itself in my throat. I gulped back the nausea in time to see my father's ghostly eyes twinkling. He was kidding.

Thank God.

"Come on. I know you're bonded to Erin, and"—he turned to River—"you've got the hots for that cute little wolf."

"For a minute there I was pretty shaken up." River laughed, sort of. It was more of a nervous chuckle.

"Just because I'm dead doesn't mean I've lost my sense of humor."

River and I stood with our mouths agape, looking at each other. What were we supposed to say to that?

"Man," my dad said, "and I thought *I* was the stiff here."

"Dad..."

"For Christ's sake, Dante. Laugh a little. Death is just a part of life. This night's activities are going to be somber enough."

"You still haven't told us what you gave Bea to do the protection spell."

"Nothing. Nothing yet, anyway. But I did tell her she'd be well compensated later."

"That can't be. She'd never agree to that."

"She did while she was inhabited with Shakespeare's ghost. I explained why we needed the spell, and she agreed. Especially when I told her what was in it for her."

"She agreed? Or Shakespeare?" I tilted my head slightly. Why would Shakespeare want to help us? And why was I even believing all of this crazy talk?

"Does it matter? As long as we're protected."

He had me there. I just hoped he was right for believing Bea. I didn't trust the so-called priestess. But I did trust my father.

River apparently agreed about Bea. "We'd better get to it. You really trust Bea's spell?"

"I do," he said. "I admit I had my doubts before I talked to the others. But she's a medium. Ghosts who have been gone a long time and can no longer appear on the earthly plane still have a conduit through her. You were right. She wasn't speaking when she quoted Shakespeare. That was Shakespeare."

"I'll be damned," River said. "Really?"

"Really. I was skeptical at first. But I was able to inhabit her and speak through her. Then I knew for sure."

"You went...*into* her?" I said.

"Don't make it sound so disgusting, Dante. You can see me, but I don't actually have a body anymore. There was no touching of any kind. And speaking of my body..."

"Yeah," I said. "Let's go."

We entered the cemetery, the moonlight streaming over the concrete vaults. It was a clear night, and with our acute vision it was almost as good as daylight. I trudged along in the lead, winding around the vault of Marie Laveau and toward the corner where Lucy, in wolf form, had stood on the grassy knoll.

We beamed our flashlights onto the area in question.

"Amazing that it doesn't look disturbed," I said.

"Makes me wonder if there's someone who didn't want your body found, Uncle Jules," River said. "The cop in me smells a rat here. You've only been dead a few weeks. If your body is truly under here somewhere, someone went to a lot of trouble to make it look like it's not."

"It's here," he said. "Vivienne knows somehow, and I trust her."

"I guess we start digging, then." I pulled my arms out of the sleeves of my duster and tossed it on the ground. "Let's take up the sod first so we can put it back down in one piece."

River and I edged our shovels around the sod and carefully pulled it away from the ground. This took some time, as we needed to put it back so it wouldn't look disturbed. When we finally got the roughly six-by-six-foot patch removed and carefully placed adjacently, we dug in.

My shoulders were cramping from the hard work. I needed to get in shape. Lying in captivity hadn't done a lot for my muscle endurance. They were still big and strong—because of the blood *she* forced me to drink, according to *her*—but they hadn't been worked in a while.

Still, I kept going, pushing myself, digging deeper and deeper, wanting to find what we were searching for...and not wanting to just as badly.

"Damn. Are you sure it's here, Uncle Jules?" River asked, wiping sweat from his brow with his shirt sleeve.

"I'm sure. Keep going."

We'd gone down about six feet at this point, my head barely able to see out of the hole, when my shovel hit something. "Hey, Riv, I got something here."

About fifteen minutes later, we were hoisting a body-sized plastic bag out of the ground.

"You ready for this?" River asked.

I turned to my father. "Are you?"

"What we see won't affect me. The body is no longer mine. You see me the way I was because that's how it makes sense to you."

"I can't deal with your noncorporeal supernatural lingo right now, Dad. Do we look or not?"

"You won't know for sure if you don't look."

"Why should we? You say it's you. Why can't we just take it to the coroner and have Riv work his magic?"

"Can you live with that?"

My father's words—the words of a ghost—shook me. Could I?

No. I needed to be sure. I needed to see my father's dead body, even knowing it would haunt me forever.

"Help me, Riv." I tugged at the plastic tarp covering the body.

His feet were revealed first. Just as well. Easy. They were bare, though, which was odd. Surely he'd worn shoes when he escaped. We hastily removed the tarp.

And I held back a heave.

My father's whole body was naked.

"Sorry," he said. "I didn't know. I was wearing clothes when I died."

His nudity didn't bother me. The injuries on his body had caused my reaction.

"No," I whispered.

"It's okay. There's no more pain where I am now, Dante."

"But they hurt you. They never touched my body in this way. They used clamps and electricity. The pain was unbearable. But this..." I choked. "You went through so much."

"And I'd do it again to save you."

Lesions covered his body. Burn marks. A jagged scar cut diagonally through his once handsome face had clearly blinded one of his eyes. His genitals had been...

I had to look away.

"It's okay, son. There is no more pain."

No. Not for him. But for me? "Who took your body, Dad? Who removed your clothes and wanted me to see this?"

"I don't know, Dante. I wish I did. I'd make sure whoever it was paid dearly."

I gulped. How could I deal with this image I would never be able to unsee?

This was what he went through because he went after me?

And God...River.

If my father's body had been battered in this way, what were they doing to Braedon's at this very moment?

"I hope he's dead," River whispered, his voice strangled. "I can't bear the thought..."

"Don't think that way," my father said. "Brae wants to live, and he's strong. Stronger perhaps even than I was. We'll find him."

"How? If you have no connection to your own body, how can you have a connection to him?"

"Because he's alive. He still has a life-force, and the connection between twins is unequaled. We'll find him, son. I promise you."

Though he used the word "son," he was talking to both River and me. Uncle Brae and he had often used the term when referring to us both.

"How –" I cleared my throat to erase the hoarseness. "How were you able to get out when you were so..." I shook my head.

"I was determined, Dante, just as you were. And I had the dream of your mother to guide me, to give me the strength I required. I knew I had to do it. For you."

"But I—"

"You'll understand when you have children of your own."

My father had said those same words to me before, and again, the image of Erin handing me a vampire child morphed in my mind.

I shook my head to clear it. I couldn't deal with that impossibility now.

"I'm sorry you have to see my body this way," he continued, "but you would have always wondered. You're strong. Both of you. The memory of what you see tonight will only make you stronger."

I swallowed down the last of my grief for what my father had endured. It was in the past now. The present was what mattered. Finding Braedon. Finding the vampire who had done this to my father, my uncle, and me.

Finding the *truth*.

THIRTEEN

Erin

I was a wreck at work most of the night. Luckily, it was a slow night. I didn't trust myself except on the easiest of cases. I could mend boo-boos all right, and I did my share of them. During my breaks, I checked in on Lucy, who slept soundly. No sirens meant I didn't have to imagine Dante's body coming in on a stretcher.

Dante.

He was in a cemetery recovering his father's body.

The shift was almost over. No vampires had come in to stalk me, and though I should want to get home, I didn't.

Not if Dante wasn't there waiting for me.

Normally on a day like this, I'd get Lucy and go to breakfast. But Lucy was in the main hospital, recovering from a stab wound—a stab wound she suffered while trying to help Dante and River.

God!

Logan walked toward me. "Breakfast, Erin?"

Dante would hate it. But I had questions for Logan, not the least of which was what had happened to him while he was gone. He claimed not to remember, but now he was back at work as if nothing had happened. Hadn't the administration had questions? The physicians? Dr. Bonneville was on vacation, but I couldn't see Dr. Thomas and the others letting his absence slide without some explanation.

Still, I couldn't be long. Dante would need to feed, especially after the night he'd had.

"Maybe just a coffee in the cafeteria," I said. "I need to be somewhere soon."

"Sure. My treat."

We walked to the cafeteria, which was pretty vacant at seven a.m. Logan brought two coffees to the table where I sat.

I took a sip. "How are you doing? I mean, how are you dealing with everything?"

"I've had physicals by two physicians, and both have declared me fine physically. I'm seeing a psychiatrist. Trying to figure out where I was and what I did. They want me to try hypnosis, which I think is beyond crap."

Hypnosis. I'd once echoed Logan's sentiment, but no longer. Hypnosis was similar to glamouring. Julian Gabriel's ghostly face popped up in my mind. He'd helped me remember my dream. Could he—or any vampire who knew how to glamour—help Logan?

"Maybe you should try it."

He scoffed, nearly spitting coffee on the table before swallowing. "Seriously, Erin? What are they teaching in nursing school these days?"

With some fortitude, I managed to ignore his nursing school comment. "What can it hurt? If it's crap, nothing will happen, and you'll be no worse off than you are now."

He shook his head. "Sorry. Not going there."

Okay, then. "Why are you back at work so soon? Didn't the admin want to know what happened?"

Again, he shook his head. "Weird, I know. But they're shorthanded, and after two docs declared me okay, that was good enough. Probably helps that Bonneville's off right now. No way would she have agreed to my coming back."

I nodded. That was certain. "Are you sure you're up to it?"

"Have you seen me make a mistake yet?" His tone was short and defensive.

"No, it's just—"

"I'm sorry. I didn't mean to snap at you. I need to work, Erin. If I don't, my mind will just go places I'm not sure I want to revisit."

"Is that why you're saying no to hypnosis?" I asked, knowing it was the wrong thing to say.

He chuckled. "Not really. I do think hypnosis is bullshit. But it's frustrating. I get fragments and images, but I can't make sense of them." He moved his hand forward and touched mine. "It helps to talk to you."

His touch burned me, and not in a good way. The feel of his flesh felt all wrong against mine. I snatched my hand away.

"Erin, I'm not coming on to you."

"I know that." Warmth flooded my cheeks.

"I just need a friend right now. If you only knew..." He closed his eyes and sighed.

But something niggled at me, prickling my neck. If I only knew *what*? Everything he'd said indicated he didn't know what had happened. Sure, he had a few fragments of memories, but no sense of what really had happened.

Was he lying to me? Did he actually know what had happened to him but was feigning memory loss?

Chills coursed through me. Something wasn't right. I needed to go.

I stood. "Thank you for the coffee, but I have an appointment I need to get to."

"You're not leaving yet."

My eyes shot open. "I assure you I am. We're off duty. I don't have to follow your orders, Dr. Crown."

"Sit down, Erin."

Without knowing why, I sat. I didn't want to, tried not to. But somehow my ass ended back down on the hard cafeteria chair.

"Thank you," he said. "I won't take much more of your time. You're just...so easy to talk to."

An hour later, I was driving home, my conversation with Logan a haze in my mind. He hadn't told me anything important, and he hadn't tried to touch me again. I had no idea why he was so adamant that I stay, or why I'd been so compelled to.

The whole thing was a puzzle, but for some reason it didn't bother me all that much. What concerned me now was getting home to Dante.

I hadn't heard a word from him, not even a short text. Had they been successful? Surely he'd have let me know. But there was so much I still didn't know about Dante and his kind.

His kind...

Logan...

Why didn't I recall anything of importance from our

conversation over coffee? Why didn't...?

I pulled over to the side of the road and stopped with a screech. Squirming, I pulled my sweats and underwear over my hips, spreading my legs to examine my thighs.

I heaved a sigh of relief.

No fresh puncture wounds.

What had I been thinking? Logan was no more a vampire than I was. Dante had completely overpowered him that morning at my place.

But I hadn't had any new wounds since he'd been gone. It was a logical—relatively speaking—assumption.

I hastily made myself right before someone could look into my car and see me with my pants down.

My mind needed to settle down. Now that I knew what was out in the world, I had to reel in my imagination. These other creatures—and I hated using that word for Dante and Lucy and their kinds, but what other word was there?—were rare, probably didn't even exist in places other than New Orleans. Maybe Transylvania.

They *weren't* everywhere.

I pulled into my parking space at my townhome and walked briskly to my door, hoping Dante would be inside.

He wasn't.

FOURTEEN

DANTE

As soon as the city offices opened at eight a.m., River and I took my father's body to the coroner, and River worked his magic. With the death certificate for Julian Gabriel in hand, we went to a nearby mortuary—River again glamouring the technician not to notice my father's extensive injuries—and arranged for his cremation. Though the process usually took five to ten business days, River arranged it so we could pick up my father's remains later the same day.

Still clutching my father's death certificate, I headed to Erin's—rather my and Erin's—place. I hadn't moved what little I owned to her home yet, but I would as soon as possible. Right now, I needed her.

Not just her blood.

I needed *her*.

I'd already known my father was dead, but seeing his battered body, holding his death certificate, had slammed it home in my mind.

River dropped me off, and I raced to the door, unlocking it with my new key.

And there she was, on the other side of the door, launching herself into my arms.

"Thank God! I was so worried about you."

"I'm okay, baby."

But I wasn't okay. I wasn't even close to okay.

I bent my face to her neck, but instead of puncturing her sweet flesh, I simply inhaled.

Inhaled the goodness that was Erin.

"Go ahead," she said. "I know you must be hungry."

I was, so I released my fangs and took just a sip, and then I licked her wounds closed. "I need you," I said gruffly.

"You have me."

"I mean I *need* you. I want to savor you. I want to savor *life*."

"Did you find—"

"Later. Please. I'll tell you everything later. Right now, I need to be with you, inside you. I need you to chase away the demons, make me whole again. Then I'll finish feeding."

"I'm here for you. Whatever you need. Always." She pressed her lips to mine in a soft kiss.

I swooped her into my arms. I was hard as a rock and my teeth remained elongated, but a quick fuck up against the wall wasn't what I craved right now.

I craved life—its very essence. Normally that would mean blood, but now? After witnessing my father's body brutalized and violated almost beyond recognition?

I needed to embed myself in Erin and remind myself that I was full of life.

I had escaped *her*, and I was alive.

I walked swiftly up the stairs and deposited her on her unmade bed. "Undress for me,"

She was wearing the standard uniform she wore to and from work—sweat pants, a T-shirt, and tennis shoes. Her hair was pulled back into a high ponytail, a few strands hanging loose around her face.

She kicked off her shoes and removed her socks quickly.

"Slow down," I said. "I want to savor this. I want to celebrate as each new inch of your flesh comes into my view."

"Are you sure?"

She was reasonably confused. Usually at feeding time I was ravenous, couldn't wait. The small taste downstairs had given me the strength I needed, and now...

"I want to savor every moment this morning. I want to make love to you slowly and sweetly and then quickly and furiously. I want to run my tongue over every part of your body, feast on you. I want to make you feel alive, and *I* want to feel alive, Erin. Totally alive."

A soft smile emerged on her beautiful face, her peridot eyes sparkling.

She understood. In that split second, she got it.

She lifted the T-shirt over her head, baring her milky shoulders, her creamy chest and cleavage. Then she unhooked her bra in the back, letting those gorgeous globes fall into my view. Her areolas were already puckered, her nipples hard in their centers.

I inhaled. Sweet musky arousal...plus the undeniable scent that was pure Erin. Erin, who I'd never be able to get enough of. Blackberries, chocolate, earthy truffles. All of it plus more today. My senses were on high alert, and I planned to use every single one of them when I made Erin mine.

Slowly she slid her sweat pants over her hips, and when they lay in a puddle on the floor, her scent wafted toward me once more, so much thicker in the room when she was covered only by her lacy thong.

She pushed her thumbs under the silky elastic, and—

"No. I'll do it." I ripped it off her with one finger.

She gasped. "I never knew underwear was so disposable. How many is this now that you've destroyed?"

I didn't answer her. Instead, I threw the torn silk on the floor next to the rest of her clothes.

Then I simply looked at her.

Her hair was still bound, and her lovely milky neck beckoned. I stayed back though, simply drinking in the sight of her. Her full breasts were swollen already, her nipples deep pink and hard like currants. Her flat tummy, with just a touch of feminine roundness, and the swell of her hips. Her trimmed black bush, and then her luscious thighs and strong calves. Even her feet were beautiful, her toenails painted a dark reddish black.

My cock was stiff inside my jeans. I'd come here straight from the mortuary, and I hadn't had time to shower. Erin deserved me clean.

I quickly stripped off my clothes. Then I gently grabbed her hand and tugged her toward the bathroom. "I need a shower," I said, my voice husky.

"All right. But you were looking at me like I was dessert."

"You're way more than dessert, love. But I've been out all night, digging in the dirt."

"You look amazing to me."

"Just like you always look amazing to me," I said. "But for what I have planned for both of us, I want to be free from dirt. Free from the tarnish of last night."

She opened her mouth, but I placed two fingers over her lips.

"I know you want to ask me. I will tell you. But not just yet. Let me have these few hours with you. Let me feel alive again."

She smiled, stood on her toes, and kissed my stubbly cheek. "Whatever you say. I'm here for you."

She opened the door to the shower and turned the water on. When the room became steamy, she led me in.

I inhaled the soothing steam infused with Erin's scent. I breathed in again and again, letting it pulse through my body. Then I stood in the gentle rain of the showerhead and brought Erin against me, lowering my head and kissing her sweet lips. She opened for me, and it was a gentle kiss. The fire and passion we always shared was still there, but this was a kiss of love. Of life.

As the water washed the tainted night off my body and I became clean, at least physically, I began to feel better. I broke the kiss and pulled Erin's beautiful long black hair free from the band that held her ponytail. I turned around, letting her stand at the stream and wet her hair. Then I squeezed some shampoo into my palm, and when I massaged it into her scalp, she giggled.

"What's the matter?" I asked.

"Nothing. I just thought you were going to wash your own hair."

"Why would I want to wash my own hair when I have your beautiful hair just waiting for me to run my fingers through it? Everything about you is beautiful, Erin. From the top of your head all the way down to your pretty little toes."

"Your words. They always make me feel so, so..."

"Turned on?"

"Well, yes, but I was going to say loved."

"You are loved. More than I'll ever be able to express."

She closed her eyes, sighing again.

"Do you like having your hair washed?"

"No. I like having my hair washed by *you*."

I was enjoying it as well. When I had all of her locks sufficiently lathered, I gently bent her head back so the shower could stream over them. When the last bit of bubbles had gone down the drain, I brought her to me again and kissed her sweet lips.

Again, it began as a gentle kiss, but as my cock burned even harder between my legs, I deepened it, taking her tongue into my mouth, swirling my own around it, sucking on it.

This time she broke the kiss. "Let me take care of you. I'll wash your hair too. Then I'll wash your whole body. I'll cleanse this night away for you, Dante, so that all that's left is just the two of us. Just our bodies."

Exactly the words I needed to hear. Her fingers caressing my scalp as she shampooed me flooded me with warmth, with love. The act wasn't important. It was the closeness, the touching. And while my cock would find its home and root itself deeply within Erin's body, that wasn't what this morning was ultimately about.

This woman had saved me in so many more ways than I could count. This morning she was saving me once again, cleansing me of the impurities of the night. Of the impurities of my life.

So much I still hadn't shared with her, hadn't even fully shared with myself.

This morning in the shower, as she washed my body, she gave me some of the absolution I longed for. If only I had been strong enough, brave enough. If only I hadn't been so stupid as to disobey my father and grandfather and go to Bourbon Street that fateful night.

Erin knew nothing of this yet, but still she granted me mercy. This shower baptized me, eradicating all wrongdoing, embracing me with forgiveness.

The feeling wouldn't last. One shower with the woman I adored could never cleanse me of all the horrors I'd endured, all the horrors I'd caused to happen to my father and uncle. But right now, the warmth and tenderness she showed me meant everything.

When we were both rinsed clean, our skin and hair squeaky, she pulled me close for a hug. No kiss this time. Just our warm bodies clamped together, no air between us, as the warm water flowed over us.

Heaven.

Just for this moment. Heaven.

Just for this moment, I was clean again.

My cock was hard and ready, and even in the shower, the fragrance of her arousal clung to the steamy air.

I was tempted to take her now, to move away from her just slightly and create the angle I needed to enter. But I couldn't. I had every intention of savoring every moment this morning. I didn't want to climax yet.

I reached behind her and turned off the shower water. Then I opened the door and stepped out onto the bathmat, bringing her with me. She grabbed a giant towel off her rack and wrapped it around both of us. When we were sufficiently dried off, she led me back into her bedroom.

I had every intention of kissing her entire body. I still would. But the smell of her arousal was too much.

"Get on the bed," I commanded. "Lie on your back and spread those pretty legs for me."

The depth of my own voice surprised even me. I knew she

wouldn't dare disobey me.

She didn't.

"Put your arms over your head and grab the rungs of your headboard." I hadn't brought the synthetic rope with me. Not something I took to a cemetery in the middle of the night—not when my purpose was to dig up a body and leave as quickly as possible.

She obeyed again, grasping two of the rungs, her knuckles whitening.

"Don't move. Don't move those hands no matter how much you want to. Pretend rope is binding you. Invisible rope formed only of my will to keep your hands in place."

She closed her eyes, and her chest moved up and down with her rapid breaths. Her nipples stuck out like hard berries, and a pink flush covered every inch of her milky-white flesh. Her blood was near the surface, warming her. It rustled softly beneath her skin.

I inhaled. Yes, her blood. I licked my lips. The scent of her arousal was stronger than ever. Her musk permeated the air around me, coating me in a cloud of fragrance. Her pussy was pink and swollen, full of blood and already glistening. She arched her back slightly.

"What are you going to do to me?" she asked, her voice low with desire.

"I'm going to eat you, baby. I'm going to suck every ounce of cream out of that pussy."

A sensual moan left her throat, swirling around the room and landing in my cock. So hard, it was. As hard as it had ever been. Maybe the hardest ever.

"Please..."

I lay on the bed and pushed her thighs forward, exposing

all of her beauty to my view. I closed my eyes and inhaled.

Once.

Twice.

One more time after that.

Then I opened my eyes and beheld the dazzling flesh before me. A feast. My cuspids were already elongated, sharp as ever, but that didn't stop me. I swiped my tongue from the sweet pucker of her anus all the way up to her clit.

She writhed beneath me, moaning. Her sounds fueled me, made me want her even more. I sucked on her clit, sucked her swollen labia into my mouth. My teeth nicked her slightly, producing tiny pops of capillaries. This only made me crazier. I shoved my tongue deep into her heat. I longed to sink my teeth into all that lusciousness and feed. She was so engorged, so filled with warm, delicious blood. My fangs scratched a few more places, and I lapped up the traces so perfectly mingled with her juices—a concoction unlike anything I'd tasted, so full of Erin, so full of life.

Her pussy had never tasted as delicious as it did this day.

"Please, Dante. Please. Let me come."

Under different circumstances, I would have commanded her not to come until I told her she could, but I could not deny her today. I sucked her clit hard and shoved two fingers into her wet pussy. The contractions started instantly, her walls suctioning around my fingers, making me vibrate all over.

"Come, Erin. Come for me, baby. Give me the first of many orgasms you're going to have today."

"I want to touch you. Want to feel your hair between my fingers, push your face into my pussy."

I couldn't help a smile. My face and chin were slick from her nectar, and my fangs sharp as ever. "Move your hands from that headboard, and you will pay."

I half expected her to move. Erin was willful, and her curiosity might get the best of her.

But she didn't. Her hands remained gripped around those rungs of cherry wood.

Too bad. I had a few ideas in mind of how I might punish her—punishment both she and I would immensely enjoy.

I slid up her body and clamped my mouth to hers, letting her taste herself on my tongue. My cock slid between her juicy folds, and though the urge to enter her was great, I held back. Still, I was determined to savor every moment before I found the ultimate climax.

This time the kiss was hard and passionate, not those gentle kisses we'd shared in the shower. I wanted to give her everything with this kiss—the taste of herself on my tongue, the love in my heart I felt for her, the life flowing through my veins that I partially owed to her. Life. I wanted to give her life. Life like she'd never known before. And when I gave it to her, I would take back my own life in part.

The raw desire in her kiss cleansed me even more, took me to another plane of existence, the plane where there was no hurt, no suffering, no brute violence.

I finally broke the kiss, and we both drew in a much-needed breath. Her body was flushed pink and warm, coated with a sheen of perspiration. Her fragrance had strengthened even more around us, cocooning us in an invisible shield of musk.

I slithered my tongue over her neck and shoulder, the saltiness of her sweat a complement to the musk already on my tongue. Her beautiful breasts awaited me, the nipples hard and straining. I took one between my lips and sucked. Hard. The other I twisted between my thumb and forefinger, relishing the moans from her throat.

"Take my blood, Dante. Suck it there. From my nipple."

FIFTEEN

Erin

Yes, those words had left my throat. I wanted it more than ever.

But his head popped up, his fangs still elongated. "Baby?"

His eyes were smoky and heavy lidded. Yes, he wanted to do it as much as I wanted him to. I'd felt his teeth scrape the lips of my vagina, felt his need to take my blood then. He'd wanted to.

"I want every part of me to be yours today. I want to feed every part of you from every part of me. Because as you feed from me, I feed from you. I become more yours, and you become more mine."

My words surprised even me, but I felt them with all my heart and soul. He needed me this morning. Though I knew why, I didn't know the extent. He would tell me later. I trusted this. And I trusted him with my body.

"Please, Dante."

He bent his head down over my nipple once more, his

fangs hovering over my flesh.

"Do it."

"I want to, baby. But I don't want to hurt you."

"You could never hurt me. Bite me. Take what I'm offering."

He sank his teeth into the edge of my areola.

No pain anymore. Only the pleasure, and a soft moan left my throat. My nipples were hard and straining as he took my blood there, and the sensations were so great that they traveled like lightning into me, into the very core of me, down to my pussy where they burst into my clit like water shooting from a geyser.

Too soon it was over. He released me and licked the small puncture wounds on the top of my breast.

"No," I said. "More. Please."

"I'll take more, but not from here. You have an entire body full of arteries and veins and capillaries. I won't be greedy."

"But I want you to. I want to feed you."

"You will. I know what you're feeling, Erin. I'm feeling it too. That raw need and desire for me to take your blood, for you to give me your blood. You believe me now, don't you? That this bond originated with you?"

"I believe it originated with both of us."

He smiled, his fangs still out, and damn, he was the sexiest man I'd ever laid eyes on. How was it that fangs could be sexy? But oh, they were. At least on this man.

At least on this *vampire*.

He moved down my abdomen, his fangs scraping me lightly. Goose bumps erupted on my flesh, and I imagined tiny rivers of blood forming in the wake of his teeth. He wasn't breaking my skin, of course, but in my mind's eye, I saw the blood, felt the blood.

Part of me wanted him to draw blood. I wanted to feel the puncture, the scratches, the intense pleasure-pain.

He continued down my left side, kissing my thigh, my knee, my calf, to the top of my foot and then to my toes. "Every part of you is delicious, Erin. Every part of me wants every part of you."

I closed my eyes on a sigh. "Take whatever you need. Please."

"I plan to." He kissed the tips of my toes on the other foot and then moved upward, kissing my calf, my knee, the top of my thigh again. He slid upward, gave me a quick kiss on my mouth, and then said, "You can release your hands now. Turn over onto your stomach and grab the headboard again."

I wasted no time following his orders. Once I was situated, gripping the rungs of my headboard once more, I turned my head to the side and closed my eyes, determined to give in to every ounce of pleasure he was willing to provide.

His lips, tongue, and teeth traveled over the back side of my body, and he nipped at my neck, my shoulders, my upper arms. Again I imagined the rivers of redness, aching for him to puncture me. He did not, but the flutter of his lips and tongue, the scraping of his fangs, sent me quickly into Nirvana. My pussy was on fire.

Empty and on fire.

"Please, Dante."

In truth, I had no idea what I was asking for. I wanted his cock, but I also wanted his lips, teeth, tongue. I ached for him to release me, so I could torture him as he was torturing me. I didn't have fangs to sink into his flesh, but I did have teeth. One day, I would bite him and take his blood. Not because I needed it, but because I wanted it.

Because I craved it.

He pressed on, making me arch when he tortured the small of my back and then the cheeks of my ass. Down my thighs his lips went once again, back up, and he stopped at the back of my knee, pressing kisses into it. Then back up to my ass, where he pressed his tongue in the crease, over my asshole.

If he'd told me he wanted to fuck my ass at that moment, I would've said yes. But upward he moved, gliding his tongue over my back and shoulders once more.

"Bring your knees up, baby," he said. "Show me what I long to see."

He lifted his body off me a bit so I could comply, and in an instant his cock was inside me.

"I want to fill every empty crevice of your body, Erin, until you want no one but me."

I already wanted no one but him. And he filled all my emptiness so exquisitely.

"God, Erin!" He pushed into me.

Again.

Again.

Again.

The climax started in my belly this time, attacking my pussy with a lightning bolt and then radiating out to my limbs so that even the tips of my fingers tingled.

He fucked me hard, as hard as he ever had, plunging and surging, taking me.

I went willingly.

And when he took me to the highest peak once more and then thrust hard into me with his own orgasm, he leaned down, his body warm against my back, and sank his teeth in the flesh of my shoulder.

I flew higher. As he took my blood, he gave me so much more in return. With each tug on my flesh, my pussy throbbed harder in climax, and as he swallowed the nourishment he craved, I was nourished as well.

Too soon, he removed his teeth.

I'd sunk deep into my pillow, still grasping my headboard. *No. Don't want to leave yet. Want to stay here, joined, where no one can hurt us, where peace and love are all that matter.*

His warm hands covered mine, slowly releasing my fists. Then he rolled off me, and I turned to face him. His lips and chin, as usual, were smeared with my blood. And as usual, I leaned toward him and kissed him. Just a peck, but I needed to touch him at that moment, touch my blood on his lips.

"That was incredible," I said.

He smiled, his fangs still elongated. My God, he was gorgeous.

"Incredible doesn't even begin to describe it."

I let out a tiny giggle. "I'm not sure there's a word in the English language that can describe that."

"I know there's not. I love you so much, Erin. Thank you for today."

"You don't ever have to thank me."

"I know. But I can't help it. You've given me so much, so much that I don't even deserve."

"What makes you think you don't deserve any of this?"

He closed his eyes, and for a second, I thought I saw the beginning of a tear in the corner of one of them.

But then he opened them, and though they were a little glazed over, they were dry. "My father. He died for me, Erin. He died so I could live. How can I be worthy of such sacrifice? How can I ever repay him for that?"

"I don't think he expects payment, Dante."

"No, I don't think he does. But he went through so much for me. Because of me. His body..." He squeezed his eyes shut, and this time I definitely saw the beginnings of a tear. But he opened his eyes and sniffed it back.

"What is it? You can tell me." I cupped his cheek.

Then I listened.

I listened as he described the condition of Julian's body. How he'd memorized every bruise, every scratch, every scar, every mutilation.

I gulped back the nausea that threatened me more than once.

If the captors had done this to Julian...

Couldn't go there. I couldn't. Not when he needed me to be strong.

Strength. He needed my strength right now, and I would not let him down.

Still no tears. He was holding them back. I could tell. I admired his determination.

"It's okay," I said, stroking his face. "Let it go, Dante. It's okay to cry for your father."

One tear fell, but he shook his head. "I can't. My father died for me. I can't let him down."

"How does grieving for his life and what he went through let him down?"

"I can't allow myself to—" He shook his head again. "I just can't."

I wasn't a psychiatric nurse, but I knew bottling something like this up inside a person never led to anything good.

But now was not the time.

Dante was strong, stronger than perhaps even *he* believed.

"I'm here for you," I said. "Tell me what you need."

"I need to sleep. Here. Next to you. For a few hours. Then I'm expecting a phone call."

The phone call came late in the afternoon. Dante and I washed up quickly, and then I accompanied him to the mortuary to pick up his father's remains.

Julian was oddly absent during this.

"Why isn't your father here?" I asked.

"Why should he be?"

"These are his remains."

"No. He doesn't think of it that way anymore. These remains aren't him. In a way, they never were. We aren't our bodies, Erin."

That was deep. A little too deep for me at the moment. I wasn't sure what to say.

"That's the only thing keeping me from freaking out now," he continued. "That the torture my father endured only happened to his body. Not to him. Not to the essence of who he is."

I nodded. Did Dante feel this way about the torture that *he* had endured? I didn't want to think about the specifics, but after he'd described the condition of his father's body, I couldn't seem to *not* think about it.

I swallowed down the thought as best I could. "Do you believe that?"

"I have to," he said somberly.

Then I understood.

He had to in order to cope right now. If he let his guard

down, if he truly mourned for what his father had endured, he wouldn't get through the next few days of filing in the probate court to claim Julian's estate.

What about after that?

What if he never mourned?

What if he never faced what had happened to his own body? Perhaps we weren't our bodies, but our flesh was part of us, at least while we were living.

Dante had to accept that eventually.

I sighed. Nothing much I could do except take things a day at a time. A minute at a time if need be. I would be there for Dante, and if he needed to suppress his pain, I'd let him.

For now.

But not forever.

He gripped the gold urn containing Julian's remains as we stood by my car in the mortuary parking lot. "Now what?" he said more to himself than to me.

"You want to scatter them somewhere?"

"Not without my sister," he said.

Then a cool rush of air at the back of my neck...and a voice.

I gasped when Julian appeared in front of us, a few milliseconds after his voice had registered in my ear.

"You and your sister may do what you wish with most of them," he said to Dante.

"Most of them?" Dante said.

"Yes. A small amount belongs to someone else."

SIXTEEN

DANTE

"Who?" I asked.

"The voodoo priestess."

"Bea?"

Julian chuckled. "You didn't think she'd cast that shield around the cemetery for nothing, did you? I told you she would be well compensated."

"With..."

"Vampire ashes are a powerful addition to any spell, at least according to Bea. And they're difficult to come by, as you can imagine."

"But if no one knows we exist..."

"Bea does. She always has, mostly because she's a medium and has been inhabited by vampires as well as by humans."

Erin scoffed. "You mean you got her to agree to help you without promising her the entire urn? Did you glamour her?"

My father smiled. "I can see why you might think that, but no, I didn't. Glamouring isn't used unless it's absolutely necessary to accomplish a greater good. For example, I glamoured the guards at the cemetery so Dante could recover my body and claim my estate. He and his sister need the money. But if Bea had refused to cast the shield, I could have found another way to protect Dante and River."

"She agreed when you offered her your ashes?" I said.

"I asked her what payment she required. She's the one who brought up the ashes. And yes," he said to Erin, "she wanted all of them. But I convinced her that my children needed to have most of my remains. Measure out one ounce and put it in a zippered plastic bag. Then take it to Bea under the bridge. She assured me they will be used only sparingly."

"I'm tempted to give her regular old ashes," I said. "How would she know the difference?"

"Give her what was promised. A man whose word is nothing is nothing himself."

"But you're...dead, Dad."

"My body is dead, Dante. I am still me, and I will not go back on my word. I taught you better than that."

I nodded. "You did, and I'm sorry. I just hate to part with any part of you."

"Those crumbs in that urn aren't me, son. Surely you know that by now, having seen me in my ghostly form."

Erin brushed her fingertips over my forearm, infusing me with her warmth. She said nothing, but the simple touch was a comfort.

I cleared my throat. "I know."

"Bea protected you and your cousin last night. Don't forget that."

"Maybe she didn't. Maybe we just got in and out quickly and no one realized we were there."

My father shook his head. "I'm sorry. You're wrong. The

dark presence was there."

Ice prickled the back of my neck. "Dad?" I rubbed at it.

"That's not me. That's your own body warning you. You believe me. Don't you?"

"I believe you, Julian," Erin said. "After everything I've seen recently, how can I *not* believe you?"

"She's a smart girl, Dante. Hold on to her."

I had no intention of ever letting Erin go, and my father knew we were bonded by blood anyway. But I got what he meant. "I won't."

"I'm coming with you to see Bea," she said.

"No. It's not safe for you there. Those vamps—"

"—don't come out during the day," she finished for me.

"That we know of. That doesn't mean they won't. What if they smell you and—"

"I'm going. I want to talk to Bea anyway."

"What for?"

"I want to find out how Abe is doing, and...I want to ask her something else too."

"What?"

She reddened. "I want to see if she has a potion for me or something."

"Are you feeling okay?"

"I'm fine. I'm a nurse, Dante. If I had a medical problem, I wouldn't be going to Bea."

"Then what do you need a potion for?"

"To disguise my scent."

I inhaled. As always, she was everywhere. All around me. Making the air sweeter and purer. "Why would you— Oh" To keep the Claiborne vamps away, of course.

"It's worth a shot." She patted the small purse on her hip.

"And I brought lots of twenties."

"But..."

"But what, Dante?" my father said. "It's a brilliant idea. Bea is quite powerful. I'd think you'd believe that by now."

But...what if *I* could no longer smell Erin?

I was being selfish. Erin's safety was all that mattered. "I'm sorry."

"Sorry for what?" she asked.

"I just don't... Your fragrance. It's so much a part of me. Of *us*. I don't want to lose that. You're the only human I can smell now. If it goes away... I just can't."

"You know how I told you that we are not our bodies?" My father smiled. "Erin is not her fragrance, Dante. Her fragrance comes from her blood, from her ancestry. You know this. But it is not *who* she is. Besides, you have a blood bond with her. You will most likely always be able to—"

"Wait, wait, wait." Erin reached out for my father's arm, but her hand whooshed into air.

"What?" he asked.

"What do you mean, from my *ancestry*?"

SEVENTEEN

Erin

"You haven't told her." Julian's words were a statement, not a question.

"No, Dad."

"Told me what? What the hell are you keeping from me?"

"Do we have to do this now?" Dante asked.

"Oh, hell, yes, we do. Honesty, Dante. Do you really think anything else will bother me at this point?"

"Not here. Not in broad daylight in a public parking lot, Erin."

"*Now*," I said through clenched teeth. "No one is here, and I refuse to go one step farther with you until you level with me."

"I should go," Julian said.

"Dad, stay," Dante said. "Please."

"If you think I won't lay into you with your father here, think again." I turned to the ghost. "You're welcome to stay or go. It doesn't matter to me either way."

"I know damned well you'll lay into me if you want to." Dante grasped the golden urn holding Julian's ashes, his knuckles tense and white. "You have every right to. I want my dad here because he knows more about our history than I do. He might be able to explain some of this better than I can."

"Fine. Then please stay, Julian."

"If you both want me to," he said. "But I do suggest we go somewhere else. Somewhere private."

A half hour later, we were back at my place, sitting—Julian stood; ghosts didn't sit, apparently—around my small kitchen table.

"Spill it," I said gruffly.

Dante inhaled, held the air with his chest puffed out for a few seconds, and then exhaled. "As kids, we're taught to distinguish scents based on certain characteristics. Blonds have a citrusy smell, for example."

"I'm not blond."

"No. Then redheads. They taste kind of like lavender. Males taste different from females. You know."

"As a matter of fact, I don't know. And I'm not a redhead."

"Tell her, Dante."

"Yes, for the love of everything holy, tell me, damn it!" I was close to pulling my hair out of every follicle in my scalp, *after* I pulled out all of Dante's.

"Dark-haired humans with light skin... Have you ever wondered why your skin is so sensitive to the sun?"

"No. I'm a medical professional. I know why it's sensitive to the sun. I'm fair. I don't have a lot of melanin. I burn easily."

"Have you ever wondered why you prefer the night shift?"

"I've always been a night owl. So is my brother. So is my—"

I clasped my hand over my mouth.

No way. No. Just no. I was *not* a vampire.

"Which one, Erin?" Julian asked. "Your mother or your father?"

"My mother. She's a cashier at a local grocery store. A local grocery store that's open twenty-four hours."

No, my mother was *not* a vampire.

"I know what you're thinking," Dante said. "It's not true. Your mother isn't a vampire. But somewhere in your ancestry, there was a vampire, most likely on your mother's side. It's part of your scent and why it's so appealing. Your vampire ancestor could have lived centuries ago. He probably did."

Julian cleared his throat.

"What?" Dante turned to him.

"That's what you were taught," he said, "and that's what we thought at the time. But my father and Jack Hebert have done quite a bit of research on this in the last ten years, some of which I've learned about recently."

I stared blankly at Dante and his father. My body went numb.

Where was this going? I was afraid to find out. I didn't want to know, yet I did. I burned for the knowledge.

Silence.

And more silence, until the ringing in my ears became unbearable.

"Would someone fucking talk, please?" I nearly screamed.

"Go, Dad," Dante said. "You obviously know more than I do. Everyone seems to these days."

"Don't," Julian said. "I only know because I was standing

over my father while he was researching one day, before he could see me. I read what was on his computer screen."

"Then he doesn't know you know?"

"No. And we need to keep it that way."

Numbness. Cold numbness. I heard the words, but I felt nothing.

I screamed. I screamed bloody murder.

Minutes after screaming, I stopped feeling. I'd just wait. Wait for Dante and his father to tell me what I already knew in the marrow of my bones.

I was part vampire.

Whether it was two generations ago or two hundred, I had a vampire in my family tree.

And because of that, my scent was irresistible to vampires, apparently.

Vampires, who couldn't smell each other.

How did any of this make sense?

"Are you listening, Erin?" Julian asked.

I popped out of my stupor. Sort of. "Sure."

"I'm sorry to lay this on you," he said.

"Yeah. I mean...what?"

"All vampire descendants have dark hair and fair skin, plus a scent that vampires find enticing. You're different, though, Erin. Your brother as well. Because your scent is so strong to vampires, it's likely that only a few generations separate you from your vampire ancestor."

"Are you saying—"

"Most likely no further than a great-grandparent. And it's possible that—"

"My mother." No emotion laced my voice. Pure monotone. Pure robot.

Julian nodded. "It's possible."

"This is still unlikely," Dante said. "Right, Dad? I mean, there aren't enough of us to..."

"To what, Dante?" Julian shook his head. "It only takes one."

My mother.

People always said I looked like her. I did. I had her dark hair, her fair skin. My eyes, though. The light green came from my blond-haired—well, gray now—father. Jay had blue eyes, like my mother. Also dark hair and fair skin.

Did my mother have the same needs as Dante? Did she drink –

Oh, God. So can't go there.

My father's blood.

The words emerged in my mind despite my will for them not to.

No, not my mother.

My grandfather. Had to be. My great-grandfather maybe.

"Erin?" Dante said gently, caressing my forearm.

"What?"

"You're a million miles away."

"Sorry. Just trying to process the fact that my mother might be a vampire."

"You would have seen clues, Erin. Can you think of any?"

I shook my head.

"What about your grandparents on her side?"

"My grandfather." I cleared my throat. "He's great. Always was there for Jay and me."

"What about your grandmother?"

"I never knew her. She died giving birth to my mom."

EIGHTEEN

DANTE

My father and I exchanged a glance, which didn't go unnoticed by Erin.

"What?" she asked.

"Does your mother have any siblings?" Julian asked.

"She's an only child. Why?" Erin bit her bottom lip.

"Tell her, son," Julian said.

"Pregnancy is difficult for vampire women. I've already told you that they're only fertile once every couple of years, so getting pregnant is difficult. But...even with advanced medicine, pregnancy is still hard on them. My own mother—" I gulped, unable to continue.

"I'm sorry," she said. "I know. You've told me, and I'm sorry."

"It's possible your grandmother was a vampire. But human women still die in childbirth, so there's no guarantee. I'm sorry, Erin."

"Sorry..." she murmured.

"Baby, are you okay?"

"She just needs a minute," my father said.

"Damn!" I brought my fist down on her table. "She had accepted me. All of me. How could I make such a stupid mistake? And now—"

Her daze seemed to fall away. And she was angry.

"How could you keep something like this from me? After all we've been through, Dante. All your talk about honesty. Was that all bullshit?"

"No, of course no—"

"How? How could you?" Erin stood, her face reddening, her hands clenched into fists.

I couldn't help inhaling. Her blood was boiling, forcing itself to the surface of her skin, making her red.

Red...and delicious.

Dark chocolate. Blackberries. Tin and copper. Milk and estrogen.

Then there were the dark-haired ones with light skin— those who, somewhere hundreds of generations ago in their family tree, were descended from a vampire. Their blood was the ultimate concoction, the Champagne of plasma. Bold and tannic yet fruity and divine. Peach, plum, blackberry. Leather, coffee, the darkest of chocolate. Tin, zinc, laced with violet and apple and estrogen. Even the men smelled of traces of milky estrogen.

And testosterone. From a woman. An angry woman.

I inhaled again, letting the fragrance infuse me with more need. More ache. More longing. More raw, primal urge.

The smell of her rage was intoxicating.

I didn't need to feed. Not until the next morning. I'd proved earlier that I was learning to control myself when I waited with Erin, waited to feed because I wanted to savor her, feel alive with her.

But something new rose within me.

Something foreign.

Something dangerous.

Something beyond my shreds of control.

"Leave," I said to my father between clenched teeth.

"Dante," he said. "I know what you're feeling. I can't smell her, but I see what her body is doing, and what it must be doing to you. This isn't you. You're stronger than this. You can control yourself. Let me teach you—"

I bared my fangs to my father's ghost.

Control? I'd learned it, found it through my love for Erin. My duty and obligation to see to her needs first, before my own. I'd shown the ultimate control this morning, when I'd taken her and fed from her slowly, evenly.

I *had* control. I'd proved it. I had it now, but I'd take what I wanted—what Erin and I both wanted. I drew in a breath. Her musk was already permeating the room.

I needed her.

What I *didn't* need was a lecture from my father.

"Leave," I said again.

"Don't do this. Don't destroy what you've—"

"Get the fuck out of here, damn it. Or watch me take her right here."

"I won't allow you to do this. You *won't* do this. Know that I would not leave if I believed it of you." He disappeared in a flash.

I inhaled once more, her steamy scent racing through my veins, my muscles, my bones.

My bare bones.

Nothing but bones supported me as I stood and grabbed her, snarling.

"Dante?"

A soft whimper.

A frightened whimper.

An *aroused* whimper.

I inhaled. Indignation. Rage. Lust. Racing blood. A potent combination I was powerless to resist.

"You're mine, Erin. Mine. And I'm going to take you the way I'm meant to take you. Violently. Forcibly. With you tied up and helpless, begging for me to take your body and your blood."

THE QUEEN

Yes, Dante. Lose control. Seize what you crave. Be what you're meant to be. Take what you want from her as I took what I wanted from you.

Everything is working.

You've asked me for answers.

Now you know the first of the questions.

The answers will come when you're ready.

My plan is underway.

Soon you will become mine.

Forever.

BLOOD BOND SAGA

PART 8

DANTE

I couldn't help inhaling. Her blood was boiling, forcing itself to the surface of her skin, making her red.

Red...and delicious.

Dark chocolate. Blackberries. Tin and copper. Milk and estrogen.

Then there were the dark-haired ones with light skin— those who, somewhere hundreds of generations ago in their family tree, were descended from a vampire. Their blood was the ultimate concoction, the Champagne of plasma. Bold and tannic yet fruity and divine. Peach, plum, blackberry. Leather, coffee, the darkest of chocolate. Tin, zinc, laced with violet and apple and estrogen. Even the men smelled of traces of milky estrogen.

And testosterone. From a woman. An angry woman.

I inhaled again, letting the fragrance infuse me with more need. More ache. More longing. More raw, primal urge.

The smell of her rage was intoxicating.

I didn't need to feed. Not until the next morning. I'd proved earlier that I was learning to control myself when I waited with Erin, waited to feed because I wanted to savor her, feel alive with her.

But something new rose within me.

Something foreign.

Something dangerous.

Something beyond my shreds of control.

"Leave," I said to my father between clenched teeth.

"Dante," he said. "I know what you're feeling. I can't smell her, but I see what her body is doing, and what it must be doing to you. This isn't you. You're stronger than this. You can control yourself. Let me teach you—"

I bared my fangs to my father's ghost.

Control? I'd learned it, found it through my love for Erin. My duty and obligation to see to her needs first, before my own. I'd shown the ultimate control this morning, when I'd taken her and fed from her slowly, evenly.

I *had* control. I'd proved it. I had it now, but I'd take what I wanted—what Erin and I both wanted. I drew in a breath. Her musk was already permeating the room.

I needed her.

What I *didn't* need was a lecture from my father.

"Leave," I said again.

"Don't do this. Don't destroy what you've—"

"Get the fuck out of here, damn it. Or watch me take her right here."

"I won't allow you to do this. You *won't* do this. Know that I would not leave if I believed it of you." He disappeared in a flash.

I inhaled once more, her steamy scent racing through my veins, my muscles, my bones.

My bare bones.

Nothing but bones supported me as I stood and grabbed her, snarling.

"Dante?"

A soft whimper.

A frightened whimper.

An *aroused* whimper.

I inhaled. Indignation. Rage. Lust. Racing blood. A potent combination I was powerless to resist.

"You're mine, Erin. Mine. And I'm going to take you the way I'm meant to take you. Violently. Forcibly. With you tied up and helpless, begging for me to take your body and your blood."

ONE

Erin

Anger boiled through my veins, turning them into rivers of raging red—rivers I could feel racing through my body, tearing through my heart.

Blood.

This was what Dante felt when he touched me. Now I felt it too.

My body blazed as if on fire. Red gold rushed through me, making me throb, toying with me, and soon I could no longer differentiate between the fury and the raw yearning, the storm and the ache.

I didn't want to want him in this moment. In fact, I wanted to hate him for keeping the secret of my ancestry from me, even more so for wanting to take me forcibly. Violently.

But I didn't.

I *couldn't*.

The pulsing between my legs was stronger than it had ever been. My nipples were so hard they could have cut glass.

Each follicle on my body tensed, forcing every hair upward. My heart pounded in a distorted rhythm—a jazzy drumbeat that buffeted me both inside and out.

Always the music when Dante and I were together, only this time the chords were disharmonic and tense...but all the more beautiful, all the more symphonious.

The peppery scent of my arousal was thick in the air, and as Dante inhaled, its effect on him was more than evident. His lips were firm and red, and his fangs protruded from his gums in sharp points. Fiery amber rimmed his irises, more pronounced than I'd ever seen. His hair was unruly as he shoved his fingers through it, sweat binding strands of it to his cheeks and forehead. The bulge in his jeans grew larger, harder, and he curled his hands into fists.

I'd never seen him look more frightening.

I'd never seen him look more magnificent.

Desire pulsed through me, raw and real.

He's insane. I need to tell him to leave. To get the hell away from me.

But the words didn't come.

I didn't want them to come.

Instead—

"You want to tie me up? Take me violently? Show me who's in charge here? Do it, Dante. Do it now."

He was on me in an instant, his tongue devouring my mouth like a sea serpent plunging through ocean waves.

Shudders racked my body, my heart hammering and my skin tingling. Yes, this was what he felt. I felt it too.

I wanted it as much as he did.

I pushed him away and drew in a deep breath. "That all you got?"

A low growl vibrated from his throat, giving me chills.

"Tell me you want this," he said, his voice low and husky. "Tell me, and I'll give you everything we both ache for."

I shivered. Partly from fear—a good fear—a fear that traveled through me at light speed, inflaming me all the way to my bones. Partly from my being so turned on I couldn't see straight.

"I already told you," I said through clenched teeth. "Do it, Dante. Give me everything. Everything you've got."

In a flash, I was in his arms, being hauled up the stairs to the bedroom.

"You're mine, Erin." He ripped the clothes from my body with his teeth, until only shreds of fabric remained.

I stood naked before him, as if I were an offering to a god. A god I wanted to please more than I wanted anything else, including my next breath.

"All mine. That blood boiling in your arteries right now is mine. This beautiful body is mine. That anger, that gorgeous rage pulsing through you—it makes you smell more divine than ever, look more beautiful than ever. It's all mine, Erin. All of it. Do you understand me?"

I nodded. "I understand."

He licked his lips. "So pink. So dazzling. Like a rose-colored diamond. Mine. I'll have you every way. Every way I want to. Gently if I want to. Violently if I want to."

I squeezed my thighs together, trying, but failing, to ease the ache between them.

Violently if I want to.

Such words shouldn't make me ache all the more.

But they did. They so did.

Was this what it meant to be part vampire? This strong

urge, this incessant longing? The attraction I felt for Dante? Was it more than a blood bond?

I wrapped my arms around his neck and pulled him toward me, our mouths meeting in a clash of lips and teeth.

The kiss was raw and hungry. He took from me with his tongue, and rather than giving him what he sought, I took from him as well. Both of us consuming in a rage of ripe desire.

A kiss of pure urgency and desperate need.

A kiss to take what we were each so willing to give.

Our lips slid against each other's, our tongues swirling, until I pushed him away once more, struggling to inhale a much-needed breath.

Dante inhaled as well, both of us panting.

"You will not push me away again, Erin. Is that clear?"

Sweat trickled down from my brow, stinging my eyes. Dante's lips were swollen from the hard kiss, his fangs still elongated and sexy. An ache emerged within me—an ache I didn't understand at first, but my body did. I nodded timidly and then closed my eyes and turned my head, exposing my neck.

A low growl.

But no puncture.

I opened my eyes.

"That's not what I'm hungry for right now." The amber around his irises glowed hot. "Get on the bed and spread your legs."

He'd said he was going to tie me up. Had he changed his mind? Disappointment vibrated through me. "Aren't you—"

"Don't make me repeat myself, Erin."

His gruff, commanding tone turned my legs to jelly, and I fell onto the bed, letting my legs fall to each side.

He knelt down between them, closed his eyes, and inhaled. "Mine," he growled once more.

"Yours," I whispered.

"I'm going to eat you, Erin. All of you. Suck every bit of honey your body has to offer me. Then I'm going to fuck you so hard and so violently and make you come again and again and again. And when you beg me to stop, I'll fuck you harder."

I groaned softly. "Yes. Please."

He clamped his lips onto my labia and sucked.

I gripped two handfuls of my comforter and arched my back. So good, how he made me feel. So fucking good.

My nipples strained, so tight and hard. As if reading my mind, Dante reached one hand forward and took a nipple between his thumb and forefinger and tugged.

"Yes, baby, please," I breathed.

More. Give me more. Take me to the highest mountaintop, to the most glorious place in the blue sky.

I fingered my other nipple, pinching it, while Dante continued his welcome assault on my pussy. His teeth nicked my sensitive flesh, but the tiny prickles only spurred me further into ecstasy, further toward that peak—the peak that I'd come to know only with this man.

Only with this *vampire*.

My rage burned a fiery crimson, and with it, my lust.

More.

More.

More.

I writhed beneath his touch, my skin prickling and my nerves—

"Dante! Erin!"

DANTE

*N*o. *Not now. Please not now.*

"Dante." Erin pushed at my head.

I reluctantly let her go, already missing the scent and taste of her. I licked my lips, relishing in her juices, and then stood. "River."

Erin's tattered clothes lay in pieces all around the room. Damn. I'd shredded them. *Shredded* them.

"Go see what he needs," she said. "I'll put something...else on."

I nodded but couldn't look away from her. She was still so pink and beautiful. Her carotid artery pulsed visibly in her neck. So enticing. Had I truly refused what she'd offered in favor of a hard fuck? A turbulent fuck? My dick was still granite in my jeans, and my teeth were still long and sharp.

Time to put that newfound self-control to work. After one more growl.

Her eyes widened at the snarl, but then she closed them halfway, showing her heavy-lidded arousal.

Now for the control.

"Erin, I hope you—"

"I'm fine, Dante. You know I'd never do anything I didn't want to do."

"I love you." I stroked her cheek gently, the blood beneath her warm pink skin nearly doing me in. "We'll definitely finish this later."

She smiled. "I love you too."

My erection hadn't gone down much, but at least it was a little more bearable. Seeing my cousin standing in the living room should do the trick. I turned, left the bedroom, and walked downstairs.

Yup. River was the antidote. But he didn't look like himself.

"What is it, Riv? And how did you get in here?"

"The door was unlocked."

Shit. Not too smart, especially with rogue vamps on the loose. I hadn't been thinking clearly when I took Erin upstairs. Hell, I hadn't been thinking at all.

"Dante," he continued, his voice tight and shaky, "it's Lucy. She's gone."

Ice chilled my veins. "What?"

"She's gone. Somehow she got out of the hospital."

"Did she get released?"

"No. She's disappeared." He raked his fingers through his hair. "Like the others. Man. I... Shit." He paced around the small living area.

"Oh my God. Erin..." This would devastate her. Lucy was her best friend.

A second later, she walked swiftly down the stairs in a pair of shorts and a tank top, her hair freshly brushed and hanging sleekly over her shoulders.

I inhaled. Her scent, still so arousing and musky.

River inhaled as well. Yeah, my fangs were definitely here to stay.

"Hi, River," she said. "What's going on?"

"Baby..." I began.

"It's Lucy," River said. "I hate to have to tell you this, but I need you guys."

"What?" Erin's voice shook. "Is she okay? Did she need more surgery?"

"She's...gone," he said. "Disappeared from the hospital. Like the others."

She clasped her hand to her mouth. "No! Oh my God. Have you called the cops?"

"He *is* the cops, baby," I said.

"Yeah. Right. But what about..."

"I went to see her at the hospital, and some blues were there, taking the report," River said, rubbing his temples. "The department is on it. I tried to call you, Dante, but you didn't pick up."

"I'm sorry. I didn't hear my phone."

Had my phone died? I should have heard it. Enhanced vampire hearing and all. On the other hand, I was all ensconced in a tryst with Erin unlike anything I'd ever experienced. He was lucky I'd heard his voice when he walked in the door.

"It's okay, man. I just don't—" He rubbed at his brow, beads of sweat emerging from his pores. "I don't know what to do."

"We'll figure it out, Riv."

Perhaps, then, you've read the most important work of all.

Bea's words. She'd uttered them right before my father told Erin and me to run. What did they mean? And why did they pop into my mind now? I gave them no further thought, though, because Erin looked absolutely petrified.

"What if..." Erin's eyes were wide.

"What, baby?"

"What if she shifts? She's fresh out of surgery. What if her control..."

"I don't know," I said. "Riv?"

"I only know shifters exist, and that they can control their shifting. The moon doesn't dictate it, as legend would have you believe. But in Lucy's condition, I don't know. She obviously shifted back after she got stabbed in the cemetery." He sank his head into his hands. "We have to find her."

"We will." My libido and teeth had finally leveled off. All it took was my cousin telling me another woman had disappeared—this one who meant so much to both Erin and River.

"You okay?" I said.

"I feel so helpless. It's crazy. We had one date. It's not like we're..." He shook his head.

"How about you, baby?" I said to Erin.

"Not even slightly. I was angry with her for keeping such a big thing from me. And now I feel shitty about that. But this isn't about me. This is about Lucy. This just got personal for all of us. We need to figure out what's going on. Why these women have been disappearing." She grasped my forearm. "Dante, we have to find her. We *have* to."

"Baby, we will. Somehow. Riv and your brother are cops. We'll get to the bottom of this."

"Jay." Erin rubbed her forehead. "I have to tell him. About everything. About you two. About Lucy. About all of it."

All of it.

Guilt lashed out at me. Erin didn't *know* all of it. She still didn't know my sister was pregnant with her brother's child. Still, I felt it was Emilia's story to tell, not mine. I wasn't sure Erin would see it the same way, though, when she ultimately found out.

I looked to River, but he was distraught, obviously thinking about Lucy.

Lucy had to be the focus right now, not Emilia and the fact that she hadn't told Jay he was going to be a father.

"I should take a few days off," Erin was saying. "But how can I? We're shorthanded as it is, and now with Lucy gone..." She shook her head. "I don't know what to do. Renee, one of the other nurses on the night shift, has already said she's looking for another job."

"You need to do what you think is right," I told her. "We'll both support you, right, Riv?"

River didn't respond.

"Riv?"

"What? Yeah, sure."

I wasn't sure he knew what he was saying yes to.

"I'm not comfortable at University anymore. Not with all the disappearances. But I can't quit. I need the money."

"No, you don't," I said. "I'm going to be a rich man when my father's estate is probated, and that will be soon. River has seen to that. Everything I have is yours."

She smiled weakly. "You're wonderful, Dante, but I can't take your money. I can't live off someone else. It's not who I am. Besides, I love nursing. I get a lot out of it, even on the days when I'm ready to throw in the towel."

"Who says it's forever?" I said. "I'd love it if you quit University, at least until we find the women who've disappeared. You can find work somewhere else. A good nurse will always be in demand."

"But I can't. I can't leave the hospital shorthanded. They're desperate right now."

"I understand, baby. I do. But your safety is so important to me. I haven't been comfortable with you there for a while now. You know that. Someone there fed on you. Sure, it seems to have stopped now—" I gasped when a thought speared into my mind.

"What?"

"That resident. The one you almost—" Couldn't even think the word. "You said he just came back, right?"

"Logan? A couple days ago, yeah."

I'd just seen her naked. There hadn't been any new marks on her thigh, or anywhere on her, for that matter. None but my own. "Never mind."

"Come on, Dante. Spill it. Why are you asking me about Logan Crown?"

Crown.

I'd seen that name. Logan Crown. No, not exactly, but similar. Shit.

"Where's your laptop, Erin?" I asked.

"Over on the sofa table."

I grabbed it, brought it into the kitchen, and fired it up.

Damn. There it was. "Check this out. Both of you."

Erin and River stood behind me, looking over my shoulders.

"Nocturnal Truth," River said. "That's the site Bill used to get information on your blood bond."

"Yeah. And they claim to have a translation of the entire *Vampyre Texts*. But that's not what concerns me at the moment. Check this out right here. The email address to contact for more information."

$\mathcal{E}rin$

"$\mathbf{L}$ucien Crown." My heart sped up a little, but over what? "Same last name as Logan."

"Right," Dante said.

"There are a lot of Crowns out there," River said.

"Are there? Maybe. But it's not like Smith or Jones."

"You think Logan is a vampire?" I asked.

"I don't know."

"How would he have gotten tied up and left in a supply closet, then? Couldn't he have glamoured..." I stopped.

"What is it?" River asked.

"There have been instances at the hospital. Instances where things have happened and no one recalls anything. Like the disappearing patients, for example. How did they get out with not a single person seeing them? It's a hospital. There's always somebody around." I shook my head. "But it still doesn't compute. He couldn't have been kidnapped and then returned tied up if he was a vampire. He would have glamoured whoever had him and gotten away."

"Not necessarily," Dante said. "Not if the person who had him was another vampire."

"There's an easy way to find out. We sniff him," River said. "If he's a vampire, he won't have a scent."

"I sure smelled his testosterone and adrenaline when he almost—" Dante cleared his throat. "*You* sniff him. I can't smell anyone but Erin, remember?"

"Can you smell those kinds of hormones on a vampire?" I asked.

"Yeah," River said. "But vampires don't have a unique scent like humans and other creatures do. At least not to us."

Logan is not a vampire. Logan is not a vampire. I repeated the mantra in my mind.

What if he was? And what if he'd been feeding on me? He hadn't since he'd returned. Dante would have known.

This was all too much to deal with. I'd wondered why they let Logan start working in the ER again so soon after he returned. Perhaps he'd glamoured the other physicians...

Perhaps he'd glamoured me...

No. Couldn't go there.

Logan is not a vampire.

"There's one way to find out. Let's find this Logan guy, and I'll give him a good sniff." River stood. "But before we do that, we need to find Lucy."

"Yes." Lucy, of course. I'd gotten so caught up in the Logan hypothesis that I hadn't given Lucy a thought for the last several minutes. Guilt hit me like a brick. "Lucy's way more important right now."

"I questioned everyone at the hospital as soon as I found out," River said. "I wasn't on duty, but they all know me anyway.

No one knew anything. No one had seen anything."

"Why didn't any of us think of this before?" Dante said. "Someone is glamouring people at the hospital. If it's not Logan, it's someone else. There's a vampire there, somewhere. Or a human who knows how to glamour."

"That's not possible," River said. "Glamouring requires vampire blood. Humans can hypnotize, but it's not exactly the same thing."

I cleared my throat. "You said glamouring requires vampire blood. Does that mean anyone with vampire blood can glamour?"

"I don't know," River said. "Why?"

"Apparently *I* have vampire blood."

"Most people with vamp blood don't even know they have it," Dante said. "For all intents and purposes, they're human."

"He's right. I didn't mean to be literal. Only full-blooded vamps can glamour. At least as far as I know."

"Oh." I wasn't sure why I felt disappointed. I had no desire to glamour anyone.

"Are you working tonight, Erin?" River asked.

"I'm supposed to."

"Is this Dr. Crown working as well?"

"Probably. Like I said, we're shorthanded all the way around."

"Good. I'll come by and check him out tonight while I'm investigating Lucy's disappearance." He shoved his hand through his short hair. "God."

"Riv, are you sure you're okay?"

"Yeah." He cleared his throat once more. "Like I said, We only had one date."

I didn't buy it. River was visibly upset. Had he fallen in

love with Lucy? "I'll go to work tonight so I'm there when you see Logan. Plus, I want to ask my own questions about Lucy. But then..." I sighed.

"What, baby?"

"I hate leaving them shorthanded. I truly do. But I have time off coming. I'm going to take it. I'm going to help you guys figure out what's going on, where these patients have been going."

"Actually," River said. "You might be able to help us more if you stay at the hospital for now. You can be our eyes and ears there."

"Not if someone glamours me, I can't."

"She has a point, Riv," Dante said. "And I can't stomach the idea of anyone glamouring her."

"Believe me. I've been watching all of these disappearances. I even went to talk to Cynthia North when she was returned. I haven't been able to find out anything by being in the hospital."

"But you have access to the records if you're there," River said.

"Doesn't do me any good if the records don't exist. All it takes is knowledge of all our backups and archives, and then a glamour, a delete, and *poof*, no more records."

"Another good point, Riv. Plus, I don't want her anywhere near any of this. I want her safe."

"If I honestly thought I'd be more good to you at work, I'd stay in a heartbeat. I've already told you how much I hate leaving them in a bind. But this has gotten personal now. Lucy is gone. We need to find her. We need to solve this mystery once and for all."

FOUR

DANTE

My father had been noticeably absent since I'd kicked him out of Erin's place.

My self-control had taken a beating when Erin's rage and testosterone had inflamed me with lust.

Shit. My father. We still had to take his ashes to Bea, as well.

In that instant, he appeared.

Erin nearly lost her footing. "Julian. You've got to stop doing that."

"Sorry. I'm not sure there's a subtle entry available for my kind."

"You can't kind of fade in, or something?" she said.

He laughed. "This isn't Hollywood. It doesn't work that way."

I felt conspicuous. The last time I'd seen my father's ghost, I'd been in a lust-fueled rage, ready to take Erin violently and forcibly.

"Dad," I said quietly.

"It's over, Dante," he said. "Life—no pun intended—is too short to rehash things that don't ultimately matter. I take it you two are all right?" He nodded to Erin.

"We're fine. Dante would never hurt me. I know that."

"I know that as well. If I thought otherwise, you wouldn't have gotten rid of me quite so easily." He turned to River. "I heard about Lucy. What do you know so far?"

"Nothing. I questioned everyone I saw at the hospital, but no one knows anything."

"A vampire might be behind this, Dad. Someone who's capable of glamouring a large group of people at one time. Is that possible?"

"I've never heard of such a thing, but elders may be able to do it. The glamouring power gets stronger with age."

River sighed. "I guess we go to Bill. Or to the *Texts*."

"Speaking of the *Texts*," my father said, "I was able to expedite the probate hearing on my will. You're my personal representative, Dante. You'll need to appear in court tomorrow. Everything else has been taken care of."

"What about the filing? The documents?" I asked.

"Taken care of."

I nodded. Glamouring did come in handy, though I still didn't like it. I regarded my father—the man who'd taught me never to glamour unless it was a life or death situation. Emilia and I getting our father's money was hardly life or death, but the rogue vamps after Erin? Lucy's disappearance? Those could very well be life or death situations, and my father's money would make it easier for River and me to investigate.

"Riv, I hate to ask you this, but—"

"Yeah. I'll do it."

"You don't even know what I'm going to ask."

"You want me to take a leave of absence from work until we figure all of this out. I'll do it. I'll use my glamour. I don't like it, but this is important enough."

"I agree," my father said solemnly.

"That's not what I was going to say. I was going to ask if Lucy said anything to you that might be a clue. You know, the last time you saw her before she disappeared."

"No. Believe me. I've gone over and over every conversation with her in my head. She slept most of the time. She was recovering from surgery."

"And you weren't in the hospital when she disappeared?"

"No. I left her room for a while to return a few phone calls. I didn't want to disturb her. And yes, I know it's a big red flag that I just happened to be out of her room when she disappeared. Whoever took her must know what I am. If it's a vamp using glamour, he'd know he couldn't glamour me."

"Precisely," my father said. "It seems pretty obvious that we're dealing with a vampire."

"What if the vampire was older and had more glamouring power?" Erin said. "Could he glamour a younger vampire?"

"No," my father said. "Glamouring doesn't work against other vampires. At least not that I've ever heard."

"Do you think it could be the same vampires who are after me?" Erin asked.

"We don't have any way of knowing," I said. "But it could be the same one who's been feeding from you." Just the thought had my fangs itching to descend.

"Control it, Dante," my father said.

"What if I don't want to control it? Someone is taking what's mine."

"Easy," Erin said. "Trust me when I say I don't like it any

more than you do. It's happening to *me*, after all. But it hasn't happened lately. We can be glad of that."

Her voice offered me solace. Not her words, but her voice. The sweetness of it.

And that's when I knew.

Erin.

Erin was the key to my self-control.

How had I not realized it before?

Was this part of the blood bond?

Had the fact that I'd been taken and hadn't learned self-control contributed to the forming of the bond?

So many questions.

Learn to ask the questions.

No! Not now. Not in my head.

"Good, son. That's it. You can learn control."

I nodded. My father was mistaken if he thought his words had had any effect on my teeth retracting.

It was all Erin.

"You still have something to do," my father said.

"I know. Bea. The ashes."

"Yes."

"And I'm going too," Erin said.

"No. Absolutely not. We had to run like hell out of there the last time. I can't have you in danger."

"What makes you think you can control me?" she demanded, hands on her hips.

I couldn't help laughing aloud. She was the key to my self-control. But control over *her*? In bed, yes. Anywhere else? Not in the slightest. I loved her all the more for it.

"Baby, I have to know you're safe."

"Dante, I'm not safe as long as those vamps are out there.

You know why I want to see Bea."

"Yes." To see if Bea had a potion or something that could mask Erin's scent. It was for Erin's own good. But if I couldn't smell her fragrance...

"We've been through this before, Dante," my father said. "Erin is not her scent."

"I know, Dad. And I know her safety is paramount."

"She may not be able to help me anyway," Erin said, "but I have to try."

I nodded. "I know."

"We'll all go." River patted his shoulder. "I'm armed. No vamp will get near Erin if I'm there."

"Thanks, Riv," I said. "You want to go tomorrow?"

"I want to go now," Erin said. "We're running out of time. Lucy's gone, and we need to get to the bottom of all of this as soon as we can. We need to get her back, Dante. Please."

"So you've forgiven your friend for keeping a secret from you?" my father said.

Erin nodded. "She's still the same person, right? I can't let anything happen to her. She's been a great friend to me. I'm scared silly for her."

"We'll find her, baby," I said, hoping I was telling her the truth. I couldn't bear to see Erin so upset. I'd move heaven and earth for her if I could.

She sniffled. "We will. We have to. Let's go now to see Bea. Do you have your father's ashes?"

I patted the pocket of my jeans. "Right here. I've got to tell you, Dad. It feels pretty weird carrying part of you around in my pocket."

"We've been through this, Dante. Those ashes aren't me. They never really were."

"Back again so soon?" Bea cackled. "And you've brought everyone with you, I see."

I fished out the bag of ashes and handed it to her. "From my father. Thank you for your help with the shield."

She snatched the sealed pouch. "You're quite welcome. I do what I can."

I resisted the urge to roll my eyes. "We appreciate it more than you know."

Erin cleared her throat. "Bea? I need a favor."

"Got any more vampire ashes?"

"No, but I have money."

She sighed. "What do you need?"

"Evidently, my smell is irresistible to a gang of vampires. Do you have something that could mask my scent?"

Bea inhaled. "I don't smell anything."

"You're not a vampire," River said. "Trust me. Her fragrance is like vampire crack."

"You might try some calendula and basil," she said, "though I can't guarantee anything."

"You don't have the answer?"

"I'm afraid not, dearie. Not being a vampire myself, I have no need of such things."

"Why calendula and basil?" Erin asked.

Bea cackled. "Those are common herbs to cover a grow."

"A grow?"

"A grow of cannabis. Marijuana."

That got River's attention. "Are you growing somewhere? That's illegal in this state."

Bea waved her hands. "Where would I be growing

cannabis? In the concrete here? Would I be living under a bridge if I had a thriving pot business?"

"That's convenient, isn't it?" River said. "You've got built-in excuses already."

Bea ignored him. "Go to any herbalist or magick shop. Have them mix you a tincture of calendula and basil. Wear it on your wrists and behind your ears. Let me know if it has the desired effect."

"Thank you." Erin pulled out a twenty.

I stopped her. "Wait until you see if it works first."

"No charge." Bea patted the bag of ashes. "This is payment enough for a long time. I know I asked for more, but I won't be greedy."

My curiosity got the best of me. "What can you do with my father's ashes?"

"What can I *not* do? These are more valuable than gold to people like me."

"Gold might get you a home of your own," I said.

Bea laughed. "Do you think I live here because I have nowhere else to go? Think again. I needed to leave everything. 'What you call bareness and poverty is to me simplicity. Not till we are lost, in other words, not till we have lost the world, do we begin to find ourselves.'"

"Thoreau," Erin said. "Two quotes. Is he with you now?"

"'It's not what you look at that matters. It's what you see.'"

"Thoreau again." Erin turned to me. "I think we're done here. Let's find a magick shop."

"Not yet," I said. "Bea, the last time we were here, you mentioned something when my father knew the book you were quoting from. You said he was a well-read vampire, and that maybe he had read the most important work of all. What book were you referring to?"

"'The library is a wilderness of books.'"

"For God's sake," I said.

"Wait," Erin said. "It's Thoreau again. That's a quote from his journal."

"Very good," Bea said.

"What is it, then? What's the most important work of all?"

"'Many men walk by day; few walk by night. It is a very different season.'"

I looked to Erin.

She nodded. "Thoreau."

"Since when do you know so much about Thoreau?" I asked her.

"I took a Thoreau seminar during the summer between high school and nursing school. I won a scholarship to attend it. It was a fluke, really. I entered an essay contest. I never expected to win, but I learned a lot. I was always drawn to the sciences, but taking a look at philosophy and literature was fun and educating." She turned back to Bea. "What are you trying to tell us?"

"I have told you."

"Wait!" Erin tugged my arm. "That last quote. 'Many men walk by day; few walk by night. It is a very different season.' Men who walk by night. You're talking about vampires, aren't you?"

Bea smiled.

"What does that have to do with the most important work of all?"

"The *Texts*," I said. "She's talking about the *Vampyre Texts*."

$\mathcal{E}rin$

Bea's smile grew wider.

"Something in the *Vampyre Texts*," Dante continued. "How do you know about that?"

"I see all. Have I not told you this before?"

"What's in the *Texts*? Why is it the most important work of all? Where do I find it?"

"That is for you to figure out. As for the second question, you already have that answer. Your father has given you what you need to succeed. He died so that you might live."

Julian's death. His body. His estate. We already knew Dante would use the money to buy the translation from that website he'd found. "You're telling us something we already know. This isn't any help at all. You're using Thoreau quotes and Shakespeare quotes and God only knows what other quotes to make it seem like you're this enlightened priestess, but you're a fraud, Bea." I turned to Dante, "We're done here. Let's find a magick shop. Though I'm doubtful calendula or basil will do any good. At least we can make a great pasta sauce with the basil."

Dante didn't move. He stared into nothingness, his eyes focused on something I couldn't see.

"Dante?" River said.

Nothing.

I touched his forearm. He was cold as ice. "Babe? What's going on?"

"She's talking to him," Bea said. "He's fighting it, but she has a grip on him."

"Who?" I had to stop myself from grabbing Bea and shaking her. "*Who* is talking to him?"

"*She* is. I'm only sensing that it's a female."

"Dante," I said, shaking his arm. "Come back to me. I'm right here."

River jumped toward him and tackled him to the ground. "Dante, come on, man. Snap out of this!"

I'd seen him like this once before, when I'd come home and found him on the floor of my living room nearly in a fetal position.

He needed me now, and I would not let him down.

"*She* knows things," Bea continued. "She knows his weaknesses. She'll stop at nothing."

Her words. I had to ignore them. Had to help the man I loved.

River held him down, shaking him, but he still wasn't back. I knelt down next to his head and cupped both cheeks. "Dante, I'm here. It's Erin. Come back to me. Please."

His vacant gaze locked onto mine, and I breathed a sigh of relief.

"Thank God," River said. "What was that?"

"I don't know, but I've seen it before."

"It's a female. She calls herself the queen." From Bea. "She's dark. And very, very powerful."

"The vampire who took him," River said. "It has to be. But vampires don't have that kind of power."

"'Uneasy lies the head that wears a crown,'" Bea said.

"Shit. Shakespeare again," River said. "I know that one. It's from *Henry IV*." He looked to Bea. "*Who* wears the crown?"

"No one, Riv," Dante said shakily. "She's no queen."

"Who are you talking about?"

"The woman. You're right. The woman who kept me captive. Had me tortured." He swallowed. "Stole my blood."

Nausea welled in my throat. So much I still didn't know.

"You'll find the answers you seek," Bea said, "in the most important work of all."

⚜

We got Dante back home to rest. River then left to take care of his leave of absence. I had to do the same thing. I'd go in tonight and work my shift, but I'd talk to admin as soon as I got in and tell them I needed to take a few personal weeks.

I hated doing it, but I had to. Not for my own safety. That was the least of my concerns. For the women who had disappeared.

For Lucy.

Dante was sleeping peacefully, and I hated to wake him, but I didn't want him waking up to find me gone. "Hey." I nudged him gently.

His eyes popped open. "Hey, baby."

He looked adorable, his dark hair mussed, his eyes glassy

with sleep, his lips full and kissable. I brushed mine against them in a soft peck. "I need to go to work."

"But—"

I placed two fingers over his lips. "I have to, Dante. I'll arrange for a week or two off, but I have to go in tonight. It's too late to call in now. They need me."

"I'll go with you, then."

"No. You need your rest."

"You might need me. I could...glamour them if I have to. Or I could try, at least."

I laughed softly. "I have plenty of vacation time saved up. Besides, you've told me you're not very good at glamouring."

"I'm not, but..."

"I'll be okay."

"I'll stay in the waiting room while you're working. Then I'll be there just in case you need me."

"Dante. Come on. You need to rest."

"I'm fine, damn it. I'm not going to let *her* dictate what I can and can't do. What I need is to protect you. That's final." His eyes burned.

I opened my mouth to argue the point, but nothing came out.

Truth was, I wanted him there. I wanted him to protect me. I needed him to do it as much as he needed to do it.

"Okay," I relented. "I need to leave. How long will you be?"

"I'm ready now." He sat up and then left the bed.

Logan wasn't in tonight, which was just as well. I didn't relish him and Dante running into each other, especially when Dante's mental state was precarious at best. I knew enough now that perhaps he'd open up to me a little about what had happened to him. But I wouldn't push. I couldn't do that to him. I texted River so he wouldn't waste a trip over here just to sniff Logan.

It was a slow night, thank goodness, so I was able to ask questions about Lucy. No one knew anything, though. It was another episode of she was here and then she wasn't. Same as the others, save for Patty Doyle and her baby, who had been transferred to a hospital in Baton Rouge by her parents.

Or had they?

I began furiously searching on my computer. Ah, yes. The transfer order. I hadn't seen it before when Patty and her baby had first disappeared. I'd looked everywhere, but it had eluded me. Had it been here all along? It could have been entered after the fact. The admins were always busy and overworked.

Shit. Speaking of the admins, I needed to get my leave taken care of. I walked out of the nurses' station and down toward the office where the night administrator worked.

"Excuse me?" I knocked lightly on her open door.

Dory Delynch looked up from her computer. "Oh, Erin, hello. What can I do for you?"

I walked into her office, clearing my throat. "I need to talk to you about some time off."

"Impossible. We're understaffed at the moment, as you know."

"I'm afraid it's serious. A family emergency. I need to fly to Ohio." The lie tasted like acid in my mouth, but this was important.

She pulled up the calendar on her computer. "I can give you two days. That's it."

That was it? For a family emergency? Granted, it was a

fake family emergency, but Dory didn't know that.

"I'm afraid that's not acceptable," I said. "I need to get home right away. I've got a flight booked in the morning."

She sighed. "How much time do you need?"

"I was hoping we could leave it open-ended."

"Erin, no. Just no. You've got to give me a—" She stopped, her gaze drifting.

"What?"

"I'm sorry. What was it that you needed, Erin?"

"I told you. I need to take some time off for a family emergency."

She looked down at her keyboard. "Of course. Whatever you need. I'll write it up. Let's leave it open-ended for now. You have personal time you can use. When that's used up, I'm sure we can work something out."

"Uh...okay. Thanks, Dory. I really appreciate this. I'm sorry for the short notice."

"No problem. If you'll excuse me, I have to get back to work."

"Yeah, of course. Me too." I turned...and my mouth dropped open.

Dante stood in the doorway of Dory's office. I signaled him to be quiet as I left her office, leaving the door slanted open.

He grinned.

"What did you do?" I asked.

"I guess I'm better at this glamouring thing than I thought."

SIX

DANTE

"How?" Erin asked.

"Truthfully, I'm not sure. I was in the waiting room, and I had this strong feeling that you needed me. I didn't even know where I was going."

"How did you even get back here? This is staff only."

"Like I said, I just knew you needed me. When I got to this office, I heard you inside. She wasn't going to give you the leave you needed, so I fixed it."

"How?" she asked again.

"Damned if I know." I ruffled my fingers through my hair. I wasn't lying to Erin. I truly had no idea. I saw what was happening, and I knew I needed to fix it. "I'll talk to my father about it and figure it out. He's supposed to teach me all the stuff I should have learned in the last ten years. We just haven't had any time to do it with everything else going on."

"Well, we'll—"

"Erin"—the administrator rustled out of her office—"what are you still doing here? Go take care of things. You're off the clock as of now."

I flattened myself as best I could against the wall. But I was a big guy. No way she wouldn't notice me.

But she whisked by, not giving me a look.

"That was strange," Erin said.

"Stranger than strange. I was invisible to her."

"Maybe part of the glamour?" Erin shrugged.

"I have no idea. I'll ask my father when I have the chance. For now, though, if you're off the clock and you're done here, let's go home."

She smiled. "I like the sound of that."

"Me too. I'm exhausted." I kissed her forehead and then bared my fangs. "And hungry."

Within seconds after we'd entered Erin's—our—townhome, I had her flattened against the wall, my teeth embedded in her milky neck.

I moaned as I drew the sustenance I needed from her body. As her creamy blood flowed down my throat, my strength returned, and though I was still fatigued, I no longer felt total exhaustion.

In fact, my dick had hardened into stone. I always got hard when I fed from Erin, but this was unexpected, given my fatigue and my spell the previous day.

I groaned when she clamped her hand onto my jean-clad erection. "Baby. I need you."

"I need you too," she said breathlessly. "Are you sure?"

"I'm always sure." I unbuttoned and unzipped my jeans, freeing my hard cock.

Just as quick, she kicked off her sneakers and shed her

sweatpants and underwear. In another second, I was inside her warmth, cozy and secure, where I needed to be.

"Dante, oh my God. You fill me so completely. I never realized how empty I was until you."

I plunged into her again and then again.

Again.

Again.

Her fingernails scraped my skin, and my balls contracted.

Once more... Oh God, and I was releasing, taking what she willingly gave to me.

As I panted, my whole body throbbing, coming down from a miraculous high, she rubbed my back in soothing circles.

And I realized she hadn't come.

What a selfish bastard I was. "I'm sorry," I said.

"For what?"

"I was thinking only of myself. You didn't come. I'll make it up to you, baby."

She smiled. "Dante, I don't care if I climax or not. I mean, I care. I love it with you. But the closeness is more important to me. Fulfilling your needs. Because when I do that, my own get fulfilled a hundred times more."

I struggled for words. How could I ever be worthy of the love and sustenance this amazing woman so willingly gave to me?

Yet I understood what she meant. I got so much by giving to her as well. And I'd give her everything I could. "Tell me," I said. "What do you want from me? What do you need? I'll give you anything within my power, love. Anything."

She smiled, and she was so fucking beautiful. Her hair was tumbling out of her ponytail, her cheeks were luscious pink with her blood rising to the surface. The soft whoosh of it buzzed in my ears

"You don't need to give me anything, Dante. I have everything I want right here."

I shook my head with vehemence. "Not good enough. I want to do something for you. Anything."

"Well... I was kind of looking forward to... Oh, this is embarrassing."

"Tell me."

"You said you would tie me up. Take me forcibly. And then River interrupted us."

"I'm sorry about that. I lost my self-control, and I never should have—"

She touched two fingers to my lips. "No, Dante. No. You were so passionate. So determined. So rogue and alpha. I loved it. Truly."

"But I—"

"You won't hurt me. I know that. I think we're together for a reason. I think we have this blood bond for a reason. We are each other's halves to an amazing whole. Whatever you need at whatever time, I will give it. It's what I was made for. I know it in the depths of my soul."

"How can you be so completely wonderful?" I wrapped her in my arms and simply held her. How amazing to just hold the person I loved more than my own life, more than anything. After a few minutes, I said, "Are you sure?"

"Totally. As long as you're sure."

God. The thought of tying her and taking her forcibly made me harden again. "I'm sure. I don't have what I need here at the moment."

"It doesn't have to be now. Just know, Dante, that when you need me, when you need to take me that way, I'm in. I'm *all* in."

I clamped my mouth to hers in a ferocious kiss.

This woman was my everything. My lover. My savior. Everything.

As our tongues swirled together, I knew I'd find out what was going on at the hospital. With Lucy. With the B positive blood. With the blood bond. With everything. I had to. Not just for me but for Erin.

For us.

Us.

We were no longer Erin and Dante.

We were *us*.

Later, after we'd slept for several hours, we went to the Quarter to find a tincture made of basil and calendula for Erin to try masking her scent. We found a little magick shop lodged in a corner, almost hidden. Goose bumps erupted on my skin.

Something was fishy here.

"What's wrong?" Erin asked.

And then I realized. We were near the manhole I'd emerged from the night I escaped. I hadn't thought I would recognize the place, but I knew. Not from anything visual or even aural. But my body knew. This was close to where I'd claimed my freedom.

"Nothing," I said. "I mean, nothing I can't handle. What made you choose this particular shop?"

"I don't know. You were leading, remember?"

She was right. I had been. Perhaps I'd subconsciously led us here.

We opened the door—it creaked softly—and walked in. A middle-aged gentleman sat behind a desk. He wore glasses and a sweater vest. Definitely not the voodoo type. The shop was cozy, but I didn't get a warm feeling.

Not a bad feeling actually, just not a warm one. Goose bumps still scattered over my arms.

"I'm Joseph, the proprietor of this fine shop. Blessed day to you. What may I help you with?" The man lowered his glasses and looked straight at me.

Erin smiled. "I need some basil and calendula."

"May I ask what for?"

"Does it matter?" I answered.

"Of course it does. I won't know how much to give you or in what ratio if I don't know what you need it for."

"To mask an odor," Erin said.

I didn't like her use of the word "odor." It sounded bad, though I knew that wasn't the actual meaning. Still, it grated on me.

"What kind of odor?"

"Well...*my* odor," she said.

He inhaled. "Beg your pardon, miss, but you don't seem to have an odor. And my olfactory sense is quite refined."

"Certain...people can smell me, apparently," she said.

Okay. Enough was enough. I bared my fangs.

Joseph nearly jumped out of his seat. "Please. Don't hurt me."

"Dante..."

"I'll take care of this," I said. "I won't hurt you. But there's a gang of vampires after my woman because of her enticing scent. I want it stopped. A voodoo priestess told us calendula and basil might be the answer. Point us in that direction, and we'll be out of your hair."

"You're a...a..."

"A vampire. Yes. A vampire who is rapidly losing patience." I showed him my teeth once more.

"No. You don't... You don't..."

"I do. And if you're smart, you'll keep that knowledge to yourself. Now mix up a potion or infusion or whatever to keep those trashy vamps away from my woman."

"Dante, please. Don't scare him."

"Too late for that, miss. Let me be honest with you." He cleared his throat as he grasped the edges of his desk, his knuckles whitening. "I'm a fraud. I don't know shit about magick or voodoo or anything. Damn. I should have closed up shop when that dead body turned up in the alley out back."

An ice pick lodged into my neck. "What?"

"A body. A man. In fact..."

I was this close to grabbing him by the collar. Erin must have felt it too, because she caressed my forearm.

Her touch calmed me. But only a little.

"In fact what?" Erin said.

"In fact, he could be your twin. Although he was probably older. And he had a nasty scar across his entire face, right over his eye."

"Julian," Erin whispered.

A wave of something foreign whipped through my body, heating my blood. "Did you make something? Leave a bottle outside a while back?"

"No. Not that I re..."

"What? Finish your damned sentence."

"I had a dream, though. A dream that I concocted some poison and left it outside the back door, in the alleyway. I swear to God it was only a dream. But the next morning..."

"The next morning what?"

"The next morning, I found the dead body out there. But I swear there was no bottle with him. Nothing. It was a dream. I swear to God it was a dream!"

"What did you do when you found the body?"

"I called the police, of course, but by the time they arrived, the body had disappeared."

"You didn't move it?"

"Of course not. Why would I call the police and then move it? I didn't want to touch a dead body."

"That's my father you're talking about," I said through clenched teeth.

"Dante." Erin's touch heated my arm. "It wasn't. He's not his body."

"You poisoned my father," I spat.

"I swear I didn't. It was a dream. A beautiful woman came to me in a dream. She was wearing a...gown of some sort. But not an evening gown. More like a—"

I finished for him. "A hospital gown."

SEVEN

Erin

"My mother," Dante said softly.

I caressed his arm again, trying to soothe him.

"This man poisoned my father."

"No, I didn't! I swear to God it was a dream. Wouldn't there be evidence if I poisoned him?"

"Dante, he doesn't remember any of this," I said.

"Look. I can't help you with masking your smell. I told you. I'm a fraud. Here"—he handed me a card—"this shop can help you. They're for real. Tell them I sent you and that I'm closing down. They'll be glad to hear it. They hate fakes."

"I need to see the place where you found the body," Dante said, baring his teeth again. "Now."

"Of course," Joseph said, his voice shaking.

He led us through the small shop to a wooden door in the back. He opened it—this one creaked even more than the front—and led us into the alley. Though it was daylight, the alley was dark with shadows.

"He was here," Dante said. "I can feel it."

"Dante," I said as soothingly as I could. "If he has no connection with his body, how can you?"

"Because I'm still a body myself. He no longer is. Maybe it doesn't make sense to you. But this is where my father died." He edged away.

"Where are you going?"

"I need to find it."

I hurried after him. "Find what?"

"The place where...." He turned to face me, his eyes dark and kind of scary. "The place where I escaped from is near here, Erin. River asked me to find it, and I didn't think I could. I didn't pay much attention that night. I was starving and scared out of my mind. But it's close."

"All right. We'll find it. We'll find it together."

"No. I can't put you in danger. I'll come back with River and my dad."

"Dante..."

"No argument, Erin. I'll do it later. Right now, we'll go to the shop the man recommended and see if they can help you." He sighed. "I know it's for the best. But not being able to smell you..." He inhaled.

"I'm sorry. But—"

"I know. I understand. Your safety is the most important thing."

"Your safety too," I said. "Not just mine. Dante, I don't want you coming back here."

"I know, baby. But I have to. For River. It might be the key to finding his father. My father died for this. I don't have a choice."

I nodded. He was right, of course. "I know. It's just—"

Dante turned abruptly and went back into the small shop. I followed quickly.

"Hey!" Dante yelled. "I need to talk to you some more."

Joseph squinted. "Not again. Please. I don't know anything."

"You said the body disappeared while you were calling the police. Can you tell me anything else? Did you see anyone? Who might have taken the body?"

He shook his head. "I've already told you everything I know."

"Think." His fangs were apparent. "Think *hard*."

"I can't—" The man went rigid.

"What is it?" I asked.

"They'll kill me." His voice was a hoarse whisper.

"Who?" Dante demanded. "Who will kill you?"

"The men. They're like you. I didn't realize until now. I've seen them before. The vampires."

"The ones who are after me," I said more to myself than anyone else.

"Vampires aren't killers," Dante said.

"These vampires are."

"And you're suddenly just remembering all of this? You're a fucking liar." Dante stalked forward, his hands balled into fists.

I couldn't let him do this. I had to do something. But what?

"They said they'd kill me. Said they'd..."

It was all making sense. Of course. The vampires had taken Julian's body and buried it at St. Louis Cemetery. They were able to glamour the guards. No one else could have gotten in.

But why?

"Dante, please. He won't be able to help us if you beat the crap out of him."

Dante's stance softened. Slightly. "You're lucky I love this woman. You're lucky I listen to her."

"Thank you, miss."

"Don't thank me." I rubbed my forehead. "I'm a nurse. I can't stand to see suffering. Besides, you're no use to us if you're messed up. We're going to need your help."

He shook his head. "No. They'll kill me."

"Do I look like I care?" Dante said.

"Dante." I touched his hand. "He doesn't remember anything. If he poisoned your father, it was because your mother told him to. Then she told your father to drink it. It brought him to you. He can't help us if he's afraid of us."

He softened once more, and I breathed a sigh of relief.

"Tell me everything," he said. "Every fucking thing. If I have a tiny inkling that you're not being completely honest with me, I'll break every bone in your body."

EIGHT

DANTE

My blood was finally calming, thanks to Erin.

I regarded the spectacled proprietor of the fraudulent magick shop. He was easily manipulated, clearly.

"Start at the beginning," I said.

"The beginning is when I had the dream. The beautiful woman in the hospital gown. She made me feel...peaceful. I told her I'd do anything she asked. She gave me a recipe. Told me to combine the ingredients and put it in a brown glass bottle on the stoop outside in back. In the alleyway. I swear to you I don't remember doing it. I don't—" He closed his eyes, squeezing them shut.

"What?" Erin said.

"I thought it was part of the dream."

"What? That *what* was part of the dream?" I demanded.

"The potion. Mixing the poison. But maybe...maybe it wasn't."

"I think it's obvious that it wasn't," I said. "Keep going. What was in the poison?"

"Hemlock. Belladonna. And...rattlesnake venom."

"Where the hell did you get rattlesnake venom?" I raked my fingers through my hair.

"I don't know. I can't afford it. It's like two thousand dollars an ounce. But it was here in my shop. At least it was in the dream. If it was a dream. No, wait..."

"What?"

"I...I milked the snake myself. In my dream."

"Where is it now? The venom? Let me see it."

"I used it all. Threw away the bottle. In my dream."

"And I suppose the trash has been hauled away since then."

"Yes. Of course."

"Rattlesnake venom is extremely dangerous," Erin said. "You're lucky you didn't harm yourself just from contact."

"I was very careful. It was almost like I wasn't doing it. Like someone was doing it through me."

"Can vampires do stuff like that?" Erin asked me. "Inhabit a person and make them do things?"

I shook my head. Vampires couldn't. But according to my father, *ghosts* could.

Ghosts could, if the person was a medium. Was Joseph a medium? Bea apparently was. Even if Joseph *was* a medium, the ghost inhabiting him would have had to know how to milk venom from a snake. Certainly not my mother.

That I knew of, anyway.

I knew very little about my mother.

Another question for my father.

"It wasn't the vampires. They didn't come until later. After I'd called the cops."

"They took the body?" I said, ire rising. Vampires. My own kind. Whoever they were, they had removed my father's clothes before they buried him.

They had wanted me to see his condition.

Fuckers. My fangs itched in anger.

Joseph nodded. "I'm sorry I lied. They said they'd kill me."

"Describe the vampires who took the body," I said. "Don't leave out a single detail."

"I... I can't."

"Why the fuck not?"

"Dante." Erin grabbed my hand.

I whisked it away. "Baby, I need answers. *We* need answers."

"You're right. We do." She turned to Joseph. "Answer his question, please."

"I can't."

"Bullshit," I said.

"No, I really can't. They were masked. I didn't see them."

"What kind of masks?"

"Black Mardi Gras masks. Ornate...and oddly beautiful, actually. I was mesmerized by them."

"You weren't mesmerized. You were glamoured."

"What?"

"Never mind." I turned to Erin. "Do you have any more questions for him?"

She shook her head. "Let's just go to the other shop and get the herbs I need. Then we can try to figure the rest of this stuff out."

"I need to talk to my dad."

In an instant, he appeared before us. I nearly jumped out of my skin. He held two fingers to his lips.

Of course, Joseph couldn't see him.

"Go to the alley behind the shop. We'll talk there," my father said.

"Thanks for everything," Erin said. "We'll be back if we have more questions."

"Please, don't—"

"We'll be back if we have more questions," I repeated. "Don't try to hide. I *will* find you."

In the alley, my father's ghost was waiting.

"This is where you died," I said. "I can feel it."

"You feel the residual energy from my body because your body came from mine."

"Semantics, Dad. Whatever. I *feel* it."

"I know, son."

"Rattlesnake venom, Dad. You were killed by rattlesnake venom."

"Was I? It was quick. That's all I know. Not a lot of pain."

At least that was a little settling. "Did Mom know how to milk venom from snakes?"

"Not that I know of," he said.

"Then I'm stumped. That guy, Joseph, said he had a dream that he milked a rattlesnake and made the bottle of poison that killed you. He said a beautiful woman came to him in a dream and told him how to do it. When he described her, she sounded an awful lot like Mom."

"It probably was. If she could come to me, she could come to others. The need was dire."

"But how the hell did she know how to make poison?"

"I don't know, Dante."

"I want answers, damn it!"

"I know you do. Sometimes there aren't any. It's possible another ghost helped Joseph make the poison. Or it's possible your mother got the information elsewhere. I'm new to the ghostly realm. I don't know all the avenues of information."

"Question after question after question." I sighed. "When are we going to find answers?"

"I don't know. But we will. The probate hearing on my estate is tomorrow. After that, you'll have access to my funds." He smiled. "Correction. *Your* funds. Well, yours and your sister's. It would be good if you both appear in court."

I hadn't talked to Em in a few days. "I'll call her."

"Good."

"Dad, the vampires who are after Erin—at least we're assuming they're the same ones—took your body and buried it in the cemetery. According to the nutjob who owns this shop, anyway."

"You know for sure they are the same vamps?"

"Not for sure, but who else would it be? Most vampires are nice people, right?"

"That's not what I mean. How did *he* know they were vampires?"

"He says he just knows."

My father began to roll his eyes but then stopped. "How does he know?"

"I don't have a clue. We got all the information out of him that we could. I figured I'd send River down here to get anything we couldn't."

"Good idea. Can he get the time off?"

"He's taking care of it. He and Erin are both on leave until we solve all these mysteries."

My father looked at Erin. "Everything worked out?"

"Yeah. With Dante's help. Apparently he can glamour after all."

He looked back to me, his brows raised.

"I'm not sure how I did it. I just knew Erin needed the time off, and she was having trouble."

"Good. You're showing good instincts. You'll be a quick study, son. You've always learned quickly."

"When can I learn more? You need to teach me, Dad."

"I know. Maybe tonight we can begin."

"Maybe? Why maybe?"

"Because I'm on constant watch. Why do you think I'm not always around? I have other things to attend to."

"What's more important than figuring this all out? We have to get Lucy back. And we have to find Uncle Brae."

"Nothing. Trust me. I'm working outside of the corporeal plane as much as I can, searching for answers."

I sighed. Always something enigmatic. If it wasn't that crackpot Bea, it was my own father. "We need to hit another shop to get the herbs for Erin."

"Good. I'll be in touch." My father vanished.

I caught Erin before her legs crumpled beneath her. "You okay?"

"Yeah. I'm fine. You'd think I'd be used to your father's disappearing act by now."

"If it helps, I'm not sure I'm used to it yet either." I pulled her to me in a tight hug. "I love you. Let's go to the other shop."

I inhaled.

Thank God!

I could still smell the luscious fragrance that was Erin. The Wiccan priestess who owned the shop had mixed up a potion for Erin, and she had placed a drop behind each ear and on each wrist.

Her scent was still thick.

As selfish as it was, I was happy her scent hadn't disappeared.

"I guess it isn't working. I can still smell you."

"That doesn't mean it hasn't disappeared to the other vampires," she said. "You might still smell me because of our bond."

"I hope so, baby. We can check with River tomorrow. If he can't smell you, we'll know it worked."

"I've cast a spell on the potion," the priestess assured us. "It should do what it is meant to do. But you can make it stronger."

"How?" Erin asked.

"Your belief. It will shield you if you believe it will."

"Okay," Erin said. "I believe it."

The priestess shook her head. "Words aren't enough, I'm afraid. But you will believe, and you will believe soon. There is one more thing that will make it even more potent."

"What?" Erin asked.

"He knows." She stared at me.

"How would I know?"

"Think about what you have in your possession. What will make every potion or spell or charm stronger."

Erin grabbed my forearm. "Your father. His remains."

"Vampire ashes are a powerful shield," the priestess said. "Add a pinch to the potion. You will see results."

We stopped at a café for a quick snack. A plate of beignets later, Erin excused herself to go to the bathroom.

I checked my phone for texts and smiled when a shadow

passed me and a body sat down across from me.

"That didn't take long," I said to Erin, still looking at my phone.

"I didn't realize you'd missed me."

The voice was not Erin's.

NINE

Erin

"**E**rin!"

I turned away from the mirror where I was reapplying my lipstick.

The blond head bobbing toward me through the restroom door belonged to Dale, one of the nurses who worked the night shift at the ER with me.

"Hi, Dale." I smiled.

"What are you doing here? We heard you had a family emergency and were headed back to Ohio."

"Oh." I cleared my throat. Just what I didn't need. Where was Dante when I needed him? Obviously he wouldn't be in the ladies' room. "I leave...soon. I couldn't get a flight until morning."

"Is everything okay?"

"As well as can be expected. Everyone is hanging in there."

"I hope it's nothing too horrible. I heard your leave was open-ended."

"Yes, for now. I hope I won't be gone for too long."

"Is your new boyfriend going with you?" She smiled. "I hear he's really hot."

"Oh?"

"Yeah. Renee told me she saw him in the ER with you last night after you came out of Dory's office."

"He's...uh...not going with me. He has business here."

"What's his name?"

Really? She thought I had some kind of family emergency, and she was worried about gossiping about my new boyfriend? "Look, Dale. I'm in kind of a hurry. And I'm really worried about...you know."

She clasped her hand over her mouth. "Oh, God. Of course! You must think I'm an unfeeling boob. I'm sorry, Erin."

I smiled. "It's okay. I'm sure everything will turn out okay. I'm just glad I was able to get the time off to be with my family. I have to run."

I whisked out of the bathroom and didn't look back as I headed back to the table Dante and I were sharing.

I stopped abruptly, my toes jamming against the tips of my shoes.

Seated at our table, across from Dante, was none other than—

"Abe Lincoln," I said.

"Erin. Hi. What are you doing here?"

I grabbed Dante's arm. "I could ask you the same thing. But I need to talk to Dante privately for a minute." I pulled him into a stand and away from the table.

"I need your help. A blond woman wearing jeans and a pink scrub shirt is going to come out of the bathroom in a minute. Can you glamour her? Make her forget she saw me here today?"

"I can try. Why?"

"She's one of the nurses in the ER. I'm supposed to be on leave for a family emergency, remember? I told Dory my flight was this morning."

"I'll do my best."

"And what's Abe doing here?"

"He said he's looking for you."

"Sheesh. Okay. If you can take care of the nurse, I'll take care of Abe."

He nodded and walked toward the restrooms. I went back to the table and sat down in Dante's seat across from Abe.

"Erin."

"That's my name. What do you want, Abe?" I eyed him. He was healing nicely from the beating he'd taken from the vampires.

"I need to talk to you. I was going to come to the hospital tonight, but then I saw your vampire friend sitting here."

"Shh!" I looked around. "Don't say the V-word so loudly."

"Sure. Sorry."

"What do you want?"

"You need to get out of town, Erin."

Funny. Everyone at the hospital thought I was doing just that. "Why?"

"They won't wait much longer. They're after you. If they can't have you, they're going to take the next best thing."

"What's that?"

"They know about your brother. They know he's a detective who works nights. They're going to sniff him out."

My heart jumped. Jay. Shit. And River had taken leave from work and wasn't there to protect him. My mind raced furiously. "Wouldn't they have noticed him by now? Like you said, he works nights, when the vampires come out."

"He's a male."

"So?"

"You're a female."

"Your vision seems to work just fine, Abe. Can you get to the point, please?"

"They're more attracted to female scents, but they'll take your brother if they have to. Erin, they think by threatening your brother, they'll get you to come to them."

I eyed his neck. Sure enough. Brand-new puncture wounds. "When was the last time you saw them?"

"Last night."

"You fed them."

"Well...sure. A guy's got to eat."

"Jesus, Abe. You're nuts. You know that? How did you end up on the street anyway? You can't be more than twenty-five or so."

"I grew up on the street, Erin. And I don't do drugs."

I flashed back to the first time I'd met Abe in the ER. I'd been convinced he'd been on something when he started talking about vampires, but his labs had come back clean. He was telling the truth. "I know you don't."

"Thank you for believing—"

Dante sat down next to me. "All taken care of. I think."

"Thank you." I squeezed his forearm.

"Can you protect Erin?" Abe asked suddenly.

"With my life," Dante said.

"Good. What about her brother?"

"Huh?"

"He says the vamps are going to go after Jay if they can't have me," I said. "And with River..."

"Shit. All right. We'll figure it out, baby. Nothing will happen to him, I promise."

Dante would never lie to me, but I feared he was making a promise he might not be able to keep. Emotion coiled in my belly. How was I supposed to—

I whipped my head around when Abe abruptly stood.

"I have to go."

"Why?"

He nodded toward a man who walked into the small café. "Get her out of here," he said to Dante, and then he fled.

Dante parted his lips to reveal his fangs. "It's one of them," he said under his breath.

My legs itched to run.

"Stay put," Dante growled. "I'll take care of this."

"No!" I grabbed his arm. "Let's just leave. Please."

"You expect me to let him go without letting him know in no uncertain terms that you are mine? I can't do that, Erin. I can*not*."

TEN

DANTE

My gums tingled as my fangs sharpened into precise points. The man had no scent. I couldn't be sure, given I couldn't scent anyone but Erin, but my whole body told me this was a vampire.

A vampire who wanted my woman.

I stalked toward him. He was clean-shaven, apparently not the leader Erin had seen in her dream.

No, he was no alpha. He was a follower. His stance made that clear.

He stood near the entrance, waiting for a host to seat him. I approached him, my blood boiling.

"Let's step outside for a minute, friend," I said in a timbre so low no one else could possibly hear.

But *he* heard.

Yes, he was a vampire. He'd heard me.

"I'm pretty sure I'm not your friend," he said.

"Don't make this harder than it has to be," I said through clenched teeth. "I'll fucking pulverize you right here if I have to."

He showed me his fangs quickly so no one else would notice.

I had to stop myself from laughing. They were nothing compared to mine. I pushed him through the café quickly and outside the back door into the alleyway.

"What the fuck?" He *oofed* as I plowed him into the brick wall.

"You stay the fuck away from my woman," I said.

"Who the fuck are you? And who the fuck is your woman?"

"The one you've been after. You and that hairy monster leader of yours. Stay away, or I'll kill each one of you with my bare hands."

"Is she...?" He inhaled. "She's not here."

The potion! It must have worked. Surely he would have smelled Erin as soon as he came near the café.

"No, she's not. And you stay the hell away from her."

"How do you even know—"

I growled, baring my teeth.

He cringed. "What the fuck?"

I cocked my head as a few homeless people walked by, their gazes riveted to the sparse remnants of food scattered here and throughout the stoned alleyway.

"Who are you? I've never seen— Oh, shit."

"What? You've never seen what?"

"You're the one. You're the one she talks about. Fuck me!"

I grabbed him by the collar and slammed him against the brick of the building.

"Fuck," he said, his voice hoarse because I was putting pressure on his throat. "I can't believe you even exist."

"You tell me what you're talking about, or your life ends right here, asshole."

"Think again."

The voice had come from behind me. I turned, releasing my hold and letting the vamp crumple to the ground.

The bearded one. Dark-blue eyes. He stood nearly as tall as I did but was wider through the shoulders.

I growled, showing my teeth.

He jarred slightly but covered himself. Only another vampire with an acute sense of sight would have noticed.

I noticed.

My teeth had frightened him.

My father had said my teeth were longer and sharper than his, and that his and his brother's were the most formidable Jack Hebert had ever seen.

I bared them once more.

This time he didn't react. But he didn't bare his own. He looked at the ground. "You okay, Giles?"

"Yeah. Fine. He says she's his woman. The one we want."

The bearded one smiled, and I could almost see the slime oozing from his lips. "Yeah? Then you can take us to her."

I snarled.

"Decker, no. He's the one. The one she talks about."

"For fuck's sake, Giles. You get hit on the head or something? She's nuts. We all know that."

"I swear to God, Deck. Didn't you see his fucking *teeth*?"

The one called Decker *had* seen my teeth. And he'd freaked, though only for a millisecond.

I whipped around and grabbed Decker by the throat, slamming him into the wall. "Start talking, shithead. What do you want with my woman? And why the fuck did you bury my father in St. Louis Cemetery?"

"I don't know what you're talking about, man. Let me go, or I'll tear you up."

"I'd like to see you try. I'm pretty sure I have the upper hand here, ass—"

Bonk!

An ache sprang up on the back of my head, and I dropped to my knees. Rage swelled inside me, and I growled as my teeth grew even longer and sharper.

"Good shot, Giles," Decker said.

I let out a huff of air when Decker landed a kick to my cheek.

No pain. Only rage as I jumped back into a stand. I would win. I always won. Losing was not an option.

Fight or die in the arena.

Adrenaline surged in my gut like a deluge of electricity, and I punched Decker square in his jaw.

He grunted, slamming back against the brick wall. I turned and swung my leg, taking Giles down with a roundhouse kick to the kidney.

I turned back, but I wasn't quick enough. Decker swept my legs, and I fell to the ground.

"Fuck!" The combination of dirt and asphalt dug into my left cheek.

Always go for the nose, especially if you're fighting another vampire. Blood will clog his sinuses, and the injury will bring tears to his eyes. You'll take out his sense of smell and sight with one punch, and the pain will bring him to his knees.

Bill had taught me that one when I was a kid.

I'd never had to use it.

Or had I?

Fight or die in the arena.

I scrambled up quickly, thrusting my fist into Decker's chin with an uppercut, and then I punched him square in the nose.

"Fucking bastard!" Blood spurted from his nostrils as he yelled out, his fangs dripping saliva and blood. He crumpled to the ground.

One down.

I turned back to Giles, who had taken a boxing stance. I thrust my leg outward in a circular motion, using an inside crescent kick to take him down. I jumped on top of him, knife-handed his neck, and then punched his nose.

He covered his nose with his hands as the blood erupted. "Damn you!"

I inhaled.

Rusted iron mixed with tarnished silver.

Vampire blood.

Most vamps thought our blood had no aroma, but they were mistaken. I'd come to know its light scent well. I'd been forced to ingest it for ten years.

Everything about it disgusted me.

I stood, rubbing the dirt off my jeans. Giles and Decker weren't unconscious, but they were in pain. Big broken nose pain. Still, they wouldn't stay down for long.

"Stay away from me, and stay away from my woman."

"You don't know what you're dealing with, man," Giles said. "She's dangerous."

Walk away, Dante. Just fucking walk away.

But I couldn't resist. I had to know.

"*Who* is dangerous?"

ELEVEN

Erin

"Dante!"

I ran toward him, Abe following me.

"No, Erin!" Abe shouted.

"Shit, Erin, get out of here! There are two of them," Dante said.

The vamps didn't make any move toward me. Perhaps Bea's remedy really was working.

Both men were down, their noses clearly broken. I didn't have to be a nurse to see that. "What have you done?"

"Get out of here!" Dante yelled again.

Even if Bea's remedy wasn't working, they couldn't possibly smell with their noses full of mucus and blood. Or maybe they could. I knew precious little about the vampire sense of smell. I knew precious little about vampire everything, other than that I was in love with one of them.

"You two get out of here," Abe Lincoln said. "I'll take care of things here."

The bearded one—God, from my dream—rose slowly. "I'm not done with you yet, vampire." He bared his teeth.

"Just go," Abe said again.

"You haven't seen the last of us," the other one said.

I grabbed Dante's arm, my nerves jumping like wasps on the attack. "Listen to him. Please. It's the one from my dream. Let's just go. Look at you. And you have court tomorrow."

That finally got him. "Shit," he said.

"Come on. I'll help you get cleaned up."

Back home, I cleaned Dante's scrapes and applied some antibacterial ointment and antiseptic.

"Ouch!"

"Sorry. What were you thinking, taking on two at once?"

"I'd have taken on more than that to protect you."

"They didn't come after me," I said.

"No. Which means the potion works, and I can still smell you. Thank God. I don't know what I'd do if I couldn't. Your scent. It's like home to me. Comfort and joy and sex and arousal and sustenance and nourishment and love. All wrapped up together in an indescribable fragrance."

I couldn't help smiling. "Do you think *they* smell all of that?"

"No. They just smell the scent your blood makes. Scents like yours are irresistible to vampires. It's a product of your ancestry."

"Oh. Right."

With all the commotion, I'd nearly forgotten that I was part vampire. That most likely my maternal grandmother had been a vampire. Yeah, I was angry about that. Angry that he hadn't told me sooner. But was it really anger? "Do you think my mother knew? About her mother, I mean."

"Probably not."

"What about my grandfather?"

"It's possible. I don't know, Erin. Is he still alive?"

"Unfortunately, no. He passed away before I came to New Orleans. I guess I'll never know."

"Not from him. No. It's always possible that your mother knows something."

My mother. Sharlene Jackson Hamilton. She was fair-skinned like Jay and me. Blue-eyed like Jay. Dark-haired like both of us. I sighed. She worked as a night cashier, hadn't gone to college but was incredibly intelligent. I'd always wondered why she never did anything more with her life. Maybe she couldn't tolerate daylight well and didn't want to go to a university. But she was an honest and hard-working woman. No fault to be found there.

She couldn't possibly know about her mother. Heck, she'd never even known her mother. My grandmother had died giving birth to her only child.

I sighed again. "We need to get some sleep."

"It's early yet."

"I know. But we were both up all night. And you have court first thing in the morning. Have you called your sister?"

"Crap." Dante rose. "I'll be right back."

I turned my arm and regarded the white skin of my inner wrist. I brought it to my nose and inhaled.

The basil overpowered the calendula, giving my skin a fresh, minty scent. I wouldn't have cared if it smelled like garbage as long as it kept those rogue vampires away, but I was glad the scent was pleasant.

My brother's image popped into my mind. I had to get to him and somehow convince him to start wearing this mixture on his skin.

How was I supposed to do that?

Dante returned. "Emilia's meeting us at the courthouse in the morning. She'll come straight from work. Good thing we're first on the docket."

"Yeah, definitely. In her condition, she needs her rest." I twisted my lips. "Dante?"

"Yeah, baby?"

"The potion seems to be working."

"Yeah. Thank God."

"But I want to make it as strong as we can. I hate to ask you this, but—"

"It's okay." He grabbed his father's urn that was sitting on the coffee table. "Let's add some."

I took the tiniest pinch of the urn's contents and added it to the brown glass bottle. I repeated with each of the five bottles the priestess had given me. "We need to tell Jay. Or at least get him to start wearing this potion like I am."

"I know, baby."

"But how?"

He shook his head. "I wish I knew."

"He's home now. Probably in bed. He's safe there, right?"

Dante nodded. "I wouldn't have left you alone here as often as I have if I didn't believe you were safe. Those vamps don't normally come out during the day."

"Why were they out today, then?"

"I don't know. But we'll find out. Neither of them will be bothering your brother or anyone else for the rest of the day, though. I saw to that."

"That was only two of them. What about the others? There were four in my dream."

"The one called Decker is their leader. They won't move without him."

"How do you know?"

"Because of how the other, Giles, acted. Decker's definitely the alpha of that crew. And he's the one we need to focus on. He knows me now, and he knows I mean business." Dante looked away for a moment, as if he were thinking.

"What is it?" I asked.

"He *knows* me," Dante said again. "Almost as if he recognized me. In fact, the other one, Giles, said I was the one she talked about. But how? I never saw anyone except... At least I don't think I did."

"Except what, Dante? What are you trying to say?"

"God, this is so hard, Erin. I don't want to be weak. I don't want to..."

"Baby." I caressed his back. "It's okay. Tell me."

"I only saw three people the whole time I was in captivity. The female vampire who took me and her two human goons."

"Are you sure they were human?"

"Oh, yeah. They had the scent. They smelled like rotten fish."

"Yuck." I scrunched up my nose.

"Not at first. They had normal human smells. I think my brain played tricks on me. I grew to hate them so much that they began to smell completely repulsive."

"What did they look like?"

"I couldn't tell you. They were always masked."

"Could you recognize them by smell?"

"Normally, yes. Probably. But I can't smell anyone but you,

baby. Not since I first encountered you in the blood bank."

"Right." I shrugged. "We have to get to Jay. Right away. This can't wait. I won't take the chance that the other two aren't out looking for him."

Dante nodded. "You're right. Let's go."

TWELVE

DANTE

We stopped off to get River before we headed to Jay's place. He lived in an apartment not too far from River's pad. Erin called him to make sure he was up.

"What did you tell him?" I asked.

"Just said we needed to talk, and that it was really important."

"Great. You probably freaked him out."

"No. I said we're all okay. Mom and Dad are okay. You know."

"The good thing is that the potion Bea suggested seems to work," River said. "I can't smell you at all."

A very slight growl emerged from my throat. A happy growl. River could no longer smell Erin.

"We added some of my dad's ashes to intensify it, though it seemed to work before then, with the two thugs."

"I'm not sure my brother is going to want to go around smelling minty fresh." Erin smiled.

We got out of the car, and Erin led us to Jay's apartment.

She let out a whoosh of a breath before knocking on the door three times.

Jay opened the door wearing nothing but lounge pants. His dark hair was mussed, and he was rubbing one eye. "Yeah, hey, Erin, River. Come on in. You want some coffee or something?"

"No thanks," Erin said. "Let's sit. We need to talk."

"Sure. Whatever. I'm exhausted, though. Work has been a pain since you took that leave of absence, Riv. What's going on, anyway?"

I resolved to stay quiet and let Erin and River explain everything. They both knew Jay better than I did, even though I'd be uncle to his child.

Of course, he didn't know about that yet, and neither did Erin.

Not telling Erin anything made my stomach queasy. I'd talk to my sister tomorrow, after court. She had to tell Jay. This had gone on long enough.

Erin fingered the small brown bottle of elixir made with basil and calendula oils and herbs. And the ashes of my father.

"What's that?" Jay asked.

"It's...fragrance. I got it in the Quarter."

"Oh?" He inhaled. "I smell mint."

"You smell basil," she said. "It's a main ingredient in the fragrance. I'm wearing it."

"Smells nice."

"Good," she continued, "because I want you to wear it. Apply it once a day to four pulse points."

"Huh? No offense, Sis, but I think minty fresh is more of a girl thing."

"But it's important that you—"

"Fuck!" Jay jerked backward against the couch where he sat.

River had bared his fangs.

"What the fu—"

"Jay, it's okay." Erin turned to River. "What the hell? You couldn't have been a tad more subtle?"

"We don't have time, Erin," River said. "I'm sorry, man, but this is who I am. I know it's hard to believe, but—"

"What makes you think I wouldn't believe it?" Jay asked. "I'm a cop in New Orleans. I've heard it all. But shit, man, did you have to go all fangs on me like that?"

Erin turned to her brother, her eyes wide. "You *knew*?"

"I've known for a while. I didn't know you were one, though." Jay shook his head. "Makes a lot of sense."

"How?" River asked. "I'm very discreet."

"Yeah, you are, but you see things before I do. I mean literally."

"Our sight is better, especially at night."

"Do you do that hypnotizing thing?"

"It's called glamouring," River said. "I *never* do it on the job unless it's absolutely necessary for our work. And before you ask, no, I've never glamoured you. At least not until recently, and that was only because I needed this leave of absence."

Jay's eyes shot wide open. "You fucking hypnotized me? You're my partner, River. We're supposed to trust each other."

"I know, man, and if it's any consolation, I feel terrible about it."

"Not terrible enough." Jay stood. "Get the hell out of my house."

"Jay," Erin began, "I know how you feel."

"*You* know how I feel?" He regarded me, anger pulsing off him in waves. "If he's one, that means you are as well, right?"

I nodded.

"And you knew all this?" He turned back to Erin.

"I know. And believe me, it was hard to deal with at first, but right now we have a big problem, Jay. That's why we're here."

"Christ. I need a drink." He walked into his small kitchen, pulled a bottle out of a high cupboard, uncorked it, and took a long swig.

"Jay..." Erin began.

"Shh," I said. "It's a lot for him to take."

"He's more upset about the glamouring than about the existence of vampires," Erin said. "On what planet does that make sense?"

"Not anywhere on this planet," I said. "Except for New Orleans. He's a cop, like he said. He's sees all kinds of shit, just like you do in the ER. Didn't you ever wonder?"

"No. Not really. I heard all kinds of stories, but I figured it was all a bunch of garbage, honestly. Until Abe Lincoln."

Jay took another long drink from the bottle and then returned to the living room and sat down. "Don't glamour me again, River."

"I won't have to, now that you know about me."

"Why'd you need the leave of absence anyway? Why couldn't you just be honest with me?"

"I had no idea you'd be so accepting," River said. "Plus, Erin is involved."

"All the more reason you should have been honest with me. She's my sister, for God's sake."

"I know. And her safety means everything to me. As much as it means to Dante. And your safety means everything to me too. That's why we're here."

"My safety? I'm not in any danger."

Erin cleared her throat. "But you are. That's why you need this." She handed him the amber bottle. "Apparently you and I have a scent that vampires find irresistible."

River quickly explained how humans all have unique scents that come from their blood. Some were better than others, depending on their ancestry. Erin flinched at the word ancestry. Was River going to tell Jay that his grandmother was most likely a vampire?

"Most of us don't feed on humans. We're taught that it's immoral, but there's a gang of rogue vampires that hang out under Claiborne Bridge— "

"Fuck. You're talking about the drug runners, aren't you?" Jay said.

"Yeah. They're thugs, and they don't give a shit about morals. They smelled Erin once and have been after her since."

"Shit."

"It's okay," Erin said, "A Wiccan priestess helped me. She made this potion out of basil and calendula oils. It keeps them away."

River nodded. "It works. I can't smell her. But I sure as hell can smell you. You need to use this shit, man. It's the only way to keep them away. Our sources say that if they can't have Erin, they're coming after you."

He took the bottle from Erin. "What do I do?"

"I told you," she said. "Put a little bit on your wrists and neck, all four pulse points. Do it every twenty-four hours."

"And...?"

"And they won't be able to find you. Even if they find you, they won't be able to smell you, and they'd rather have someone they can smell. That's how our noses work," River said.

"Unbelievable." But he opened the brown bottle and

applied the stuff. "Good enough?"

"Yeah. Just do it every twenty-four hours, and you'll be good," Erin said. "Let me know when you're going to run out. I have a lady in the Quarter who's making it for me."

"How much does this shit cost?" he asked.

"Not too much. About ten dollars an ounce."

"Whatever." Jay shook his head. "Level with me, River. Why the leave of absence?"

"Dante and I are working on something."

Erin cleared her throat. "And I am too."

"What?"

"The disappearances from the hospital. We're all taking leave until we figure it out."

"Then work your hypnotic magic for me and get me a leave too. If my little sister is involved, you can count me in."

"Jay..." Erin began.

I touched her shoulder. "Let him. We could use the help. As long as he uses the potion, he won't be in any more danger than you are."

"But why would you want him involved?"

I couldn't tell her one of the reasons, which was so he could get to know River and me and our family. That way, when he found out he was going to be a father to Em's baby, maybe it wouldn't be much of a shock. But there was another damned good reason as well—an even more important one. "He's a cop, baby. We need him."

"And if you think you're taking my baby sister into this without me, think again."

"Easy, Jay," Erin said. "He's in favor of it. You don't have to fight him."

"He's a vampire. And you're...with him. You're... Christ."

"I love her, man," I said. "I'll protect her with my life if I have to."

"You damned well better." He turned to his sister. "I'm just as glad you're out of that hospital for now, with all those women disappearing."

She nodded. "Yeah. Me too. I'm really worried about Lucy, though."

"We'll find her, baby," I said. "I promise. We'll find all of them."

"I know, Dante. But I'd prefer to find them alive."

⚜

I borrowed a suit from River for court the next morning. Emilia showed up looking a little green.

Make that *really* green.

"Morning sickness?" I asked.

She nodded. "All nine months for a vampire woman. So not fair."

Still, I didn't remember my mother looking nearly so bad. Em's skin truly did have an emerald tinge to it. "Have you talked to the doc?"

"Yeah. Jack says it's normal."

"Has he *seen* you?"

"Not for about a week. My next appointment is in a few days."

"Call him today. This is ridiculous."

"Hey, guys." River walked into the courtroom and sat down next to us. "Here to 'work my magic,' as Jay says."

"Jay?" Emilia reddened. Or browned, when the blush hit her greenish skin. "What about Jay?"

River and I exchanged a glance. "Jay knows what we are," I said. "You have no reason to keep this from him any longer."

"I don't know. He doesn't know I'm your sister. Or anything else."

"You don't look too good," River said.

"Thanks," Em shot back with sarcasm. "Is Dad going to be here?"

"He didn't say," I said.

"All rise!" the bailiff said.

We stood. In a few hours, I'd be a rich man.

The judge entered and sat down at his bench.

"First case on the docket is the estate of Julian Guillaume Gabriel." Then the judge looked straight at Emilia and me. "I'm afraid we have a problem with this case."

THIRTEEN

Erin

I lay on my couch. Dante and River were in court. I'd decided not to go along because I'd just be in the way. Dante had fed, and I was relaxed. I yawned, stretching my arms above my head and closing my eyes.

Until my doorbell rang.

So much for a little time for relaxation. I stretched again and rose, making my way to the door. Thank goodness I'd showered.

I gasped when I opened the door.

There, in all her glory, stood Dr. Zabrina Bonneville. Her long blond hair was twisted on top of her head into a severe bun, and her fair skin was still fair. No tan at all. Wasn't she supposed to be vacationing in the tropics?

"Doctor," I said. "I thought you were in Barbados."

"Doctor? Who are you talking to, dearie?"

I blinked.

Not Dr. Bonneville, but Bea stood in my doorway. Her

dark-brown dreads were pulled up into a messy mass on top of her head, and her skin was the usual mocha color. She wore her red gypsy skirt that was tattered, and on her fingers were the cymbals she'd worn the day she'd found Dante and me at the café in the Quarter. Had she been playing them? I hadn't heard anything.

I shook my head to clear it. How had I mistaken Bea for Dr. Bonneville? Bonneville was, of course, on vacation as she said she was.

And what in the world was Bea doing here? At my home, no less?

"How did you find me?"

"A little bird," she said, cackling.

"Seriously. How did you get this address?"

"Bea sees all."

Of course. I wasn't going to get an answer. But I was sure as hell going to change all my privacy profiles and passwords as soon as I got rid of her.

"What do you want, Bea?"

"I need to give you some information."

"About the most important work of all?" I asked, hoping. The *Vampyre Texts* still sat on my coffee table. "Come in, please."

"Not about that."

"Please, sit down." I led her to the couch I'd just vacated— the couch adjacent to the coffee table where the *Vampyre Texts* were on full display. I'd see for sure if she knew that book. "Can I get you something? A glass of water?"

"Fruit juice, if you have it, with a shot of vodka."

"It's nine in the morning," I said.

She cackled. "It's five o'clock somewhere."

Bea had never struck me as a drunk. What the hell? I poured a glass of orange juice, added a tiny amount of vodka—when had I bought vodka?—and handed it to her. "Here you go."

"Obliged." She took a sip. "Delicious."

"What can I do for you, Bea?"

"It's not what you can do for me. It's what I can do for you. Or what I've done for you."

Of course. She'd somehow heard that her advice had worked, and she wanted payment. I reached for my purse on the coffee table, nudging the book as I did. I pulled out a twenty. "I appreciate your advice. Thank you."

She took the twenty and stuffed it into her cleavage. "Obliged," she said again, "but that's not the only reason I came. I won't turn it down, but I meant what I said. The ashes are payment for some time."

"Oh." Still, her advice had been well worth the twenty bucks. "What have you come to do for me then?"

"I have news for you. But first things first. There's a vampire woman who's breeding. Your boyfriend's sister."

"Emilia. Yes, I know."

"She's ill. Very ill. If she's not treated, she will be in danger of losing her baby and her life."

"Oh!" I touched my fingers to my lips. "I've heard pregnancy and childbirth are sometimes difficult for vampire women. Is there anything we can do to help her?"

The grandmother I'd never known popped into my mind. She'd been beautiful, at least in the photos I'd seen of her when she was young.

"Yes," Bea said. "She's suffering from severe morning sickness. It's worse than usual because the baby she carries has

B positive blood. She's B negative. The baby's blood is attacking her and making her ill. She needs relief."

B positive. That blood type again. But Bea had her information wrong. "That's not how it works. When a mother is negative and a baby is positive, the mother's immune system attacks the Rh positive cells as a foreign substance, which destroys the baby's red blood cells and causes hemolytic anemia. This is Emilia's first baby, so she's probably not affected. It's more of an issue with her next baby. Even so, treatment with immunoglobulins will take care of the problem. She's under the care of a physician. I'm sure he's taking care of her and following protocol."

"But this is a vampire pregnancy, dearie. Things are different. Everything comes down to blood with vampires," Bea said. "'We are all sculptors and painters, and our material is our own flesh and blood and bones.'"

"Thoreau again," I said.

"A genius," Bea said. "Women are sculptors. They create life within them and bring forth art from their bodies. Their material is their flesh, blood, and bones. But vampire women are prisoners of blood at times. You can help, dearie."

"How can I help? It sounds like *you* can help."

"You will help through me. If I show up at this woman's home with a remedy, she won't accept it. But if you show up, as a nurse, she will."

"Why doesn't she just ask her doctor?"

"Her doctor is a learned man, but this remedy is new."

"How do you know about it, then?"

"I see all."

She'd been quoting Thoreau again. Was he inhabiting her? Probably not. Thoreau was a writer and philosopher, not a physician or scientist. He wouldn't know anything about vampire medicine.

"Who is with you, Bea?"

"No one is with me."

What the hell? It couldn't hurt. "What is the remedy for Emilia?"

She pulled out a crumpled piece of paper from a pocket in her skirt and placed it in my hand. "Give her this. It will help with the sickness and help her to carry her child to term."

I flattened the paper and glanced at it.

Nettle leaves, gingerroot, peppermint, chamomile. Wild yam.

Wild yam?

"But—"

She stood. "It will help." When she got to the doorway, she turned. "I almost forgot. I have news for you. That book on the table? It's a fake. Someone has been here. Someone stole the real one."

The paper fluttered from my hand.

She hadn't come to give me a remedy for Emilia. Emilia was under a physician's care and was most likely fine.

She'd come to warn me that someone had stolen the *Vampyre Texts*.

FOURTEEN

DANTE

My heart pounded. "A problem?"

"Someone has contested this will," the judge said.

I looked to River. *Can you fix this?* I hoped he understood.

"I'm trying," he whispered so only I could hear. "Nothing is happening."

What was going on? Was this judge a vampire?

"Who would contest the will? My sister and I are our father's only heirs."

The door to the courtroom opened, and a whoosh of energy hit me like a bolt of lightning.

"Mr. Guillaume Tyrus Gabriel," the judge said.

Emilia, River, and I all stiffened as Bill entered.

"Mr. Gabriel is the deceased's father," I said. "No provision was made for him in the will."

Bill waved a hand, and all the humans in the courtroom went glassy-eyed. "Really, Dante," he said. "Did you think you'd get away with this?"

Emilia, River, and I stared at him, our eyes wide.

"What did you just do?" Emilia asked.

My father had said he'd never heard of a vampire being able to glamour a group of people. But Bill had done it, and if Bill could do it, perhaps another vampire, an elder, could also do it. Not only a courtroom of people, but a hospital full of people.

Bill ignored Em's question. "You *won't* get away with this."

I bristled. "Get away with what? Claiming our father's estate? He's dead, Bill. You know that as well as we do."

"That's not the issue. The money is yours. I'm not denying that. But I can't let you have it."

"You have no power over it. It's what our father wanted. He helped us find his body so we could get the money."

"Yes. I'm aware of what has gone on. Did you really think you could keep everything from me?"

"Dad?" I said.

"Your father is otherwise occupied," Bill said.

"What the hell did you do to him?" I said, baring my teeth.

"Nothing. He's my son. I would never bring any harm to him. Not that I could in his current state anyway. I just made sure he was out of the way for this little session this morning." He came closer, meeting my gaze. "Formidable, Dante. Very nice. But those teeth will do you no good until you can control them and learn to use them properly."

"Dante..." Emilia urged.

"Stay out of this, Em. In fact, River, get her out of here."

"Uh...hell, no," Em said, whipping her hands onto her hips.

"I'm staying too," River said. "Look, Bill, you have no right to do this. We need Uncle Jules's money. He wants us to have it. People are disappearing. The woman I love has disappeared!"

He loved? River loved Lucy? "Riv?"

"Sometimes it takes losing someone to realize it," River continued. "We're going to find out what's going on, and we're going to find out the secrets behind what is happening."

"I've told you the *Texts* will bring you only darkness," Bill said. "Why didn't you listen to me?"

"Because you're different," I said. "You've been different since I returned. River and Em even see it now. My father sees it. Whatever you saw in that book changed you, Bill. We need to find out why. And how. I need to understand what's happening between Erin and me, and I need to find out why women are going missing from hospitals. Women who all have the same blood type. B positive. You know who else has that blood type, Bill? *I* do."

"Why does that matter?" he asked.

"Because it's genetically impossible for me to have it. That's why it matters. When's the last time you talked to Jack Hebert? Both my mother and father were Rh negative. Em is Rh negative. It's genetically impossible for two Rh negative parents to produce an Rh positive child. Jack swears I am my parents' child, and I look just like my father, so he can't explain it. If the answer is in that damned book, I am damned well going to find it."

"Dante, the book will not give you any answers."

"No, Bill, the book didn't give *you* any answers. Maybe it led you to darkness, but it won't lead me there."

"It will, Dante."

"It won't. I've *been* to hell. Nothing in that book can be any worse than what I've already been forced to endure. And if it is? Then I'll find my way out. I've found my way out of darkness before. You have no idea what I've been through, and my father went through worse and got out."

"Your father *died,* Dante." He sighed. "I can't lose the three of you as well."

My heart softened. A little. "Is that what this is about? You losing us? We're not going anywhere."

"That's right. Which is why I'm contesting this will. I'll tie it up in court for years to keep you from getting your father's money. And when time runs out for me there, I'll glamour the administrators to keep it going. I can't allow you to pursue this dark path."

"Too late. Fuck up my father's will if you have to, but I still have the book, and I'll find the money to translate it one way or the other. Count on that."

"You won't. You no longer have the book, Dante."

"It's sitting on Erin's coffee table as we speak. I saw it before I left this morning."

"It's not. Never will you find out the secrets of the *Texts.* For your own good. The book in your home is counterfeit. I had the real one stolen."

Rage surged inside me, and my blood turned to boiling plasma in my veins. "You *what?*" I growled, my gums itching and tingling more than they ever had. Every fraction of every millimeter they lengthened forced more electricity through my body, currents charged with anger and madness.

I snarled at my grandfather, a man without whom I wouldn't exist.

For an instant, I felt regret.

Only for an instant.

He would not keep me from the truth.

He would *not.*

I balled up all the electric energy inside me and hurled it at the judge sitting on the bench. I thought not in words but in images, showing him what I needed him to do, forcing him to do my bidding.

The people in the courtroom began moving, their gazes no longer glassy.

"As no contests have been filed concerning the estate of Julian Guillaume Gabriel," the judge said, "all assets are now the legal property of his heirs, Dante Julian Gabriel and Emilia Vivienne Gabriel, in equal shares."

Outside the courtroom, Bill grabbed my arm and pulled me aside.

"What happened in there isn't possible," he said.

"Apparently it is."

"This isn't you, Dante. I won't allow you to continue."

My fangs were still descended, and I snarled. "You have no fucking choice."

"Don't let this be who you are. Please."

The look in his eyes startled me, unnerved me even.

I'd expected to see anger, determination. Maybe pleading. But I didn't.

Bill's eyes held something I'd rarely seen him emote. *Fear*.

FIFTEEN

Erin

I awoke with a start. My body was stiff from lying on the couch.

What a dream! Dr. Bonneville had come to my door, and then she had morphed into Bea. It had been so real. Bea had quoted Thoreau again, and she'd been talking about Dante's sister and her pregnancy. She asked for vodka, and then she'd told me she had a remedy, and she'd given me—

I looked in my hand.

No crumpled piece of paper.

I looked at the floor.

No paper there either.

Yes, definitely a dream.

Nettle leaves, gingerroot, peppermint, chamomile. Wild yam.

Words—words that had been written on the piece of paper in my dream.

But it was only a dream. Those things couldn't possibly

help Emilia have a healthy and successful pregnancy. I'd never heard of wild yam, anyway. Was there such a thing? Sweet potatoes growing in the wild? Probably not.

I drew in a deep breath and looked at the clock on my phone. Dante would probably be home soon. The rest of the day would be spent wading through red tape and getting Julian's assets transferred.

I jolted when Dante burst through the door, followed by River and Emilia.

"Hey," I said. "Did everything go okay?"

"You could say that," River said. "We got the will through probate, anyway."

"What's the problem, then?"

Dante walked toward me and grabbed me in a tight embrace. When he finally pulled away, he looked at me, his face unreadable.

"What is it?" I asked.

"I'm not sure. Remember how I was able to glamour the night administrator to help get your leave of absence?"

I nodded.

"Today I apparently glamoured a judge."

River shook his head. "You did way more than that, Dante. You reversed a glamour on an entire courtroom, as well. You reversed the glamour of a vampire elder. What you did is technically not possible."

"Okay. Start at the beginning," I said.

"If you'll excuse me," Emilia said, "I need to go throw up."

For the first time since the three of them had walked in, I took a good look at her. She was green. Truly green. This was bad morning sickness.

I looked at my hand, where Bea had put the piece of paper

in my dream. "Are you feeling okay?"

"I'll be better after I puke."

I nodded. No use talking to her until she did what she had to do.

I turned back to Dante and River. "Tell me everything."

Dante opened his mouth but then shook his head. "You tell it, Riv. I still can't even believe it."

"None of us can," River said. "But it happened. Bill showed up at court to contest the will."

My brows shot up.

"Apparently he didn't want us getting the *Texts* translated because it would lead us to darkness, so he decided to tie up Uncle Jules's money so Dante and Em couldn't afford to do it. Dante got angry. I mean, really angry, and somehow he reversed Bill's glamour on the judge and the entire courtroom."

"Dante?" I said.

He shrugged. "I don't know how I did it. I know I couldn't do it again."

"What he did isn't possible," River said. "A vampire's glamour gets stronger with age. I can't glamour a roomful of people yet, but Bill apparently can, and he did it today. Everyone in the courtroom went glassy-eyed when Bill entered and started talking to us about why he was contesting the will."

"Where was Julian?" I asked.

"Bill had him tied up doing something. We'll find out what it was when we see him next, I guess." River shook his head. "I still can't fucking believe it."

I touched Dante's arm. He was cold as ice. "What did you do?"

"I have no idea. I was just really angry. So angry."

"Your teeth were frightening, man," River said. "I've never seen them like that."

I cupped Dante's cheek. His teeth were completely retracted. I'd seen them sharp and ferocious. And they'd been even more so earlier?

"Can you remember anything you did?" I asked.

"I can't. I don't think I was thinking at all. I was reacting purely on instinct, and I managed to get what we needed."

"By doing the impossible," River said again.

"Clearly it's not impossible if he did it," I offered.

"I'll never be able to repeat it. I have no idea how."

"You *will* be able to repeat it."

I jolted at Julian's voice. He stood before us as he always did, wearing the same clothing.

"Dad, where have you been?" Dante asked. "We could have used you this morning."

"Obviously you didn't need my help," the ghost said. "You're coming into a strange new power, Dante. One I don't have. River doesn't have. Bill doesn't have. I can't explain it, but I can try to help you learn to control it."

"How, if you don't have the power?"

"I'll teach you how to control your glamour. Once you know how to do that, you should be able to control any glamour power, no matter how intense."

"We need to get started then," Dante said. "What happened today was pretty daunting. Where were you, by the way?"

"My father sent me on a wild-goose chase. I should have seen what he was up to, and I'm sorry I didn't. You learn at an early age to trust your parents, and until now, my father has never been unworthy of my trust. I also didn't expect him to try to contest my will."

"No one's blaming you, Uncle Jules," River said.

Emilia emerged from the bathroom. "Hi, Daddy."

"Hi, sweet pea. Are you all right?"

"Not especially. This pregnancy sickness is the worst."

"Your mother had it bad both times," Julian said. "It's normal for our kind. Although...have you seen Jack lately? I don't like your skin tone."

"I see him in a few days."

"I think we should take you in now," River said. "I agree. You don't look good."

She scoffed. "Thanks."

Bea's face emerged in my mind. Maybe she had truly come to me in a dream to help Emilia, not just to warn me that the *Texts* had been stolen.

Nettle leaves, gingerroot, peppermint, chamomile. Wild yam.

Would those things help her? I had no idea. "Try some saltine crackers," I said. "You need to stay hydrated too. I know it's hard when you feel sick all the time, but you have to think of the baby's health."

"Believe me, none of that ever leaves my mind. But saltines don't help. I throw up everything I eat. It's been that way for the past week."

"I don't like the sound of this," Julian said. "Let's get you to the doctor."

"I agree with your dad," I said. "It sounds like you have hyperemesis gravidarum."

"Hyper what?"

"Just a fancy term for severe morning sickness. You might need IV fluids."

"It's normal for our kind," Julian said again.

"The sickness? Or her color?" River asked.

"I admit neither of your mothers ever turned green," Julian said.

"She needs to keep hydrated," I said. "Look at her. She's miserable."

"Thanks." Emilia rolled her eyes. "Who here hasn't told me how shitty I look?"

"I'll take her to see Jack," River said. "Dante, you can take care of the transfers yourself, can't you?"

"I'll try. I might need Em's signature, but I'll tell them she's ill today, which she is. She can always go in and sign later."

"Use your glamour," River said.

"What glamour? I may have this amazing power, but I have no idea how to control it or even to get it to come out at will. This is fucked up."

"A little," River agreed.

"I'll go with him," Julian said. "If any glamours are necessary, I can take care of it."

"Cool." River took Emilia's arm. "Let's go."

"I'm fine," she protested.

"You're green," River said. "That's *not* fine, at least not on this planet." He ushered her out the door.

Dante picked up the *Vampyre Texts* and held it. "It looks the same to me." He opened the book.

"What do you mean?" I asked.

"Apparently Bill had someone break in and steal the book. This is presumably a fake, according to him."

Chills crawled up my spine like tiny insects.

That book on the table? It's a fake. Someone has been here. Someone stole the real one.

My dream.

"What is it, Erin?" Julian asked.

I clamped my jaw shut after it had dropped open. "Nothing. At least I don't think it's anything." I quickly told them about my dream.

"Bea couldn't have made her way into my dream," I said.

"No. But a ghost could. A ghost that was inhabiting Bea, perhaps," Julian said. "Remember, she's a medium."

"She was quoting Thoreau again. But what would Thoreau know about morning sickness in vampires or whether the book was real?"

"Another ghost could have been quoting Thoreau," Dante offered.

"Oh! I almost forgot. When Bea first came to the door in my dream, she wasn't Bea. She was one of the ER doctors from University. Dr. Zabrina Bonneville."

"A doctor might know about morning sickness remedies," Dante said, "but how would she know about the book?"

"She could only get into your dream if she's dead, Erin," Julian said.

Dead? Dr. Bonneville? "She's not dead. She's on vacation with her husband."

SIXTEEN

DANTE

*A*sk the queen, Dante. Ask me what you want to know.

I clamped my hands over my ears in an attempt to shut *her* out. Not now. I had too much to do.

"Dante?" Erin said.

I removed my hands from my ears. "I'm okay."

"Are you sure, son?"

I nodded to my father. "Yeah."

Erin cleared her throat. "I suppose Dr. Bonneville could be dead. I should probably feel worse than I do about that possibility. Anyway, I'm sure she's fine. She's on a three-week vacation. I haven't seen her in a week or more."

"It could be anyone," Julian said. "A ghost will take the shape of whatever is familiar to you. Are you and this doctor close?"

"Ha!" Erin shook her head. "Not at all. She's an excellent physician, but on the niceness scale? She's a zero."

"If it's not someone close to you, it's doubtful it was her. It could have just been a random dream," Julian said.

"It didn't seem very random," Erin said. "I remember it so vividly. I remember the herbs that Bea had written down on the piece of paper. One I'd never even heard of. Wild yam." She grabbed her phone and punched on the keyboard. "I'll be damned. Here it is. Wild yam." Her eyes moved rapidly as she read. "There are conflicting views about whether it's safe during pregnancy. Some sources say it can cause miscarriage, but others say it helps morning sickness and can prevent miscarriage. Some say— Oh!"

"What?" Dante asked.

"Wild yam contains a substance that can be converted to progesterone in the body. Progesterone is a female hormone that we make naturally, but supplements of it are often given to women to *prevent* miscarriage."

"Maybe we should tell Jack," Dante said.

"We can tell him if you want," Erin said, "but I'd advise against using it. None of this is substantiated that I can see, and if it's associated with a risk of miscarriage, I'd stay away from it."

"What about the other ingredients?" Julian asked. "Are they safe?"

Erin did some quick typing. "Yeah, they all appear to be safe during pregnancy and can help with morning sickness. Nettle leaves, gingerroot, peppermint, chamomile."

I sent a quick text to River to relay the information to Jack. "Now, about the phony book."

Ask the queen. Ask what you wish to know.

"Damn it!"

"What is it, babe?" Erin asked.

I cleared her out of my head. "Nothing. I'm fine. Bill says the book is a fake. If I still had my sense of smell, I'd be able to tell if anyone had been here."

"Bea told me in my dream that the book had been stolen," Erin said. "Funny, it looks the same to me. Just as heavy as it always was. I never would have imagined it had been stolen and replaced."

"I guess we'll never know for sure," I said. "Bill could be lying."

"Then Bea would be lying as well"—Erin shrugged—"though admittedly it was a dream."

Julian shook his head. "I don't think so. Whatever is in the book has my father good and spooked, and this is a man who was never scared of anything. I'm wondering..."

"What?" I asked.

"Don't hate me for suggesting this, but maybe we should leave well enough alone."

"Are you serious, Dad? After all we've been through to get to this point? I had to see your dead body, for God's sake, with everything those creatures did to it. I'll never be able to scour that image from my mind."

"I know, son. I'm sorry. But my father isn't easily frightened, and he's clearly willing to move heaven and earth so we don't uncover what's hidden in the *Texts*."

"No. No. Just no." If I could have grabbed my father by the collar, I would have. "We have to. I have to understand the blood bond. And now, I have to understand what's happening to me, why I can apparently out-glamour an elder. It must all be in there. And damn it, we're going to figure it out."

Ask the queen. Just ask me.

She *was lying, of course.* She *never told me anything, just got me anxious enough to ask and then denied me any answers.*

As she *sucked the blood from my body,* she *sucked the life from my soul.*

Or so it felt, anyway.

As determined as I was to retain my strength, to escape someday, sometimes I nearly gave up.

Sometimes, I wished the unthinkable.

I wished for death.

It never lasted long, and I erased the thought as quickly as I could, but sometimes...

Mostly during torture. I refused to cry out, and I kept the promise to myself. But inside the deepest recesses of my brain, I sometimes let go.

I wished to cease existing.

What might death feel like? The process could be painful, but I'd endured horrific pain already.

And once the process was complete?

No pain.

Only peace.

How do you know that? Death might be eternal hellfire.

Her again. *In my head. I'd begun noticing it during her feedings. Somehow,* she *got into my head.*

Unless it was my imagination.

Not your imagination, Dante. I'm part of you now. As you are part of me.

I winced, though I was not in pain at the moment. I'd long since gotten used to her feedings, but while they were not exactly painful, they were far from enjoyable.

She *took.*

She *took without my consent.*

Then she *forced me to take from* her.

Those were the worst times. I needed blood. Without it, I would die. Hers was my only choice.

She *detached her teeth from my body, licking the puncture wounds closed.*

Then—

What? She *stood and began removing my leather bindings. I held back a gasp. Would* she *let me go?*

No. Of course not. She *had an ulterior motive.*

I soon found out what it was.

SEVENTEEN

Erin

"Dante?" Julian's voice dripped with concern.

Dante had stood immobile for several seconds after his tirade about figuring everything out. I tentatively touched his arm.

He broke from whatever kind of trance he was in and met my gaze. "I'm all right."

"You seemed a million miles away, son."

"Sometimes I just...remember. Does that happen to you, Dad?"

"Not anymore. But I'm not bound by the limitations of a physical brain. You still are. Memories are created in the brain, and they sometimes come when you don't want them."

Dante let out a sarcastic laugh. "You make it sound like it's better to be dead."

"In some ways, I suppose it is," Julian said. "But I can never again enjoy the crisp tannins of a glass of Bordeaux or the softness of a Pinot Noir. I can no longer let a piece of salmon sashimi melt on my tongue. I can never stroke the soft fur of a pet or smell the sweet fragrance of flowers in the spring. I can no longer run until my legs ache and feel the endorphins afterward. I can never again caress the warm skin of someone I love, Dante. I can't hug you or your sister." He shook his head. "In many more ways, it's so much better to be alive."

"But you can no longer feel pain."

"Part of the upside, though I guarantee you life is better. Embrace it while you have it. It's fleeting."

"Yet you chose death." Dante rubbed the back of his neck.

"I chose death for *you*. I've said this before, but you'll understand when you have a child of your own. I'd do it again a thousand times."

Dante seemed far off again for an instant. Then he sighed. "I know, Dad. I don't know how I'll be able to thank you enough."

"Together, we'll figure out what's going on. I'm sorry I suggested otherwise. I shouldn't have. Your life means so much to me that I allowed myself to be overprotective for an instant." He turned to me. "We'll find your friend too. We won't stop until all these mysteries are solved."

"What about Bill?" Dante asked.

"I will deal with my father. He may be the most powerful vampire in the world right now, but I'm no longer bound by the confines of the physical plane. I have a few tricks up my sleeve."

"It's nice to have a ghost on our side." I couldn't help smiling. "I can't believe those words just came out of my mouth."

That got a laugh out of Dante. "You rock, Dad."

"I'll take that as a compliment. But know this. My father might be the most powerful vampire in existence, but I have a feeling that will change very soon."

"How?" Dante gasped. "You don't mean..."

"No. No. Bill is in excellent health. But from what you and River described today, I think your power, once you learn to harness and control it, will blow your grandfather's away."

"That's impossible. I'm not even thirty. Bill is a hundred and two years old."

"Nothing is impossible, Dante. I'll admit it's improbable, but there is no explanation that I know of for what you were able to accomplish this morning. We'll look into it together. For now, though, I need to go. I want to peek in on Emilia at the doctor's."

"Let us know what's going on," Dante said.

"Absolutely." He disappeared.

I shook my head. "I'm not sure I'll ever get used to that. He's here, and then he's gone. No poof of smoke or fading out or anything."

Dante chuckled. "This is reality, Erin."

I burst into laughter. "Do you realize what you just said? Both of our realities have recently been turned upside down."

"True that. In fact, I don't know how I'd be getting through all this without you, baby."

I cupped his cheek, letting his dark stubble run roughly under my fingertips. "I know exactly what you mean." I stood on my toes and brushed my lips lightly over his. "You don't happen to have your rope, do you?"

He smiled against my lips. "I've moved what little I own here, love. I'm sure it's around somewhere."

I winked at him. "Let's find it."

❖

As I pulled on the rope binding my wrists to the rungs of the headboard, Dante tantalized my pussy with his tongue. His strokes were soft and teasing, not raw and untamed. That would come another time, when we both needed it.

For now, I was good with sweet and sultry, lounging on my bed, bound for his pleasure.

For *my* pleasure.

I writhed beneath him, grinding into his face as best I could without the benefit of my arms and hands. He continued to suck on my clit and then nipped my inner thigh, teasing me almost to climax.

"Dante! God!"

"Easy, baby. You'll get what you want when *I* decide it's time."

Tingles ran through me. The command in his voice always made me hot, made me want him all the more. As he tongued my pussy, I closed my eyes and let myself whirl inside the deepest recesses of my soul, where only Dante and I existed.

Only Dante and I...

He thrust two fingers into my wet channel, and the climax surged through me like a lightning bolt, hurling me further into my imaginary plane.

Images swirled in my mind... Dante, pounding into me. Dante, at my side as we exchanged rings and vows. Dante, as I struggled giving birth and then holding a beautiful black-haired newborn.

Our baby.

We'd have a baby someday.

A baby that...

My eyes popped open.

My body was still shaking, my pussy still pulsing, Dante's fingers still thrusting.

But the baby.

The baby.

Something was different.

Something was different yet wonderful.

Our baby—Dante's and mine—was a vampire.

EIGHTEEN

DANTE

Erin's body tensed.

She had clearly climaxed, and was enjoying it.

Now she was tense, her pussy walls no longer pulsing but gripping my fingers.

I withdrew them and looked up at her. "Baby?"

"Untie me, Dante. Untie me."

I was hard as a rock, ready to jam my cock into her heat, but the tone of her voice made me hesitate.

"Please," she said again. "Untie me."

I quickly released her from the headboard. "What's wrong, love?"

"Nothing. Nothing. I just saw something... I mean, it's okay, really. You're one. You're sister's one. River's one. Lucy's...well, not one, but something else. So what if we make another one? What's the big deal?"

"Erin, love"—I caressed her cheek—"what are you talking about?"

"Our baby, Dante." She closed her mouth quickly. "Shit. I

mean...I don't presume that you...that you and I..."

"Erin, it's okay. I know you're not presuming anything. What has you freaked out?"

"I was so happy, feeling so good, floating on a cloud, and then I climaxed, and it was perfect, and I saw us in my mind. I saw us"—she reddened—"getting married. And then..."

"What?"

"I saw our baby. He was beautiful, Dante."

"Any baby that comes out of you would have to be. It was a boy?"

"Yeah. It was. I think. But he..." She shook her head. "It can't be, according to what you've told me, but it was clear as day. I don't know how I knew it, but I did. He was a vampire, Dante."

The image I'd seen a few times landed back in my mind.

Erin handing me a bundle. The baby crying...and the tiny white nubs where his canines would grow in.

"I'm sorry," she continued. "I know it was just a fantasy. I was coming, and my mind was just going to beautiful stuff. Please don't think I expect—"

I placed two fingers over her lips. "Shh. It's okay. I know you don't expect anything. And for what it's worth, if I ever get married, it will be to you. I've always known that."

She smiled, sighing. "Me too. To you, I mean."

"Now tell me. Was there something about the baby?"

"No. I just knew. He was beautiful. Perfect red lips in the shape of a pout. A big tuft of black hair on his head. He was tiny and beautiful. And he couldn't be a vampire. You said a human and a vampire mating always results in a human baby."

"Yes. That's why there are so few of us left."

"So how...?"

I shook my head. "I don't know. It could be just your imagination playing tricks on you. Or it could be..."

"What?"

"I don't know. But I've seen the same thing, Erin. I've seen our baby, and he is vampire."

Once Erin had fallen asleep, I called out to my father. He appeared instantly.

"I need a good way to summon you," I said.

"Summon me?" He laughed.

"I didn't mean that to sound condescending, but I do need to know how to get in touch with you. Sometimes you come when I call, and sometimes you don't."

"I don't always hear you. And sometimes I do hear you, but I can't come."

"Okay, then. We need to figure out a communication system. You need to be able to let me know if you hear me, and if you can't come."

"I can't exactly carry a cell phone, Dante."

"I don't get that. You're wearing clothes, aren't you? Put it in your pocket."

"These clothes don't exist. You're seeing me the way it makes sense to you. There are no pockets because there are no clothes."

I sighed. "Great. All right. What do you suggest, then?"

"You're not a medium, so I can't speak to your mind."

"You did before I could see you. Remember?"

"I was speaking directly to you. It only felt like it was in your mind because you couldn't see or hear me yet. You weren't letting yourself."

"That is such a crock! Emilia and River saw you right away. Why the hell couldn't I?"

"We've been through this. I don't know."

"Fuck. That doesn't help, Dad."

"I know it doesn't. But you see and hear me now. Why does it matter?"

"It just does. It just fucking does." But why did it? He was right. I could see and hear him now.

"You have something your sister and your cousin don't have. There's something inside you, something that gave you the power to reverse your grandfather's glamour and get what you wanted. I've never seen or heard of anything like that before. All the more reason why we need to decipher the *Texts*."

"Bill took our only copy."

"Then we'll find another."

I regarded my father. He looked as real as he ever had when he was alive. "How did you get so optimistic?"

"How can I not be? Anything is possible now. I'd always thought that death meant the end of uniqueness. Now I know it doesn't. The body may perish, but the spirit lives on, Dante. The unique spirit lives on."

I smiled. "It is pretty amazing. But that's not what has you so enamored with life, no pun intended, right now."

"True. We got some good news for your sister. I got to Jack's right at the end of her appointment. Her illness is severe, but still in the range of normal for our kind, and both she and the baby are progressing well."

"That's great news."

"River gave Jack the list of herbs Erin recalled from her dream. Jack's going to look into it. He said it's possible they could give Em some relief."

"More great news, if it pans out."

"Let's be optimistic, son. It can't hurt. Positivity is a powerful tool."

I sighed. He was right, of course. "It's difficult to be positive when with every step forward, we seem to take two steps backward. We finally got the money to take the time and figure out what's going on, but now we don't have the book."

"We find another copy. And we try the website you found. They may have the translation, as they claim."

I rubbed my forehead to keep an ache from springing up. It vibrated just on the surface. If I could ease the tension just a bit...

Climaxing would have helped, but I could hardly do that at the moment.

"Do you believe Bill?" I asked. "I mean, do you believe that a man can be led to darkness by a book?"

"I believe in the inherent virtue of all men. Can some be led astray? Of course. We have positive proof of that with the many criminals among us. But I feel very strongly that you will not be. You have an internal strength that most only hope to have, Dante. You survived your captivity, and you survived it intact, both physically and mentally."

"I don't always feel mentally intact, Dad."

"No one does. But your inner strength, your good heart, got you through. You knew you were meant for something better, and you were determined not to let yourself be broken."

My father had ingested rattlesnake venom for me. No one was more determined than the ghost before me. "I think I got that from you."

He smiled. "Maybe you did. But I had a reason more powerful than you can yet imagine to get me through. You and your sister."

"That's not true. I wanted to get back for Em, for you, for River and Bill."

"I'm sure you did, but one day you'll know a much fiercer love. Think about how you feel for Erin, and then multiply that by the idea that you brought an individual into the world who is not yet self-aware—an individual who, but for you, would not exist. The bond a parent feels for a child is indescribable. It's as intense as a love for your partner, yet in a wholly different way."

"I'm trying to understand."

"You will someday. I feel very strongly that you and Erin will have children."

Children.

A son.

A vampire son.

"Dad?"

"Hmm?"

"I had a... I'm not sure what it was. I wouldn't call it a vision. Just a picture in my mind. Of Erin handing me a baby. A vampire baby, Dad."

"That would be wonderful, but it's not possible."

"I know. And the weird thing is that she had the same vision earlier today."

"In a dream?"

"No, not really." I didn't want to tell my father that she had it during an orgasm. TMI.

"It could mean absolutely nothing."

"I know that. But what seems significant, to me at least, is that we both saw the same thing."

"It's puzzling. I won't deny that. But physiology is physiology. A vampire and human always produce a human baby."

"Why is that?"

"I don't know. Some kind of genetic dominance on the human's part, obviously."

"But hasn't anyone ever studied it?"

"I'm sure they have. We could ask Jack."

Jack. My blood. My B positive blood.

"There's something else," I said.

"What?"

"I had some blood work done, to find out my blood type. I'm B positive."

"And?"

"I'm your son, right? I look like you. And you watched me come out of Mom, right?"

"I did."

"Jack says he did some genetic testing when I was born, and you two are definitely my parents. The problem is, both of you are Rh negative, and it's genetically impossible for two Rh negative parents to produce an Rh positive child. Something happened to me while I was in captivity, Dad. Someone changed my physiology."

"I'm no scientist, but that doesn't seem likely."

"I know. Jack couldn't explain it, beyond calling it a spontaneous mutation."

"I suppose that's possible."

"Yeah, but unlikely." I shoved my fingers through my hair. "I remember some things about my time in captivity. I remember some of the torture, the pain. I remember her feeding from me, and then forcing me to feed from her. We always learned that drinking vampire blood could cause unwanted side effects. Could spontaneous Rh factor change be one of them?"

"That's hardly an unwanted side effect. It has no effect on your life at all."

"I know, but— What about this strange ability I have for glamouring? I out-glamoured Bill, for God's sake, and I have no idea how. I just knew what had to happen, and I made it happen. Could that be a side effect?"

"I don't know. It's been some time since you drank her blood."

"True. I'm drinking Erin's blood now. The blood bond..." My mind raced. "Maybe the bond. We're taught not to drink from humans. Maybe there's a reason beyond it being immoral. Maybe human blood gives us something..."

"Dante, despite what we're taught, some vampires survive on human blood."

"Not the blood of someone they're bonded to."

"True. Not that we know of, at least."

I walked to the coffee table and picked up the counterfeit *Vampyre Texts.* "Damn you, stupid fake book. I want the secrets. I need the secrets."

You will have them, Dante. You will have them all.

When you learn to ask.

NINETEEN

Erin

I awoke with a start, sweat dripping down my cheeks. I sat up, and the perspiration poured from my forehead into my eyes. I squinted away the sting.

My heart hammered and my palms were clammy.

I'd dreamed something. Something big.

Something I struggled now to recall.

A baby had been crying—alone and crying.

A vampire baby.

But not Dante's and mine, like I'd seen before. This was a different baby. A baby I knew, somehow, I had some sort of connection to.

Emilia's baby, maybe? I rubbed my brow.

I could call Julian, have him glamour me to remember the dream better like he had before.

No. For some reason that I couldn't articulate, it was important that I remember this dream without any prompting.

It was necessary.

Vital, even.

I rose, went to the bathroom, and splashed some water on my face to get rid of the perspiration. Then I lay back down and closed my eyes.

I breathed in, out, back in again.

Relax. Relax. Relax.

The baby again. She was crying. Yes, it was a little girl. I just knew. She was crying.

Someone help her! She's hungry! She needs her diaper changed.

Still she cried.

Still no one came.

Then a voice.

"I want my baby!"

A voice I recognized.

Who was it?

"Be quiet."

A male voice. Another voice I recognized.

Logan.

Logan was keeping this mother from her baby.

My heart sped up and the images dispersed. No!

Easy, Erin. Just relax.

"Can't move. Help me. Help me, please. I want my baby."

The woman's voice again. She was lying in a hospital bed. She couldn't move. God, she was in pain. She'd had some kind of surgery.

Logan.

I think I might have done some surgeries.

He'd said that when I found him.

He'd performed surgery on this woman.

The baby still wailed.

Why wasn't anyone taking care of the baby?

"Help me!" the woman cried. *"Help me, please!"*

I shot my eyes open.

The woman. I recognized her.

The young mother who had been transferred to a hospital in Baton Rouge.

"Help me," she said again. *"Please help me, Erin!"*

THE QUEEN

Your powers are emerging, Dante. You are more formidable than your father or uncle could hope to be. And your grandfather? He's an old fool whose time is at an end. He won't torment you for much longer.

The answers you seek are within you. You don't need to decode a book to find them.

The darkness your grandfather fears is real.

You don't need to fear it, Dante.

You must embrace it.

BLOOD BOND SAGA

PART 9

PROLOGUE

Erin

I rose, went to the bathroom, and splashed some water on my face to get rid of the perspiration. Then I lay back down and closed my eyes.

I breathed in, out, back in again.

Relax. Relax. Relax.

The baby again. She was crying. Yes, it was a little girl. I just knew. She was crying.

Someone help her! She's hungry! She needs her diaper changed.

Still she cried.

Still no one came.

Then a voice.

"I want my baby!"

A voice I recognized.

Who was it?

"Be quiet."

A male voice. Another voice I recognized.

Logan.

Logan was keeping this mother from her baby.

My heart sped up and the images dispersed. No!

Easy, Erin. Just relax.

"Can't move. Help me. Help me, please. I want my baby."

The woman's voice again. She was lying in a hospital bed. She couldn't move. God, she was in pain. She'd had some kind of surgery.

Logan.

I think I might have done some surgeries.

He'd said that when I found him.

He'd performed surgery on this woman.

The baby still wailed.

Why wasn't anyone taking care of the baby?

"Help me!" the woman cried. "Help me, please!"

I shot my eyes open.

The woman. I recognized her.

The young mother who had been transferred to a hospital in Baton Rouge.

"Help me," she said again. "Please help me, Erin!"

ONE

DANTE

I walked to the coffee table and picked up the counterfeit *Vampyre Texts*. "Damn you, stupid fake book. I want the secrets. I *need* the secrets."

You will have them, Dante. You will have them all.

When you learn to ask.

Bitch was still in my head, talking in riddles as usual. So many questions, none of which the book in my hands could answer given that it was a counterfeit of the original.

But was it?

Bill said it was, but I no longer trusted Bill. Bea had told Erin in a dream that it was. But how much stock could be put in a dream?

"I understand your frustration, son."

My father's ghostly form still stood in the room. He looked so perfect. So healthy. So...*real*. The image of his battered and partially decomposed body erupted in my mind.

No son should have to see his father look the way my father had.

Yet here he stood before me, as young and vibrant as I remembered him. Problem was? It was all an illusion.

"Do you?" I asked. "Do ghosts feel frustration? Do ghosts feel...anything?"

"Of course we do. Do you think I would be here if I didn't?"

"I'm sorry. You must feel. I know you're here to protect me. To protect Erin, River, and Emilia. You would have no desire to protect us if you couldn't feel. It was a stupid question, Dad. Forgive me."

"There's nothing to forgive, Dante. As I said, I understand your frustration."

"You said you would teach me everything you should've taught me in the last ten years."

"I will, although I think you might be the one to teach me."

"What do you mean by that? I know nothing, Dad. Nothing."

"Perhaps you don't have knowledge in the formal sense, but Dante, you have abilities I never had. That Braedon never had. You sent Bill to his knees in the courtroom. Your grandfather is scared, Dante. Not just by what he read in the book. He's scared of *you*."

Tiny invisible feet scampered up my spine. "Are *you* scared of me?"

My father smiled. "No, I'm not. I'm a ghost. You can't hurt me."

"Does Bill think I would hurt him? I would never—"

"Not intentionally. Of course you wouldn't. I will teach you what I can. You've already learned a lot of control, but when times are dire, you come close to losing it. I don't believe you would hurt Bill. I don't believe you have ever hurt Erin, which is why I left when you demanded I do so the other day.

You have control, Dante. The problem is...neither of us knows exactly what we're dealing with here. These newfound powers you've exhibited are unlike anything I've ever seen. We should probably talk to Jack about them."

"We can do that. But before we do, I need you to begin teaching me. Bill said fathers teach their children through symbolry and example. Can you still do that? I mean, being a ghost now?"

"I'll do my best. Would you like to begin now? Or would you rather get some sleep?"

"I'd like to do it—"

"Dante!"

Erin. The scream was shrill and full of fright. I raced right through my father's form—the feeling was intensely odd, like a combination of gelatin and seawater—up the stairs and into the bedroom.

"Baby?"

She sat up in bed, her spine straight as a board, her eyes wide as dinner plates.

"Erin, love, what is it? Are you all right?"

She swallowed, the gulp registering in my ears. "I had another one of those bizarre dreams, Dante. Why is it that every dream I have lately seems so real? Seems to be telling me something?"

"I don't know, baby. What was the dream about?"

She closed her eyes. "A patient was calling for my help. Her baby was crying. She was a seventeen-year-old young woman who gave birth in the ER a week or so ago. Her parents transferred her to Baton Rouge."

"Is she still hospitalized somewhere there?"

"I don't know. The baby was a bit premature, but her lungs

were good." Erin smiled. "She wanted to name her daughter after me. Isabelle Erin."

"Do you remember her name?"

"Patty Doyle."

"We can have River and Jay check it out. Make sure she's all right."

She let out a relieved sigh. "That's a great idea. I could find out if I were at the hospital, but I no longer have access to those databases now that I'm on leave. I just want to make sure she and the baby girl are okay. We kind of bonded, and then she was transferred. I never got to check back in with her and make sure they were okay."

"I'll text Riv." I pulled out my phone and sent the text.

"What next then? River, Jay, and I are all on leave. To help you. Where do we go from here?"

Damned good question. I had no answer.

"Dante?"

"I love you, Erin."

"I love you too. But what—"

I stopped her soft lips with a gentle touch of my fingers. "We need to sit down with my dad and figure out what our next step is."

He appeared, jolting Erin.

"Shit, Julian!"

"I'm sorry. Are you all right?"

"Yeah. Just another weird dream."

"Anything I should know about?"

"No. It was about a patient who was transferred to Baton Rouge. I'm sure she's fine. I'm much more concerned with the patients who've disappeared, beginning with Lucy."

"We have two mysteries to solve," I said. "The missing

women and finding Uncle Brae. Make that three. The blood bond. No, four. The secrets of the *Texts*."

"We do have our work cut out for us," my father said.

"Plus, you're supposed to teach me what I missed. We were going to begin when Erin screamed."

"I'm sorry I interrupted you. I don't know why I dreamed about this particular patient. She can be accounted for, according to Dr. Bonneville. I should be more concerned about Lucy and the others. I *am*. So why would I dream about a patient who doesn't need me?"

"I don't know, Erin." My father sighed. "At times like these, I really wish I could sit down next to you. Share your physical world again for a moment."

"You thought my dream about the vampires in the ER could be a premonition. What about this dream?"

"It could be, but I doubt it. You said yourself that this patient isn't in any danger. She's safe in Baton Rouge. It could be just a fear of yours manifesting itself."

"But everything about this dream—the images and the emotion they invoked—felt so *real*."

"Dreams can feel that way," he said, "especially when you wake up in the middle of one."

"I'm going to have Riv and Jay check it out," I said. "For her peace of mind."

"Good idea."

"I feel so ridiculous," Erin said. "We have so much more important stuff to deal with, and I'm taking up time with a silly dream about a patient and her crying baby. Then I had this really strong feeling that Logan had performed some kind of surgery."

Ice chilled my veins. "Wait a minute. Logan Crown was in the dream?"

"No. He wasn't there. It was just a feeling. A really strong feeling that he'd operated on the woman or her baby. Maybe both."

"But he's back at the hospital now," my father said.

"Yes. He came back. You know that."

"So he can't be in Baton Rouge operating on the woman or the child, then."

Erin shook her head, laughing lightly. "I've lost it, haven't I?"

"No more so than the rest of us, baby." I smoothed her hair. "We've all had more than our share to deal with lately."

I wanted to soothe her, make her feel better. But the mention of Logan Crown had me tensed up like the skin of a drum. Maybe it was because I'd caught him about to fuck Erin.

Maybe it was because the very sound of his name made me want to throw heavy objects.

Or maybe it was something else. Something I couldn't define. Something I didn't even know yet.

Whatever it was, I knew in the marrow of my bones that something was sinister about him.

"So," my father was saying, "we need to decide whether we'll be working days or nights, now that everyone is free."

"We're all used to working nights," Erin said.

"But you're not as safe at night, when the Claiborne vamps are out," I reminded her.

"Hello?" She held out her wrist. "Did you forget my anti-scent perfume?"

"We don't know for sure—"

"Dante, River couldn't smell me. What more proof do you need?"

"Son," my father said, "nights are a good idea. You know

that as well as I do."

"Yeah, I know." I sighed. "I just want her safe, Dad."

"You will protect her. You, River, and her brother."

"We don't even know what we're dealing with," I said.

"I know. Which is why it's time to contact Nocturnal Truth. It's time to find out what's in the *Texts*."

Without warning, Erin gasped and took a quick step back, her lips dropping into an O.

TWO

Erin

A lightning bolt hit me. "Julian? Remember how you helped me remember my dream? Could you help someone remember something that happened while they were awake?"

"Yes. But the person would have to be open to it."

"What are you getting at, baby?"

"The first woman who disappeared and then returned. Her name is Cynthia North. She couldn't recall anything when I talked to her. Could you help her even if she'd been kept in a drug-induced coma?"

"I don't know," Julian said. "I've never tried that before. It would require a really strong glamour. Stronger than any ghostly glamour. The only one who could probably produce a result is an elder."

"Bill," Dante said.

"But Dante, you reversed Bill's glamour," I said. "Maybe *you* could do it!"

He shook his head, sighing. "I have no idea how I

accomplished what I did, love. I doubt I could repeat it."

"Probably not," Julian agreed. "From what you've told me, you were acting purely from emotion due to the situation. It was instinctive. That will be difficult to replicate if you're not feeling the same intensity."

"But you could teach me," Dante said.

"I can teach you what I know about glamouring," Julian said. "I don't have the ability to do what you did in the courtroom. No one does."

"Can't we at least try?" I begged. "Cynthia is our only chance to find out where Lucy and the others might be."

"We can always try," Dante said. "But I can't guarantee anything. And we'd need her permission."

"Leave that to me," I said.

"I'm here to see Cynthia North," I told the receptionist at Elyssa's Beauty Salon and Spa.

"Do you have an appointment?" she asked.

"No, I'm sorry."

"Well, you're in luck. Cynthia has an opening in fifteen minutes. Would you like to take it?"

"An opening for what?"

"For a facial. She's one of our estheticians."

Jay, who had found out where Cynthia worked, hadn't been able to tell me what her job was at the spa. A facial didn't sound half bad. I'd never had one before. Why not pamper myself a little while I talked to her? Plus, I'd have her undivided attention for an hour. "Yeah, that sounds great. Pencil me in."

"Perfect." She handed me a clipboard. "Fill out this

paperwork, and then I'll take you back to the relaxation room."

Relaxation room. Any room that could produce relaxation in me at this moment would be a true miracle. I absently answered the questions about my skin type and general health and then handed the questionnaire back to the receptionist.

"Thank you," she said with a pasted-on smile. "Let's get you back to the lounge." She led me through a narrow hallway to a dark room. Several women in robes sat in cushy chairs. "Since you're having a facial rather than a massage, you can undress in the treatment room, but if you'd like, I can give you a locker and a robe."

"No. I'm fine. But thanks."

"Then have a seat. Cynthia will be with you soon."

I sat down and absently pulled a magazine from a pile on the table in front of me. I opened it and couldn't read a thing due to the darkness in the room. Interesting. Did they have a lot of vampire clients? I nearly laughed aloud. No one else could possibly read in this room.

The woman across from me leafed quickly through a magazine, while the one next to her had leaned back and closed her eyes.

Me? I had the jitters. For a minute, I thought about actually trying to relax and enjoy the facial.

But that wasn't why I'd come here.

The lit clock on the wall showed five minutes to four p.m. This was probably Cynthia's last facial of the day, unless she worked a swing shift.

The second hand moved around the clockface.

Tick Tock.

Sometimes time seemed to stand still.

"Erin?"

I jerked in my chair. Cynthia North stood in the doorway of the room, looking much better than the last time I'd seen her. Her cheeks were rosy, and she sported what looked like a genuine smile.

I stood. "That's me."

Cynthia held out her hand. "I'm Cynthia. I'll be doing your facial today."

She didn't recognize me. Why should she? We'd talked for only a few minutes when she'd been recovering from a drug-induced coma.

"We've actually met," I said.

"I'm sorry. Have you been in before? Your paperwork says you've never had a facial."

I cleared my throat. "No, not here. I'm an ER nurse at University."

Her knuckles whitened as she grabbed the doorknob to what I presumed was our treatment room. "Were you there the night I was...shot?"

"Yes."

"And then when I..."

"Came back. Yes. I came to see you. Do you remember?"

"I don't like to talk about that." She pressed her lips into a firm line.

"I understand." I bit my lower lip. No lie there. I *did* understand. Problem was, I had come here to make her talk about it, to convince her to talk to Julian, a ghost. Or River.

For a split second, I considered just enjoying the treatment.

But Lucy. And the others. They needed me desperately. I had come here to get information, and I would do my best.

Cynthia turned to me, smiling. Sort of. She handed me a wraparound towel. "Please take off your shirt and bra and put

this on. Then lie face up on the table. I'll give you a few minutes."
She left the room.

Native American flute music drifted around the confined space, and the fresh scent of lavender wafted toward me. I drew in a breath and touched the table. The cushioning was soft and warm. Heated.

The perfect equation for relaxation.

Too bad that wasn't in the cards.

I undressed, donned the wrap, and lay on the table, covering myself with the warm cotton sheet.

And I waited.

And waited.

Had she forgotten about me?

Then a knock on the door. "Ready?"

"Yeah. Come on in."

"Hi, Erin. I'm Sheree. Cynthia had an emergency and had to leave, so I'll be doing your treatment today."

I looked into the face of an attractive African American woman. "Oh? Is everything all right?"

"Yes. She said not to worry."

She'd run. Cynthia had run rather than talk to someone who'd been at the hospital when she'd arrived and when she'd returned.

Which meant one of two things. Either she was trying to escape the entire ordeal, or she was afraid I was going to ask her something she didn't want to talk about.

I was betting on the latter.

"So you've never had a facial before?" Sheree continued.

"No."

"Then close your eyes. You're in for a treat."

"I really needed to..."

"What?" Sheree asked.

Talk to Cynthia, I finished in my mind. But I didn't want to be rude to Sheree. She was here to do a job, and she was helping out a coworker. "Could you do me a favor?"

"If I can."

"I'm going to give you my phone number. Could you see that Cynthia gets it?"

"Of course. I'll get it from you when we're done. Now, close your eyes and relax."

Relax.

Sure.

If only that were possible.

THREE

DANTE

"Glamouring is all about energy," my father said.

"What kind of energy?"

"All living beings are made of energy. A lot of it goes to support the body, but vampires have the ability to harness their excess energy and force it onto others. That's how we glamour."

"Why can't humans do it?"

"They most likely can. They just don't realize it. Some people have learned to tap into those excess stores of energy and produce results. Telepaths, for example. And telekinetics. As for why it's easier for vampires to glamour? History tells us the power was used to subdue prey to feed on their blood."

"Like I subdued the homeless man—Abe—that first night."

"Exactly. Your need for blood forced the glamour on him. You acted on instinct, as you have each time you've been able to glamour. I will teach you how to harness the energy and produce it whenever you need it. But there's a caveat."

"What's that?"

"You have much more power than any vampire I've seen

or heard of. You've got your grandfather scared, Dante. He's scared of what he read in that book. And now he's scared of *you*."

The thought should have frightened me. Should have. Instead, it emboldened me. "I never thought I'd see Bill be afraid of anything."

"Neither did I. I can't help but wonder..."

"What?"

"If the two are related somehow. That this power you're exhibiting is somehow related to what he read in the *Texts*."

"I don't know. I doubt it. Why would it be?"

"It's unlikely, true, but worth looking into."

"Well, we're going to get the *Texts* translated one way or another. I guess we'll find out then. But Dad, do you think..." Unwanted thoughts muddled my mind.

"Do I think what?"

My shoulders tightened. "Do you think I'm capable of harming anyone with this weird power I seem to have?"

His eyes softened as he looked at me. "Dante, all living beings are capable of harming another, no matter what power they hold. Remember that. It will serve you well. Your power is not a weapon in and of itself. Only *you* can make it one."

"Control," I said softly.

"Precisely."

Control. Strength. Everything came down to those two things. "I tried to be strong, Dad. When I was...*there*. With *her*. I made a promise to myself that I wouldn't cry out when they tortured me, wouldn't give them the satisfaction. I kept that promise."

"That shows amazing self-control."

"But I did say one thing that I regret. That I wish I could take back."

"What's that?"

"I called her 'my queen.'" Humiliation threatened to strangle me. This was my father. Even though he was dead, I still respected him more than any other man I knew. "I tried. I resisted as much as I could, but the pain was unbearable. She was willing to go to any length to get me to say it."

"They're only words, Dante. Did you mean them?"

"Of course not."

"Then they mean nothing. They were said under duress. Hold a gun to someone's head, and you can get him to say just about anything."

"But *you* didn't. You didn't call her a queen."

"Why would you think that?"

"She told me. In a...vision or something." I lowered my voice. "She gets into my head sometimes."

"Dante, I don't know whether she told you that or not, but I never saw this queen you speak of when I was in captivity, and I certainly never referred to anyone as such." He paused a moment.

He had a look about him, a look I recognized. If he'd still been wearing his wedding ring—which he wore for several years after my mother died—he'd be twisting it on his finger. Something was making him nervous.

Then, "What do you mean she gets into your head?"

I darted my gaze around the room.

"Look at me, son."

I faced him. Faced what was left of my father. All because of me. All because of *her*.

"Now tell me. How does she get into your head?"

How to put it into words? I sighed.

"You said you had a vision," my father said.

"More like auditory hallucinations."

"You hear her?"

"Not exactly. She's in my head. I can't really describe it."

"Do you think she's communicating with you telepathically?"

"That's what it seems like. Sometimes. Are vampires telepaths?"

"Not usually, but like humans, a small percentage can have that gift. So few of us are left, though, that you'd be hard-pressed to find one."

"I can chase her out most of the time, but sometimes I can't."

"When you're feeling more vulnerable?"

"Maybe. Or..." I sighed. "I have so many questions, Dad, and I believe she has answers. Sometimes I... I think I actually *let* her in."

"First of all, it might be in your mind. You've been through a lot of trauma, and you haven't fully healed from it. But let's say for the sake of argument that she *is* communicating with you. She lied to you about me, son. She's probably lying to you about having answers as well. Never trust a liar." He smiled. It was tentative, but it was a smile.

I let out a nervous laugh. "Those seem like reasonable words to live by."

Then he got serious. "Dante, listen to me. If you never take any more advice from me, take what I'm about to say."

I nodded.

"Whether she's getting into your head or whether it's your own imagination doesn't matter."

"It doesn't?"

"No. The important thing—the *most* important thing—is

that you do *not* succumb. Do you understand me?"

"I would never succumb to her!" My gums prickled as my teeth grew.

"Son, you just told me that sometimes you let her in."

"Only because I want answers. I need answers."

"I understand, and it may be your imagination, like I said. But if it's her, she's manipulating you. She already lied to you about me. That is how evil works. It gains your trust with manipulation. Don't let her do that to you. You're stronger than that."

As my teeth continued to descend, my blood moved through my veins, nourishing my muscles. "I'm stronger than that," I repeated.

"I don't know what kind of power this female vampire has, son, but know this. You can withstand anything. I've never seen the kind of power you possess."

"What if I can never learn to control it?"

"No more questions. There is only what you and I both know in our hearts. You *will* control it."

"I *will* control it."

"Good. Now let's begin your training."

I was lying on the couch, my eyes closed, when Erin returned from seeing Cynthia North. My father had put me through some vigorous mental exercises, and I was exhausted.

"Hi, baby," she said, closing the door.

I opened my eyes. She looked radiant. Her skin was glowing.

"Hey, beautiful. How did it go?"

She sighed and plunked down on a chair, holding a red gift bag. "It didn't. Turns out Cynthia's an esthetician at a nearby salon, and she had an appointment open. I grabbed it, but as soon as she realized who I was, she had another girl fill in for her. I made sure to give her stand-in my number so she could give it to Cynthia, though I doubt she'll reach out, since she ran away today. Great facial, though. Not that I have anything to compare it to."

"That's why your skin looks so amazing."

"You mean it doesn't always look amazing?" She smiled tiredly.

"Of course it does."

"Sheree—the girl who did the facial—recommended this new cream with natural herbs that block the sun's rays. She said it would be great for someone as fair as I am. So of course I buckled under the pressure and bought the skin care line." She held up the bag. "Now that I'm not working, apparently I think it's okay to spend three hundred dollars on moisturizer and eye cream."

I laughed. "She must have been a great salesperson."

"She massaged my hands and arms into jelly. I probably would have bought swampland from her." She sighed. "I'll take the products back tomorrow."

"Like hell you will. You deserve something nice for yourself."

"Dante, I can't afford this kind of stuff."

"You can now. I'm rich, remember? Or at least I will be when all the assets transfer."

She reddened. "I'm not."

"What's mine is yours, love. You know that. In the meantime, I got approved for a credit card that just came in the mail today, so we're good until the money hits."

"Not to pry, but...just how rich are you?"

"Suffice it to say that neither one of us has to work another day in our lives. Even after we pay to get the *Texts* translated."

She dropped her jaw open. "Wow."

"Yeah. I know. My mom came from vampire royalty."

"You said there wasn't any vampire royalty."

"Not *real* royalty. Just old money, you know, like the Kennedys."

"I had no idea."

"Now you know. And you're keeping the stuff you bought, okay?"

"Okay. Just this once. We're not going to become spendthrifts, Dante."

"Of course not, but we can splurge every now and then. In fact, I'd love to splurge on you right now, but I'm afraid I'm too exhausted. My dad gave me the mental workout of a lifetime while you were gone."

"You started your training, huh?"

"Training? I feel like I just ran a double marathon with no training at all."

"It'll get easier, Dante."

"Whether it does or not, I'm all in. I have to be."

She rose. "You hungry?"

"I could eat."

"I'll whip us up something." She headed to the kitchen.

I lay back down and closed my eyes, when my phone buzzed in my back pocket. I looked to the kitchen. Erin was pulling frozen hamburgers out of the freezer.

I read the text. "Shit."

"What is it?" she asked.

"I hope you've got more of those. River and Jay are on their way over here."

"What for?"

"They say they have news. That's it." I hurriedly texted River back, asking for details.

Erin opened the freezer. "I only have four more burgers. Jay always eats two. I guess I can have a hot dog. My George Foreman grill will get a workout tonight."

"Whatever you want, baby." I listened to her with one ear. "Damn. Riv isn't responding."

"I'm sure we'll hear everything when they get here. What do you want to drink?"

"Just water is good. Scratch that. Make it bourbon if you've got it. My head is exploding from my father's exercises."

A few minutes later, she handed me a bourbon on the rocks.

"You actually have it?"

"Yeah. I picked it up after my dream about Bea. She asked me for vodka in the dream, and for some reason I felt like I needed to have some in the house. I got bourbon too, since I know you like it."

"Thanks, baby." I took a long sip. "This is what I was drinking the night we danced at the bar. Remember?"

"How could I forget? We'd both had more than a few that night." She smiled. "The music."

"The music that wasn't there," I said. "Except that it was."

"I know."

Even now, I heard the faint jazzy tune. No, I didn't hear it so much as *feel* it. It was second nature to me now whenever Erin and I were together, so much so that I'd gotten used to its omnipresence.

Erin walked back into the kitchen while I furiously began another text.

Then—

No knock. Just two big men barreling through the front door.

"We've got trouble," River said. "Right here in New Orleans."

FOUR

Erin

The facial had relaxed me more than I thought possible, but River's words negated the entire effect. I poured myself a bourbon and headed to the living area.

"What's going on?" Dante asked.

"Bill." River shook his head. "Fucking Bill. He did something to the boss down at the station. He denied our requests for leaves of absence. So we either go back to work... or we lose our jobs. For good."

"Do you know for sure it was Bill?" I asked.

"Who the hell else could it be, Erin?" River said. "No one else has the power to reverse my glamours."

They all looked to Dante.

"Hey, why would *I* do that? I need you guys helping on this shit."

"He's been here with me since we got back," I said. "And when I went out, Julian was here with him."

"Sorry, cuz. I know you had nothing to do with it. Can you

fix it? Jay and I need our jobs."

"I can try, but I can't guarantee anything. I have no idea how I did that shit in the courtroom. You know that."

"You said you were with Uncle Jules. Isn't he helping you?"

"Yeah, and my mind is fucking fried. I can't do anything tonight."

"There's really not a problem here," I said.

"Just how do you see it that way, baby sis?" Jay said.

"Quit your jobs."

"And live on what? Our good looks?" Jay scoffed. "No one's paying us for being studs."

I rolled my eyes. "Don't be ridiculous. Just quit for now, and when this is all over and Dante learns to control this glamour thing, he can get you your jobs back."

River burst out in laughter, which irked me.

"What's so damned funny?" I stood with my hands on my hips, indignant.

"It's brilliant. Jay and I were so pissed off, we didn't see what was right in front of our eyes."

"That's my little sis." Jay whomped me on the back, nearly knocking me off my feet.

"One small issue, though," Dante said. "Bill won't back down. He's freaked out, and he's going to do everything he can to get us to stop pursuing this."

"Then we'll have to stop him from stopping us," River said. "And you're the only one who can do that, Dante."

"Not right now I can't," he said. "I can't just will myself to act on instinct."

"Get mad enough, and you'll be able to do it."

"I *am* mad. But that's clearly not enough, or I'd be doing it right now."

"Anger's not the only trigger," I said. "When I was having trouble getting my leave at work, you did it. You weren't angry then, were you?"

"No. I just knew you needed that leave, so I made it happen."

"So maybe anger doesn't trigger it. Maybe need does."

"That's true," River said. "You needed Uncle Jules's money to research the *Texts*. Bill's contest of the will was in the way. You eliminated it by doing...well, whatever it is you apparently can do."

"This is still so much to deal with." Jay sat down with a plunk. "I'll take one of those bourbons, Sis, if you don't mind."

"Me too," River said.

I filled two more glasses and brought them out.

"Thanks." Jay took a long drink. "Good thing we're not working tonight."

"Ditto, partner." River took an even longer drink and then let out a sigh. "At least one good thing happened today. I've been so pissed at Bill that I haven't ruminated on Lucy's disappearance. But now I feel guilty."

"We'll find her, partner," Jay said. "We'll find all of them."

"Except we no longer have the resources of the department," River said.

"The department hasn't found jack shit on those cases," Jay said. "Who needs them?"

Dante was eerily quiet.

"Babe?" I said.

His eyes were glassy.

"No. Is she with you?"

He shook his head. "But something is. That darkness. I felt it the first time I came here. Something is here. Can't any of you guys feel it?"

I felt creepy crawlies on my neck, but those were from Dante's words. At least I thought they were, since I hadn't felt them before. "Maybe we should go out to dinner."

"No." Dante shook his head vehemently. "We won't be chased out of our own home. Not by whatever the hell this is. Come and get me, you piece of shit! You want to target me? Come take what you want."

I laughed nervously. "I was trying to get out of cooking."

"Seriously? None of you feel that?"

"What exactly are you feeling?" River asked.

"I'm not sure I can describe it. Just a feeling of unease. Like the beginnings of evil. Something dark. This is the third time I've felt it here, I think. Maybe the fourth."

"Do you always feel it *here*?" I asked. "That's freaky."

"No. I felt it that night in the restaurant, when we left quickly. That night my dad was there to warn me."

"If it was really here, wouldn't he be warning you now?" I said.

"Maybe." He sighed. "Maybe it's just the mental exhaustion. He really worked me out today."

"You know what?" River said. "I like Erin's idea. Let's go out to dinner. We can hit the Quarter, have a few hurricanes. God knows we deserve a night out. We can talk strategy. We need a plan."

"Yeah, we do," I said. "I tried to talk to Cynthia North today, but she bailed, and she's our only lead."

"What about the other woman from the free clinic?" Jay asked.

"Bella Lundy?" I said. "We could try. You guys will need to track her down."

"Again, we need the department's resources." River held

up his hand. "Don't say it."

"How else can we get the information?" Jay asked.

River huffed. "Fine. I'll get the address. I hate doing it this way, but it's for Lucy." His eyes softened. "I'll do anything for Lucy. God, I hope she's okay."

Fear laced with sadness welled in me. I could use my best friend right about now. She was alive. We had to hold on to that. She was alive. If Cynthia, Bella, and Logan had all been returned, whoever was taking people didn't have an interest in killing them.

I pasted on a smile. Someone had to try to lighten us up, or we'd get nothing done. "I'd die for a Pimm's Cup. Let's go to Napoleon House. For one evening, maybe we can let loose. We all need it."

"But Lucy..." River shook his head.

"I know. She's my best friend. But we've got to eat."

"We can't leave, not until—" Dante stopped abruptly.

"What is it?" I asked.

"The thing. The darkness. It's gone."

"Just like that?"

"I know. I can't believe it either. But it's gone." He shrugged. "Still more I don't understand. We might as well go out. Baby, if you want a Pimm's Cup, you'll have a Pimm's Cup."

Napoleon House was crowded, but we managed to get a small table for four. Dante and I ordered Pimm's Cups—a crisp cocktail of gin liqueur, lemonade, and cucumber—while River and Jay opted to continue with the bourbon.

"What about the hurricanes?" I asked.

"Nah, too sweet," River said. "I was kidding."

The server came, and we ordered our sandwiches and another round of drinks.

"All right," River began. "We need a plan. Let's—"

"The four of you are difficult to find."

I jerked in my chair. Dante's grandfather had appeared at our table.

"What do you want?" Dante growled.

"Easy, son. I'm not here to fight with you."

Silence for a few seconds that seemed like an eternity.

I couldn't take it any longer. "This is my brother, Jay," I said. "This is Bill, Dante and River's grandfather."

"I know who you are," Bill said, holding out his hand.

Jay shook it, but I wondered for a moment whether he would. Things seemed to be going in slow motion.

"Let us eat in peace, please," River said.

"May I join you?"

"Are you kidding?" Dante stood.

"You're younger, bigger, and apparently stronger than I am, Dante," Bill said. "But I'm a hell of a lot more stubborn than you are."

"We'll see about that," Dante said.

Bill didn't wait for an affirmative response. He pulled a chair from the corner and sat down at our table. "Have you ordered yet?"

"Are you really going to sit here and act like everything's fine?" River said. "You just got Jay and me kicked off the force."

"I simply got your leaves of absence revoked. No one kicked you off the force."

I opened my mouth but then shut it quickly.

"Something to say, Erin?" Bill asked.

I was going to comment that it didn't matter, that Dante would get them their jobs back when this was all over, but then thought better of it. Bill wasn't stupid. He probably knew that would be the plan.

"No." I took a sip of my sweet gin drink.

"What are you all having?" Bill signaled to our server. "I think I'm going to have the grilled alligator sausage po' boy."

I downed the rest of my drink. The server was on his way. He distributed our second round of drinks and took Bill's order.

I nearly downed my second Pimm's Cup in one draught.

Could this get any more awkward?

I glanced to the doorway.

Oh, yes.

It could.

FIVE

DANTE

I gripped the tall glass holding my drink, my knuckles white.

"Easy," River said. "Remember what happened the last time you did that."

I flashed back to the night Erin and I had danced. Before she'd shown up, I'd crushed a lead crystal glass with my bare hands.

I set the drink down on the table with a clomp.

Erin cleared her throat loudly and gestured toward the doorway. I twisted my neck.

Shit.

Abe Lincoln headed toward us. In what appeared to be new jeans and a plaid shirt. He stopped at our table. "Erin. I knew you'd be here."

"Exactly how did you know? We didn't decide to go to dinner until the last minute."

"Bea told me."

"You know this young man, Erin?" Bill said.

"This is Abe Lincoln," she said.

"Indeed?" Bill cocked his head. "Like the president?"

"Yeah. He's a former patient of mine."

For a minute, I thought Erin was going to do formal introductions, but thankfully she chose a more direct approach.

"What do you want, Abe?"

He looked around, his gaze shifting nervously. "Can we speak alone?"

"You can speak right here to her or not at all." I squeezed my glass once more.

"Easy," River whispered so only I could hear.

Well, Bill probably heard.

Shit. Bill. Whatever Abe had to say, Bill didn't need to know. I didn't want him anywhere near our situation, especially considering how determined he was to stop us.

"I changed my mind," I said, standing. "Erin and I will talk to you. Outside."

"You *do* know I can find out whatever you speak to him about," Bill said.

"*Can* you?" I snarled.

"Of course. I'll just glam—"

My fangs tore through my gums at rapid speed, and I welcomed the pain. "Try it. Just try it. I fucking *dare* you."

"You're being childish, Dante." Bill took a sip of water.

"We *will* find what we seek, Bill. Not you—not anyone— will stop us." I grabbed Erin's hand as she stood. "Come on." I led her briskly through the dining room and out the front door.

Abe followed us.

"What is it, Abe?" I said.

"The vampires. They're plenty pissed off at you. Both of you."

"Do I look like I care?" I showed my teeth.

"Dante"—Erin caressed my arm—"he's a friend, remember?"

"Is he? I'm not so sure. He's been hanging with those thugs for God knows how long."

"They give me hot meals, man. That's gold for people like me."

"You could just get a fucking jo—"

"Dante"—Erin patted my arm—"we don't know his circumstances. It's not that easy."

I drew in a breath and counted to ten. Then, "What do you want, Abe? Or is it Rover?"

"Abe. Red Rover was Bea's nickname."

"Then how come you responded to it that day in the Quarter?"

"Because everyone calls me that now. No one even remembers my real name. It's annoying, but what can I do?"

"You can tell them to stop if you don't like it," Erin said.

I didn't wait for him to respond to Erin. "What the hell do you want? What are they angry about?"

"You broke Decker's and Giles's noses."

"They're lucky that's all I did," I growled, my teeth descending.

"It's affecting their sense of smell."

"And again...so?"

"They're pissed. They want blood."

"Don't they get enough of yours?"

"You know what he means, Dante," Erin said soothingly.

"They've lost Erin's scent, and they can't pick up her brother's."

"Their noses will heal," Erin said.

"That's not the big problem," Abe said. "The other two can't pick up your scent either."

Good. The basil potion was working. For now, at least.

"And again...so? That's a good thing. You've already tried to protect Erin. You don't want them to have her."

"No, I don't. But if they can't have her, they're going to come after you."

I broke into a heaving guffaw. "Tell them to bring it on, then."

"Dante," Erin said. "No. You can't take on all four of them."

"Want to bet on that, baby?"

"You're angry right now. Insanely protective of me. But think about it. Seriously."

I didn't have to think about it. My hands curled into fists of their own volition, and my fangs sharpened. The pit of my stomach gave birth to red rage, and it radiated through me.

Those vamps were history.

An electric bolt jarred me back to normal.

The darkness.

It was here.

I grabbed Erin's hand. "We need to leave."

"What is it?"

"Let's go. We need to get out of here now."

"But—"

"Now!" I pulled her down the street, nearly tripping over a guitar case filled with coins.

"Dante? What's going on?"

I pulled her behind a shop and into the back alleyway.

To my astonishment, Abe had followed us.

"I felt it," he said.

I widened my eyes. "*You* did?"

"Yeah. You were getting really mad, and it was like a...a... shadow or something hovering over us."

Yes. Exactly. But how could he feel it, when no one else but I had— No. Not true. Bea had felt it. My father had felt it.

But Erin and River had not.

"It's the bad ghost," he said.

"What do you mean, the 'bad ghost'?"

"Remember that day in Café Amelie, when I left quickly? I told you it was a bad ghost who told me to leave. This was the same feeling."

"This isn't a ghost. If it were, my father would know about it. He'd be able to see it."

"Oh?"

"It's a long story, Abe," Erin said, smoothing her jeans. "I didn't feel anything."

"Did you see this ghost?"

"Of course not. You can't see ghosts," Abe said.

"Then how do you know it was a ghost?"

"I just know."

I rolled my eyes. "It's not a ghost, then. But you definitely felt it. I didn't feel it that day at Café Amelie. Are you sure it's the same thing?"

"It sure felt the same."

"At Café Amelie," Erin said, "you told us that the ghost told you to leave."

"Yeah. But not in actual words. I just knew I had to get out of there."

"We're arguing over semantics," Erin said to me. "If you felt the darkness, and he did too, you were probably feeling the same thing."

Abe darted his gaze around erratically. "I need to go. I just wanted to let you know that the vampires are angry. Really angry."

"You tell them that *I'm* really angry. How's that?"

"Dante, please." Erin tugged on my arm.

"We need to find answers, Erin. We can't let four rogue vampire thugs scare us. River and I are pretty formidable ourselves. Plus we have my dad."

She nodded, swallowing. "Abe, please stay away from them. If it's a hot meal you want, I'll buy you one each day."

"No. I can't take something for nothing, at least not from you. I owe you a lot."

An idea popped into my head. "How about this, then? We give you money for three meals a day, and you do something for us in return."

"What's that?" he asked.

"Spy for us. Find out where these vamps live. Who they work for. Why they stole my father's body."

His eyes turned into circles. "What?"

"Dante, he doesn't know—"

"Just anything," I continued. "Anything you can find out about them will help us." I pulled my wallet out of my back pocket and extracted three twenties courtesy of a cash advance on my credit card. "This will feed you for a day or two. Find out what you can."

Abe took the money. "I'll do it," he said. "For Erin." In a flash he was gone.

"How do you plan to get money to him?" Erin asked.

"We'll find him at night." I smiled. "Exactly when the vamps find him."

SIX

Erin

"Where the hell have you two been?" Bill demanded when we rejoined the others at Napoleon House.

Our meals sat undisturbed at our places. The others were eating slowly, tension filling the air.

"None of your damned business." Dante took a huge bite of his sandwich.

"Abe just wanted me to know he was okay," I said. "He was in the ER a while back and needed a transfusion. He left before I could check in on him."

"Nice try, Erin," Bill said. "You're a lousy liar."

"Don't call her a liar," Dante said, his mouth full of muffuletta.

I cleared my throat and looked to my brother. "What did we miss here?"

"Not much," he said. "Just a new level of me being uncomfortable."

I let out a nervous laugh. "I'll bet."

"Bill has been trying to talk us out of going after the translation," River said. "I told him we'd think about it."

"Think about it? Are you insane?" Dante threw his sandwich on his plate.

"Yeah. *Think* about it. Right now our priority has to be Lucy and the others. Right?"

"That's right," I said, pleading to Dante with my eyes not to push it. He was on edge. I could tell. Tension radiated from him in waves.

"I'm just as interested as the rest of you are in getting the missing women returned," Bill said.

"Thanks, but we're good," Dante said.

"Maybe he can help, cuz," River said.

"How?"

"He's a powerful vampire elder."

"So?"

"So..." River's voice took on a strange tone, one I hadn't heard before. "Maybe he can help."

Dante went rigid, his facial expression pensive. "Maybe..."

"Would the two of you care to let us in on what the hell you're talking about?" Jay said. "I'm feeling like the odd one out here."

"What do you have to offer, Bill?" River asked.

"Give up your quest to translate the *Texts*," Bill said. "And I guarantee you that you'll find those missing women."

I stiffened, my skin going numb. How could he guarantee anything? Unless he *knew* something.

I stood. "Damn it. She's my best friend! Where is she?"

River joined me. "Erin's right. You must know something. These are *people*, Bill."

"Sit down, both of you."

We both remained standing.

"Have it your way. I don't know anything, but I have sources that you don't." He turned to Jay. "That the police don't."

"What kind of sources?" River demanded.

"The council. I'm the eldest member, as you know. I can get their cooperation."

"To find missing human women?" River said. "I don't think so. What could they do anyway?"

"You're forgetting something very important, son," Bill said.

"Yeah?" Dante said. "What's that?"

A voice sounded out of nowhere. "Say one more word, Gabriel, and you're off the council."

"Who was that?" I asked, looking around. No one was near our table. Waitstaff trickled in and out of the room, and other guests were eating and talking among themselves.

"What was what?" Dante said.

"Didn't you hear it? Someone said, 'Say one more word, Gabriel, and you're off the council.'"

"I didn't hear it," River said. "Jay?"

"Nope."

"*You* must have heard it." I gestured to Bill.

"I heard nothing."

Was I truly going batty?

"What is it?" River said. "What were you going to say, Bill?"

"Nothing."

"Not nothing. You said, 'You're forgetting one important thing, son.'"

"Nonsense. You misheard me."

"Bullshit." Dante said. "We all heard it. Right, Erin?"

"Yeah. I heard it. And right after he said it, someone said, 'Say one more word, Gabriel, and you're off the council.'"

Bill's lips twitched slightly. So slightly that I wondered if I was seeing things. I looked to Dante, and he nodded at me negligibly.

He'd noticed. Bravo for acute vampire vision.

Bill had heard the voice too.

The only question was—why hadn't the others?

SEVEN

DANTE

Bill smiled, but something was off. Erin would never lie to me, so either she had imagined the voice, or she had indeed heard it. Judging from Bill's reaction, I was betting the latter.

His desire for us to stop our quest for translating the *Texts* was strong—strong enough that he was willing to let go of some other secret to help us find the missing women.

Which meant he knew how to find them, or at least had sources that we didn't know about.

I'd never imagined I'd have any interest in the council's secrets. I'd never imagined they had any. But they did, and they most likely all involved the *Texts*.

Yes, the council might have its secrets, but Bill had a secret of his own. One he didn't want the council knowing about.

He had read a portion of the *Texts*, a portion that scared him so much he was willing to divulge other secrets now to stop us.

I opened my mouth to remind him of his own secret but

shut it abruptly. If indeed Erin had heard someone, we weren't alone. Bill's secret was our leverage. If the council knew about it, they'd most likely ban him, and then he'd be no use to us at all.

"I need to speak to my father," I said.

"Not now," Bill said through clenched teeth.

"Why not?"

"He's busy."

Bullshit. Bill didn't want him here for one reason and one reason only. He'd be able to see whomever Erin had heard.

Dad! I called to him in my mind, hoping it would work.

No luck. He didn't come.

Damn.

"Can you still help us?" River asked. "If we agree to abandon the *Texts*, can you help us find Lucy and the others?"

"River, no," I said, seething.

"It's Lucy, Dante. Lucy and other innocent women. Erin's patients. They need to be our first priority."

Erin rubbed my arm. "He's right."

"What makes you think the same people aren't involved?" I said. "Erin said these patients just disappeared. In a busy hospital like University, how likely is that? Unless glamouring was involved."

"I agree that vampires are probably involved with the missing women," River said. "But why would you think it's the same vampires?"

"There are so few of us, and most of us are good people," I said. "It stands to reason—"

"Enough!" Bill slammed his palm down on the table.

Erin and Jay jerked in their chairs, and then their faces went blank.

A glamour.

"You fucking son of a bitch." I rose.

"Sit down, Dante." Bill's voice was stern. He turned to River. "And before you go all animalistic on me, you stay seated too."

Instinct. I'd acted on instinct in the courtroom when I'd reversed Bill's glamour and gotten what I needed.

I curled my hands into fists and concentrated, trying to conjure the energy necessary to overtake my grandfather. I closed my eyes, focusing. Thinking. Praying.

And—

Nothing.

Fucking nothing.

You're overthinking it, son.

My father! My eyes popped open.

Don't. Don't make it known that I'm here. I'm staying invisible and inaudible to everyone else.

I nodded slightly.

"Are you okay, Dante?" River said tentatively.

I unclenched and tried to relax my body. "I'm fine."

"You have no control over your newfound power, Dante," Bill said. "Let me help you."

"Are you kidding? You tried to keep me from my inheritance. I don't want your help. I have my father."

"Your father is a ghost."

"He still has his knowledge. He's already begun teaching me."

"He hasn't done a very good job. You can't unglamour Erin and Jay."

I opened my mouth—

Let it go, son. Don't give him any ammunition to use against you.

Then I closed it at my father's words.

"Say what you want to say, Bill," River said. "Say it and get it over with."

"Vampires indeed are involved in the disappearance of the women."

"We already had that figured out." I scoffed. "Staff were glamoured when the women disappeared. There's no other explanation."

"Dante's right. It's obvious. What else you got?"

"I have my knowledge, my wisdom, and my experience. I've been around for a century, boys. I've seen evil at work before. Don't underestimate the help I can give you."

Tell him you'll hear him out but not here. You need to go back to his house.

My father again. I couldn't let Bill know that he was here.

"I have two conditions," I said.

"Two conditions for what?" River asked.

"For hearing him out. Feel free to add any more that you want."

"What are they?" Bill asked.

"Number one, you don't glamour Erin or her brother again. They are part of this, and they need to be involved. Number two, we go back to your house to discuss this. Discussing it here isn't safe."

"Do you have anything to add, River?" Bill asked.

"I'm good. I think."

"Good," I said. "Now let them go, and we'll discuss this at your home."

"Done." Bill waved his hand subtly.

"It stands to reason... What, Dante?" Erin asked.

Right. I'd been in the middle of talking when Bill

glamoured Erin and Jay.

"Sorry. It stands to reason that the same vampires that are after you are also involved in the disappearances."

"That's a far cry from hard evidence," River said, "but you have a point."

"Bill, if you truly have information that can help us, it's probably not a good idea to discuss it here. Why don't we go back to the Heartsong?" I smiled for Erin and Jay's benefit.

"Agreed." Bill pressed his lips into a thin line. "I'll meet you there." He stood and left the Napoleon House.

Our server brought the check, and I grabbed it. "I got it." My money worries were over, thank goodness. Being able to treat felt damned good after I'd sponged off Bill and River for so long—even if it was inherited money, not money I'd earned.

"Nice of you to buy his dinner." River sighed, rolling his eyes.

"Yeah, he conveniently left right before the check came," Jay said. "Let me help you with that."

"No, we're good. You can get the next one."

"You got it." Jay stood. "I'm going to hit the can, and I guess we'll go to the Heartsong. Why are we going to that old mansion?"

"That's where Bill lives," I said.

"Why not somewhere else?" Erin asked.

"I'll explain on the way," I said. "Let's go."

"Spill it, please," Erin said once we were on the road.

"I heard from my dad while we were at Napoleon House," I said. "He was speaking only to me. He told us not to talk about this stuff while we were there."

"Can he stay invisible to other ghosts?" Erin asked. "Because I know I heard something, and I think your grandfather heard it too. Someone told him not to say anything more to us. Bill was getting ready to divulge some kind of secret."

"I'm pretty sure you're right, baby. We need to talk to my dad before we get to Bill's."

"I'm here, son."

Erin jerked in her seat. "Did anyone else hear that?"

"Yeah, I heard it," River said. "Where are you, Uncle Jules?"

Jay sat uneasily in the back. "I hear you too. Uh...Uncle Jules."

"I can't manifest in a moving vehicle, but I'm here. There was a ghost at the restaurant. It was Levi Gaston, an elder I remember from before I was taken. He must have passed away while we were gone, Dante."

"Did he see you?" I asked.

"I don't think so. I was careful. That's the voice you heard, Erin. You seem to be well tuned in to ghosts. It's doubtful he thought about making himself inaudible to you. He just assumed no one else would hear him."

"Was Levi Gaston a good guy?" River asked.

"As far as I know," my father said. "The elders keep to themselves."

"Um...no one else is here in the car with us, right?" Erin said.

My father chuckled. "No. It's just us."

"Good," I said. "We have some leverage with Bill. We and only we know that he secretly read the *Texts*. If the other elders knew, he'd be kicked off the council. We can use that."

"Yes, I think we can," my father agreed.

"So this elder ghost won't be able to follow us into Bill's house?" Erin asked timidly.

"No. I arranged for Bea to cast a shield around the mansion. The only ghost who can get past it is me."

"How is that possible?"

"Because she used my ashes to help form the shield. Even though I have no further connection to my earthly remains, my energy will allow me to pass through them."

"Are you sure it will work?" I asked.

"It will work. She protected you and River the night you retrieved my body, didn't she?"

"True. Or maybe that was just a coincidence."

"Dante, for God's sake," Erin said. "I know I called her a fraud, but maybe it's time to start believing in Bea. Her advice is keeping the rogue vampires from smelling Jay and me."

"All right. I give in," I said. "She does seem very wise. Though I have to wonder—if she's that smart, why does she live on the streets?"

"Simplicity, like she said." Erin smiled.

"You mean like Thoreau said. Wasn't she quoting him?"

"The words might not be hers, but she can still agree with them."

"Okay, okay. I give up. Again. Bea will keep the elder ghost out."

"Bea is a remarkable person. I've never met anyone quite like her," my father said. "I feel certain that the shield will work."

"Good," River said. "Bill can tell us what he was going to tell us at the restaurant."

"He might, but he'll have no idea the house is shielded.

That's not why we're going there, anyway," my father said.

"Then why?" I asked.

"We're going to recover the *Vampyre Texts*."

EIGHT

Erin

"But first," Julian continued, "you need to drop Erin and Jay off at their places."

"Excuse me?" I said.

"This is vampire business, Erin," Julian said. "We don't mean to leave you out, but Bill will glamour you and you won't be any help anyway. If you're at home, we'll know you're safe."

"He's right, baby," Dante said. "This could get ugly."

"Fine." I harrumphed. "Drop us both off at my place."

"Good idea," River said. "You two should stick together. In fact, you should move in with me, partner, until this is all cleared up."

"What the hell for?"

"For your own protection. That mixture is working for now, but we can't take the chance that the thugs won't sniff you out."

"I'm a cop. I can take care of myself."

"Not against these types," I said. "River's right. You can

stay with us if you'd rather. I have an extra bedroom."

"Thanks, but no thanks. I'll take River's couch. No offense, Sis, but I don't want to be under the same roof while the two of you...you know."

Dante dropped Jay and me off at home.

I pulled him to me at the door and squeezed him in a giant hug. "Please be careful."

He tipped my chin and kissed my lips softly. "We will. This will work, Erin. It has to."

I nodded, blowing him a kiss as he walked back to the car where River waited.

Jay had already gone inside.

And I had something to tell him.

It wasn't every day a person got to tell her brother that he was part vampire.

Maybe it could wait until all this shit was over.

I sighed. No. He deserved to know. He had a right to know. Then he and I would decide whether to approach our parents.

"I think I'm going to need another bourbon."

"You've already had—" I stood and went to the kitchen. Not a great time to lecture my big brother on drinking.

We'd all had a lot tonight, but one more wouldn't hurt. Not when I'd just told him our grandmother had most likely been a vampire.

"Is it really that surprising?" I said. "Mom works nights. She always has. You and I work the night shift. We both have fair skin that needs a lot of sunscreen. It adds up in a bizarre way."

"Why does being descended from vampires make us smell really good to them, though? When they can't smell each other? That doesn't make sense."

"After everything you've seen, you've decided to get logical? None of this makes any sense."

"You're wrong, Sis. A lot of it *does* make sense. Here. In New Orleans. Remember, I've been here longer than you have. I'm a cop who works the night shift. I see a lot of weird shit."

"Have you ever seen a ghost?"

"It's possible. Almost all the old buildings in the Quarter and in the Garden District have stories of hauntings associated with them. Ghosts are a fact of life here."

"Dante said that vampires are taught to believe that ghosts don't exist. That any manifestations are the result of the strong veil of supernatural energy that covers New Orleans. He was surprised to find out that ghosts do exist and do retain their unique identities."

"We're all taught not to believe in ghosts. We're taught not to believe in vampires too. Then again, this is New Orleans. Weird shit happens here. Maybe that's why I like it so much."

"I suppose it could be why we're both drawn here. I never expected to stay after Corey and I broke up, but I couldn't bring myself to leave."

"I couldn't either when I finished school. Going back to Ohio never entered my mind."

"Ohio's pretty drab compared to this." I laughed. "But I'm glad I didn't leave. You were here. And then I met Dante..." I closed my eyes.

"Please, spare me the mush."

"I will. Suffice it to say that I didn't know a connection like we have even existed. I hope you can find the same thing one day."

"Yeah. I don't think so. Not with a vampire, anyway. Does he..."

Drink your blood.

The words were clear, though he didn't say them.

"Yeah," I said. "I don't expect you to understand. But it's really meaningful. For both of us."

"TMI, Sis."

"Hey, you brought it up."

"Yeah, sorry. It's like a train wreck. I don't want to know, but I had to know."

"I get it." I picked up his empty glass. "You want another?"

"Nah. I've had more than enough. I think I'll lie down."

"Take the couch. Or the extra bedroom. Your choice."

"The couch is fine. I'll just wait here for River to pick me up." He crossed his arms over his chest. "I really hate having to be on the lookout like this."

"You're a detective. You're on the lookout all the time."

"Yeah. For clues. For criminals. I watch my own back. I don't like the idea of someone else watching it for me."

"Come on. You and River are partners. You have each other's backs. How is this any different?"

"It just is. I have a weakness, and I don't like it."

"Not being able to glamour isn't a weakness."

"No. But being able to be glamoured is."

He had a point. "I don't like it any more than you do. But you need to be safe, and so do I. We both need to be our best selves so we can find Lucy and the others."

Jay got comfortable on the couch while I tidied up the kitchen from my earlier attempt to make dinner. Seemed like a lifetime ago.

I jarred when a knock sounded on the door.

I eyed the clock on the wall. Ten p.m.
Who would be knocking this late?

NINE

DANTE

"It's simple," I said to my grandfather. "You give us back the *Texts*, or we tell the council what you did. How do you think they'll react when they find out you took it upon yourself to read the *Texts* when it's forbidden?"

"They won't believe you."

"Won't they?" I scoffed. "We know you heard the ghost of Levi Gaston at the restaurant. Erin heard it too."

"It's true, Dad," my father said, standing nearby. "He was there."

"How would you know?"

"I was there too. I can control whether you see me. And no, Gaston didn't see me."

"You were about to tell us some council secret, something that would help us find Lucy and the others," River said. "The ghost stopped you."

My grandfather looked around nervously. "Is he here now?"

My father shook his head slightly at River and me—code

I assumed meant not to tell my grandfather about the shield.

"No, Dad. I'd be able to see him if he were."

"He's not here," I said. "So spill it. How can you help us?"

"I'll do nothing. Nothing. Not if you're determined to translate the *Texts*."

"That's not negotiable," River said. "Dante needs them. He needs to find out what's happening. Not just between him and Erin, but *to* him as well. You saw what he did in the courtroom."

"No. I can't. Not in good conscience."

"Would you have a little faith in us, for God's sake?" I stood. "Whatever you read didn't turn you to the dark side. Why would it do so to any of us?"

"Because you're both young. Young and at the height of your potency. You're ruled more by instinct and emotion than by logic." He shook his head vehemently. "I absolutely cannot allow it."

"Are you fucking kidding—" River started.

"Then give them to me, Dad."

"To a ghost? You can't even carry them. How can I do that?"

"You give them to Dante and River, and you take their word that they'll attempt to translate them only so *I* can read them. Trust *me* to make the decision as to what they can know."

"Julian..."

"You raised me. You taught me. I'm no longer a slave to the hormones and chemicals of a body. Who better to trust with the *Texts*?"

He had a good point.

"Julian..." Bill said again.

"Do you want to find Braedon?" my father asked.

"Of course. More than anything."

"Then give us the *Texts*. Something is happening to Dante. He has a power unheard of for vampires. If the *Texts* can give us the key, he can use this energy he has to help us find Braedon."

"He might be dead." Bill lowered his head so his chin touched his chest.

"He's alive, Dad. He's alive. But he doesn't have much time. We need those *Texts*."

"I'm sorry, Julian. I can't. And as long as you continue on this quest to get information out of that book, I will not help you find the women who have disappeared."

"You fucking son of a bitch." I growled, baring my fangs. "These are *people*. One of them is Erin's best friend. River's girlfriend. If you have sources no one else has, you need to use them."

"You may think my position callous." Bill sighed. "But if you had read what I've read, you would understand."

"You're willing to sacrifice innocent people to keep your secrets?" River shook his head. "You're not the grandfather who looked after me when my father disappeared, who taught me our history and how to glamour. Who taught me how to be a moral, ethical vampire. A moral and ethical man. No moral or ethical man would leave innocent women to rot when he could help them. What's happened to you?"

My cousin paced across the Persian carpet swiftly. He was angry. Angry, anxious, and full of nervous energy. Why weren't his teeth descending?

Control. He'd been taught the control I lacked.

Fine with me. I wasn't a big fan of control at this moment.

"What happened to me?" Bill, the ultimate in control, bared his own fangs this time, his voice rumbling into a growl. "That damned book happened, and I'm willing to face the wrath of my sons and grandchildren to keep its secrets. *For your own damned good.*"

My own bigger and longer teeth pulsated. "We are adults. Grown men."

"You're a grown man who can't control your own teeth, Dante," Bill said.

"What about you? Why are you baring your teeth at your son and grandsons?" River asked. "Don't talk to us about control."

"I was talking to Dante."

That bolt of electricity, that red rage of anger, all of it boiled in the pit of my stomach. "Say goodbye to your seat on the council, *Grandpa*," I snarled. "Come on, Riv. We have some phone calls to make."

River regarded me, his eyes unreadable.

"Let's go, Riv," I said through clenched teeth.

"Yeah. Sure. After I use the john." River stood and left the room.

Bill sighed, his countenance returning to normal, though his cuspids were still descended. "I don't know what they'll do to me. It won't be pretty. But I'm old. I've lived an amazing life. Go ahead, Dante. Tell the council. I can't risk letting the secrets of the *Texts* get out."

"Have it your way. Let's go, Dad. Riv," I yelled. "Meet us outside."

"Got it." His voice was muffled.

I walked out of the living room, through the foyer, and out the door. I stood still for a moment on the porch, waiting to see if Bill was watching.

He wasn't.

I walked quickly to the side of the house, to the window of

Bill's study. River was there, as we'd planned after dropping Jay and Erin off. He handed me the heavy tome. "Be quick," he said, "now I really do have to use the john."

"Great job. See you in the car."

"Nicely done," my father said out of thin air while we were driving away from Bill's house.

"Thanks for telling me where to look, Uncle Jules," River said. "The book was right where you said it'd be. So much for Bill trying to keep it hidden."

"I just happened to see where he hid it," my father said. "He'll realize it's gone quickly enough. I hope he didn't hear you. He used to be able to hear Brae and me even thinking about sneaking out. His ears take acute vampire hearing to a new level."

"I was quiet as a mouse," River said. "I couldn't even hear myself. If we'd had more time to plan, we could have replaced it with the fake."

"Let's make sure he can't get to this one," I said. "We'll have to hide it well."

"I've got that covered," my father said.

"What do you mean?"

"You'll see."

"I still don't understand," River said. "If this book is as dangerous as he thinks, why does he keep it?"

"I don't get the feeling he's lying about that," my father said. "It's our history. It's been part of our culture for so long. He can't part with it. What if Christians found something dark and evil hiding in the *New Testament*, or Jews in the *Torah* or

Hindus in the *Bhagavad Gita*? They wouldn't destroy them. They couldn't."

We pulled into the townhome complex and—

"Oh, God," River said. "Jay's in there."

Oh, God was right. Emilia stood on Erin's stoop, her fist poised to knock on the door.

"Now's not the time," I agreed.

"I've got this," my father said. "I'll make sure she's okay."

She tapped on the door twice before my father appeared at her side and apparently convinced her to move away quickly.

A few seconds later, Jay opened the door, holding his pistol. "Huh," he said and then looked toward us. "Good. You guys are back."

"Did you hear us?" River said.

"No. Someone knocked on the door. Must be kids playing tricks or something." He shoved his gun back into his shoulder holster. "I see you got the book back."

We walked into the townhome.

What had Emilia come here for? To see me, no doubt. She looked better than she had a few days ago, thank goodness. Whatever she needed, my father would see that she got it.

Right now, with Jay here, Emilia couldn't be. Though Jay had every right to know about her pregnancy, it was Emilia's call, and the stress of seeing Jay wouldn't be good for her or the baby.

This pregnancy had to progress smoothly. I wasn't ready to lose my baby sister.

I set the book on the coffee table next to the fake. They looked identical.

"I wonder what's different about the fake?" Erin said. "I guess we could compare them page to page."

"That's not a bad idea," River said.

"It sounds like it will take hours and hours and lead to nothing," I said.

"That's where you're wrong. It might lead us to exactly what we need."

"Good thinking, partner," Jay said. "Find the discrepancies, and you find the parts your grandfather doesn't want you to see."

"But we can't read it. We'd have to go through word for word until we find a word that doesn't match. Sounds ridiculous."

Erin was looking at both books, open to page one. "I don't think that will help," she said. "From what I can see, every word is different. This phony one appears to be Old French gibberish."

"How would you know it's gibberish if you can't read Old French?"

"Because the words are all here on the page. They're just out of order. I noticed it when I got to the second paragraph. The first sentence has all the same words, just in jumbled-up order." She turned the page. "Yeah, it looks like the same thing here."

"I guess Nocturnal Truth is our only chance," I said. "Good thing we have the money now."

"Still," River said. "We don't know who this Lucien Crown is and whether he's legit. I'd feel better if we could read these damned things ourselves."

"Me too," I said, "but we don't have time for that. It's time to contact the site."

Erin lay in bed, her eyes closed, while I undressed. A few minutes later, I slid into bed and snuggled against her warm body.

"Did you send the request?" she asked.

"Yeah. I waited for my dad to get his input."

"Julian's here?"

"Not anymore. He left when River and Jay left."

"Quite a night," she said. "I'm beat, which is weird, because I'd be at work right about now."

"I don't think any of us are going to be keeping normal hours until we figure everything out."

She sighed. "I get so distracted sometimes with everything else. Then I feel guilty because I haven't been thinking about Lucy."

"Shh. Don't beat yourself up about that. There's a lot going on. We're going to find Lucy. I promise."

My cock hardened, and I slid it between her soft ass cheeks.

"Mmm," she said, wiggling into me. "Please."

I entered her slowly, impeded a little because she wasn't quite ready.

I smiled. This was the first time we'd made love without both of us being completely aroused.

But that wasn't what this was about.

This was closeness.

Closeness after a rough day.

She moaned softly as I continued to pump into her, slowly and gently.

We climaxed together, and I reveled in the sheer sweetness

and soft intensity of it.

Then we fell asleep, still joined.

TEN

Erin

Mmm. Something felt good. Really good.

I opened one eye. Dante was between my legs, licking me.

He smiled, his lips shining with my juices. "Sorry, baby. Couldn't wait." He sank two fingers in me while simultaneously spearing his teeth into the flesh of my thigh.

I soared.

So quickly yet so completely.

I'd come to know that Dante's feedings were another kind of lovemaking between us. I looked forward to them, relished them.

Needed them as much as he did.

As he took the blood his body needed, he also gave to me—his strength, his courage, his magnificence.

I'd grown stronger because of his feedings. Because of his love.

When I came down from my orgasm, he was lapping at the wounds, helping them coagulate and close. Then he slid slowly upward and plunged his cock into me.

I was tight from the orgasm, and now, as he intruded into the tightness, he created a good, slow burn.

Heavenly burn.

"So snug, baby," he whispered against my neck.

"Mmm. Feels good." I closed my eyes, my hard nipples pushing against his chest.

He thrust once more, grunting and exploding in orgasm.

Then a knock on the door downstairs.

"Shit," he said.

"At least you finished." I chuckled.

"I'm not ready to get up yet."

"Neither am I. We can ignore it."

"We can't. It might be River and Jay. Or it might be—" He stopped abruptly.

"Might be...who?" I asked.

"Nothing. I'll go take care of it."

"Not without me, you won't." I followed him out of bed and hurriedly put on shorts and a tank top.

Dante pulled a pair of jeans over his hips, and we walked downstairs.

The knocking became more persistent.

"For God's sake," Dante said, opening the door. "Oh. Good morning, Bill."

Bill stood rigid, dressed in black pants and a tan shirt. The man looked too good to be a hundred and two. Too bad he was a jerk who wouldn't help us.

"What do you want?" Dante asked.

"You know why I'm here, Dante. May I come in?"

"I don't think so."

"Do you think I didn't hear River sneaking into my office?

I'm taking the book."

"Think again."

Bill pushed Dante out of the way and entered. A low growl emerged from Dante's throat, and he turned and plastered his grandfather against the wall.

I stood, motionless.

"Good morning, Erin," Bill said, as if his grandson weren't holding him against the wall. "I'm sorry to barge in like this, but Dante and River stole something from my home last night. I've come to retrieve it."

What could I say? I had no idea, so I said nothing.

"Let go of me, Dante."

Dante, to my surprise, released Bill. "You're not taking anything from this house."

Bill walked toward the coffee table, where both books sat. "I assure you I am. I could have you and River arrested for theft, you know. I'll call the police."

"River's one of them, even though you forced him and Jay to quit. They'll never arrest him, no matter how much you glamour the department."

"I don't want to resort to that. I'll just take the book. Which one is it?"

"You want it?" Dante said. "You're the one who planted the fake. You figure it out."

"I'll take both, then." He picked up one of the books—the phony—and then reached for the other—

"Ouch! What the hell did you do?"

My heart lurched. "What happened?"

"I didn't even touch it. Damn thing shocked me or something."

"I did nothing." Dante reached toward the book hesitantly and touched it.

Nothing happened.

Then he picked it up, holding it out. "You want it? Take it."

Bill put the fake down and reached for it once more. "Damn! What is that?"

Dante chuckled. "Looks like the book doesn't want to go with you, Bill."

"I don't know what you're doing, Dante, but I beg you to stop it. You're dealing with powers you don't understand."

"Ha! I did nothing. If someone put some kind of hex on the book, it wasn't me. I don't know shit about things like that."

"Erin." Bill turned to me. "You need to talk to him. Talk some sense into him. He doesn't know what he's dealing with."

"He just told you he didn't do anything." I reached toward the book, touching it lightly.

Nothing.

Thank God.

Whatever was going on seemed only to affect Bill.

Bea. Bea and another shield. Julian had arranged this. I'd bet everything I owned on it.

"Since you won't be taking the book," Dante said, "I suggest you leave. Erin and I need to get some breakfast." He smiled sarcastically. "Unless you'd care to join us?"

"This isn't over, Dante." Bill strode toward the door. "Whatever you've done to that book, it won't work. Not in the long run."

"At the risk of repeating myself, I did nothing. Don't let the door hit your ass on the way out."

Bill left.

"He won't stop," I said. "He's determined in a way I'll never understand. He's willing to risk those missing women to protect the secrets in that book."

"I know. What do you think is going on with the book? Bea?"

I nodded. "That's my guess. Julian must have had her shield it from him."

Julian appeared. "That's exactly right. We have to take precautions now. My father is on a quest to stop us. I promised Bea a little more of my ashes, even though she didn't ask for payment. You still have them, I hope?"

Dante nodded. "Yeah. Em and I haven't had the chance to talk about what to do with them. I was thinking we'd scatter them where Mom, Grandma, and Aunt Simone are buried."

"At this point," Julian said, "I'd advise against scattering them. They're clearly very valuable, and they can help you."

"But they're—"

"No. They're not me. We've had this discussion."

"I know." Dante rubbed his temples. "It's just hard."

"I know, son. But right now, they're a commodity, and we need all the help we can get solving these mysteries."

My stomach growled. "Breakfast?" I said.

"None for me." Julian laughed.

"Dante?"

"Yeah, baby."

"Eggs, bacon, and coffee?"

"Perfect. I'm going to log on to your computer—"

"*Our* computer. Everything's ours now."

He smiled. "You're so sweet. Okay. Our computer. To see if Nocturnal Truth has gotten back to me."

"You just sent the request last night," Julian said.

"I know, Dad, but you never know. If he's a vampire, he was probably up."

I laid six strips of bacon in a cast-iron frying pan and

turned on the stove. While the bacon sizzled, I made a pot of coffee and cracked four eggs into a bowl, whisking them until they were frothy.

I looked into the living room. Julian stood behind Dante, who was tapping on my laptop.

"Anything yet?" I asked.

"The Wi-Fi is slow this morning. It's taking me a min-- Oh, fuck!"

ELEVEN

DANTE

*T*he domain *nocturnaltruth.com has expired. If you are the owner, please log in to your domain manager for more details.*

"Fuck, fuck, fuck!"

"Bill," my father said. "He must have gotten to them and forced them to take the site down. At least you sent your email before it was down. It may have gotten through to the owner."

"And it may not have," I said. "I sent it through the site."

"Try again," Erin said, coming toward us. "Maybe we can find a cache."

"What's that?"

"Saved data from a site or page."

"How do you know about all that?" Again, being gone for ten years reared its ugly head. Plus, I'd never been a tech wiz.

"We use them at the hospital. Caches are created so future requests can be served faster. Maybe this Lucien Crown guy created a cache."

"It's worth a try, son."

"How do I do it?"

"Let me try."

I handed the laptop to Erin.

"Watch the bacon, okay?" She began tapping keys.

I headed to the kitchen and turned the slices of bacon. Then I went back and watched over Erin's shoulder.

"Nothing yet." She continued typing.

"It was a small site," my father said. "Not like what you must use at the hospital."

She sighed. "Yeah. It was worth a try. I'm sorry. At least we have a name. Lucien Crown."

"There could be a million Lucien Crowns," I said.

"In New Orleans? Probably not," she said.

"We don't know he's here in New Orleans," I said.

"No, but where else would he be? Where do vampires live?"

"Everywhere and anywhere," my father said. "Your grandmother obviously lived in Ohio."

Erin sighed. "Well, I know a *Logan* Crown. Dr. Logan Crown."

"You're not going near him," I said, my hackles rising.

"Dante..."

"Son, it's a decent lead."

"Lead? It's nothing. I'm sure lots of people have that surname. She's not going near him."

"Maybe I'm not," she agreed. "He currently thinks I'm on a family emergency in Ohio."

"River can go with you," my father said. "He can glamour the doctor into not remembering you were there, and he'll be there to protect you if you need it."

"Good plan," Erin said.

"Good plan? Are you fucking insane? This guy tried to—" I stopped. My father was here.

"I was a willing participant at the time," she said. "And River will be with me."

"We need to follow every potential source, Dante," my father said. "If it makes you feel better, I'll tag along as well."

"No. No. Riv will protect her. It just pisses me off that I can't." My teeth itched to descend.

"Control," he said. "We'll do some more work on glamouring today."

"I was mentally exhausted after yesterday."

"That's good. It means you're working hard."

"Shit!" Erin ran to the kitchen. "I hope you like extra-crispy bacon."

"Yeah. Fine."

"Coffee's ready too. Just give me two minutes for the eggs."

I walked to the kitchen and poured two cups of coffee.

"I miss the taste of coffee," my father said.

"Do you miss blood?" I asked.

He shook his head. "Blood was just sustenance for me. I lived on bagged steer and sheep's blood, remember? It fulfilled a physiological need, but the flavor was nothing special."

In that moment, I felt sorry for my father. He'd never tasted blood as sweet as Erin's. Never had a blood bond. Indeed, had probably never fed from a human.

"How did you do it, all those years? All those smells of the humans around you."

"Control, Dante. Simple control."

Control. Everything came down to control. I still didn't possess the control a vampire of my age should.

I'd come a long way, but the path was far from its end.

Erin and I had slept off and on the rest of the day. Now she was on her way to the ER with River, hoping to speak to Logan Crown.

I was alone, staring at the *Vampyre Texts*.

The actual *Vampyre Texts*, not the phony, though we'd decided to keep it in case River and Erin's original idea ended up having any merit. Something within these pages had scared my grandfather—my strong and powerful grandfather. Had scared him so much he was willing to risk his seat on the council and risk the lives of Lucy and the others to keep us from learning what it was.

Seek, and ye shall find.

Stay out of my head!

Knock, and it shall be opened unto you.

I'd never been overly religious, but I recognized the language. It was from the *New Testament*, from one of the Gospels, though I couldn't remember which one.

She was quoting the bible.

Unreal.

How did someone so evil quote the bible?

Evil is in the eye of the beholder.

I think that's beauty, you bitch.

Good. You're learning. You're speaking to me without casting me away and without succumbing. Your strength is increasing.

Get out!

I'd show *her* I could cast *her* away.

She said no more, but *she* was still there. I felt *her* in my head—that shapeless thought that hung out with me when *she* wanted to.

Anger mounted in me, and I screamed silently. *Get the fuck out!*

And—

She was gone.

Just like that, *she* was gone.

I'd enjoy the reprieve.

For I knew better than to believe *she* was gone forever.

TWELVE

Erin

"I don't even know if he's coming in tonight," I said to River. "We may be chasing ghosts."

"Can you go in and ask?"

"I'm not supposed to be in town, remember?"

"I know. That's why I'm here, remember?"

"Glamouring Logan is one thing. If we go in there, you'll have to glamour everyone who sees me."

He laughed. "You make that sound difficult."

"Isn't it?"

"I may not have the glamouring power Dante seems to have, but I've got ten years on him in experience. I can handle anyone who crosses your path."

"All right. Let's do it." We got out of my car and headed into the ER, bypassing the main entrance and sneaking in the staff door. "I just need to check the schedule."

I looked down, trying to remain inconspicuous, until I got to the scheduling board. Yes! Logan was on duty tonight, due to come in soon. I signaled to River, and we walked back out just as quickly.

"That was strange," I said. "No one seemed to notice me at all."

"I didn't let them."

"You glamoured them? All of them?"

"I just sent out a glamour that made the two of us invisible. Well, not so much invisible as unnoticeable. I can't actually make things vanish."

"Amazing. How exactly does glamouring work?"

"It's difficult to explain. Imagine trying to explain to someone how to walk. You'd say, 'put one foot in front of the other,' but to someone who has never used his legs in that way, those instructions mean nothing."

"Okay... Then what can you do?"

"There are varying degrees, which are also hard to explain. I can glamour someone into not seeing me. I can glamour someone into forgetting something or into telling me the truth. I can also glamour someone into a catatonic state, so he goes numb and doesn't know what's going on in any particular time."

"Amazing."

"Just a different part of the brain. Humans probably have the ability. They just never needed to evolve into it. We needed it to feed."

"I think it would have done humans a lot of good as well, back in the day when they were out in the wild."

"They didn't need it. They could kill their food. We needed to drink from live beings back then, according to our history. Our bodies evolved generations later so we could exist on stored blood."

"Oh. I see." Though I really didn't. "Logan's coming.

Remember to get a good sniff too. I don't think he's a vampire, but you never know."

"Logan, hi." I walked toward him.

"Hi, Erin. What are you doing here? I thought you were out of town."

"I am. But I need to talk to you."

"What do you mean you are—"

"Come with us." River appeared almost out of nowhere and grabbed Logan's arm. He inhaled, his expression a conflicting mixture of pleasure and extreme distaste. "My God. Unbelievable."

"What?" I said.

"Get your hands off me!" Logan tried to yank his arm away.

River held fast. "We're not here to hurt you. We just need some information."

"Who the fuck are you? You look like Shit. I'm so out of here."

"Sorry, but you're not," River said. "We're just going to go back to Erin's car and get in, and you're going to answer some questions. It won't take long."

"The hell I am—" His eyes went glassy. "Sure. No problem. Lead the way."

I let River and Logan have the front seat. I was happy to sit in back, away from the glamouring. I rubbed my arms to keep from shivering. I was completely freaked out.

"I have to be at work soon," Logan said.

"Don't worry. You'll be on time," River said.

"What do you want from me?"

"Do you have any living relatives?"

"No. My parents are both gone. I'm an only child."

"Did your mother by any chance die in childbirth?"

"What? No. She died two years ago. Breast cancer."

"I'm sorry to hear that. What about grandparents?"

"No. All dead."

"Do you know anyone named Lucien Crown?"

He furrowed his brow. "Sounds familiar, actually. I think it was my great-grandfather's name. On my father's side, obviously."

"Is he alive?"

"No."

"Are you sure?"

"I never met the man, but he'd be well over a hundred years old by now, so yeah, I'm pretty sure."

"Do you know where he lived when he was alive?"

"No. But my whole family is from here. Probably somewhere in Louisiana. Why do you care?"

River cleared his throat. "Genealogy is a hobby of mine."

"*My* genealogy?" Logan turned around to meet my gaze. "Erin, what is this about?"

What the hell? He wouldn't remember any of this anyway. "We think you might be descended from a vampire named Lucien Crown."

"A vamp—" He stopped, staring into nothingness.

The catatonic state?

"Erin," River said, "exactly what are you doing?"

"He won't remember any of this, right?"

"Yeah, but—"

"So let's find out exactly what he knows."

"I've been a cop for seven years, Erin. Only twice have I resorted to glamouring when questioning a perp, and then only because I knew the fuckers were guilty as sin. But I'm doing it now because we need the information. There's something weird going on here. He shouldn't be able to question what I'm asking."

My skin went cold. "What are you saying?"

"I'm not sure. He's not responding to the glamour."

"River, he's comatose right now. Clearly he's responding."

River shook his head. "Something's not right."

I swatted at the invisible bugs on the back of my neck. "Have you ever come across someone who couldn't be glamoured?"

"I haven't. But I haven't glamoured a lot. I've heard some humans can't be glamoured."

More chills surged through me. "I'm not sure what to tell you."

"We're in this now," he said. "I'll continue."

I nodded. "Let's just see what he knows. He was gone for over a week, and he has B positive blood, just like all the other missing women. He claims he might have performed surgery while he was gone, but he can't quite remember. There's something in his head that we need to get out."

"He might be playing us, but I'll try." River waved his hand.

"—pire. What the hell are you talking about?"

"Come on, Doctor," River urged. "You've lived here all your life. This is New Orleans. Surely you know about vampires."

"Yeah. Of course. But I'm not related to any."

"I assure you that you are."

"Why the fuck are you so interested in my genealogy?"

"Because I can tell you have a vampire in your lineage. I can tell by your scent." River bared his fangs.

"Oh, fuck," Logan said.

"Hey, wait a minute," I said from the back seat. "You don't seem all that surprised to see that River here is a vampire."

"He reminds me of— Never mind."

"I know," I said. "He reminds you of the guy who kicked you out of my bedroom that day. That was my boyfriend, Dante. River is his cousin. Their dads are identical twins, so Dante and River look a lot alike."

"Yeah, yeah. That must be it." Logan squinted.

"So about your great-grandfather," River continued.

"I seriously know nothing about the man. He has to be dead. And how do you know I'm related to a vampire?"

"You have a certain scent. I can't describe it, because you won't understand it anyway. Trust me, though. You are."

"And you think it's my great-grandfather?"

"I don't know. I just know we're looking for a Lucien Crown who used to have a website called Nocturnal Truth. It was taken down recently. Do you know anything about that?"

Logan shook his head.

"Are you sure?"

"Yeah, I'm sure. Do you really think I'd lie to you, when you're looking at me like I'm lunch?"

River chuckled. "I assure you I have no intention of taking your blood."

"You'd better not, or I'll have you arrested for assault and battery."

"You won't, actually."

"Want to bet?"

"I'd bet the moon, except that you won't remember any of this in about five minutes."

"The hell I won't. Oh, shit."

"What?"

"I don't remember much about when I was taken. Just bits and pieces. Not memories. More like fragmented images that may or may not have occurred. Do you think..."

"Vampires had something to do with it?" River rubbed his jawline. "They might have."

"Logan," I asked. "Why are you on lithium?"

"Mood disorder," he said absently. Then, "How the fuck do you know that?"

River waved his hand over Logan's face, and Logan lapsed into the suspended state again.

"What was that, Erin?" River said.

"I checked his medical records at the hospital."

"I don't have to tell you how illegal that is," River said.

"I know. But there's something about him, River. Something off. It's more than that, even. He knows something. I just don't know what."

"What does any of that have to do with the fact that he's on lithium?"

"Lithium is used mostly to treat bipolar disorder or, more specifically, the manic episodes associated with bipolar disorder, including manic rage."

"I see what you're getting at," River said. "What if he was denied his lithium while he was gone?"

"Exactly. If he was taken by vampires, and it seems likely that he was, given that he has no recollection, and also given that the other patients disappeared without anyone realizing it, we want to know why. Was it to perform surgery? Probably. He thinks he did. Was it because he has B positive blood? Probably. All the rest of the missing people have it. What if there was a third reason? What if—"

Logan turned to me, his pupils dilated.

"What if you're right, Erin? What if you're fucking right?"

THIRTEEN

DANTE

*S*ometimes, I wished the unthinkable.

I wished for death.

It never lasted long, and I erased the thought as quickly as I could, but sometimes...

Mostly during torture. I refused to cry out, and I kept the promise to myself. But inside the deepest recesses of my brain, I sometimes let go.

I wished to cease existing.

What might death feel like? The process could be painful, but I'd endured horrific pain already.

And once the process was complete?

No pain.

Only peace.

How do you know that? Death might be eternal hellfire.

Her *again. In my head. I'd begun noticing it during* her *feedings. Somehow,* she *got into my head.*

Unless it was my imagination.

Not your imagination, Dante. I'm part of you now. As you are part of me.

I winced, though I was not in pain at the moment. I'd long since gotten used to her feedings, but while they were not exactly painful, they were far from enjoyable.

She took.

She took without my consent.

Then she forced me to take from her.

Those were the worst times. I needed blood. Without it, I would die. Hers was my only choice.

She detached her teeth from my body, licking the puncture wounds closed.

Then—

What? She stood and began removing my leather bindings. I held back a gasp. Would she let me go?

No. Of course not. She had an ulterior motive.

In came her two human goons.

I inhaled despite myself. Their stench had become unbearable. I'd never imagined a human being could smell heinous to a vampire, but these two did.

They stood over me, their pupils dilated as they always were. She had them in some kind of trance. Were they truly sadists? Or had she made them so?

Didn't fucking matter.

They were here to torture me.

"How strong are you, Dante?" she said. "How truly strong are you, son of Julian? Are your teeth as sharp as your father's?"

Were my father's teeth abnormally sharp? Were mine? I didn't know. We were peaceful vampires. We didn't use our teeth.

"You tell me," I said. "You're the only one I've bitten."

"Touché." She smiled her evil smile, her eyes blue and icy behind her mask. "I don't know, then, for your father has never bitten me."

Of course he hadn't. He was home, probably trying to find me.

Had he given up?

Had Uncle Brae, Bill, Em, Riv...all of them given up?

I'd been here for so long. Days had morphed into weeks, into months, into years. Possibly decades. All I knew was hell.

Pure hell.

"They've forgotten about you, Dante."

No. Never. They'd never forget.

"They've stopped looking. They think you're dead."

No! Not dead! Never dead!

"They have forsaken you. They no longer care. They've gone on with their lives."

My wrists were now free. I rubbed at them furiously, trying but failing to ease the ache.

"How strong are you?" she *asked again.*

"I don't know."

"We will find out." She *unbound one of my feet.* "Only the strongest survive."

I had survived so far. I'd resisted the urge to cry out during torture.

What more was expected of me?

She *unbound my other foot.* "Stand, Dante. Stand straight and tall. Proud and tall."

I was released several times daily to eat and go to the bathroom. But the goons hovering over me were the ones who released me.

Never had she *released me.*

Why today?

Why?

"In Rome, the gladiators fought for survival. Fight or die in the arena."

The two goons oozed disgust. Treacherousness. Did she *mean for me to fight* them*? With my arms and legs free, I could destroy them in minutes. My muscles were big and strong, not atrophied from my time in captivity.*

"*That's from my blood. My blood keeps you strong.*"

Get out of my head!

"*You won't fight* them." She *eyed the goons.* "*Wouldn't be a fair fight, after all. You'll have a more worthy opponent.*"

I shot up into a sitting position on the couch.

I'd fallen asleep, or so I thought.

Then I'd flashed back. A new memory of those abhorrent years with her.

I'd fought. *She*'d trained me. No. Not *her. Someone* had trained me. Someone I couldn't remember.

I flashed back to the day in the alley with the two Claiborne vampires, Decker and Giles. I'd taken them both down easily.

A roundhouse. An upper cut. An inside crescent kick. A knife hand. Martial arts moves.

I'd never studied martial arts, but my muscles had rushed straight into the movements, had *remembered* the movements.

Yet I had...

The first fight, before training. *She* dropped me in a dirty pit with...

With whom? I didn't know then. Still didn't know now.

I'd nearly gotten the shit kicked out of me, until...

Until...

Something had unleashed inside me.

Something feral and wild.

I lay back down, closing my eyes.

Come on. Take me back there. What happened? What did I do?

Nothing.

Nothing.

Nothing.

Damn it! Come back! Show me what I did! How I did it!

You knew I wouldn't stay away forever. You knew you wouldn't want me to.

Her again.

The reprieve had been restful. Those few hours on the couch, no *her*. Sleep. Pure sleep.

Then the flashback dream.

That had been me. All me. *She* hadn't been there. Hadn't shown me.

I can show you more.

No. No. No. Out of my head. Give me peace again!

Dante, dear Dante. I didn't come back of my own accord. I came back because you wished it so.

You brought me back, Dante. You. You. You.

FOURTEEN

Erin

"River," I said timidly, "what's going on?"

"I don't know. I didn't release him."

His pupils were so dilated, his entire iris looked black. He looked...

No. The word I was thinking. Couldn't go there.

"Logan?" I said tentatively.

He snapped back into his glamour, his eyes glassy.

"What the hell was that?" River said.

"I have no idea. Let's get the rest of what we need from him and get back." A shiver raced through me. "This is freaky."

"Logan," River said, waving his hand in front of the doctor's face, "are you okay?"

"Yeah. Sure."

"Okay. Good. While you were gone, do you remember seeing any of the missing women? The ones who were taken from the hospital?"

"No. I just remember... Yeah, a baby. A baby was there."

My stomach dropped. Patty's baby. Isabelle. From my dream. I'd felt sure that Logan had operated on her. "Was it a girl?"

"The baby? Maybe. Either a boy or a girl."

River rolled his eyes. "That's helpful."

"Did you recognize the baby?" I asked.

"No."

Stupid question. Logan had already disappeared by the time Patty and her baby came into the ER. I silently berated myself. I needed to get it together.

"What about anyone else? Did you recognize anyone else?"

Logan squeezed his eyes shut. "It was... There was another doctor there. A woman. Her name was... Damn!" He opened his eyes. "I can't remember, but she definitely told me her name."

"Okay, good," River said. "A female doctor."

"What about your blood?" I asked. "Did they take any of your blood for testing?"

"I don't know."

River huffed. "This is going nowhere. Look, Logan, let's attack this from a different angle. Did you ever have an issue with manic rage?"

"Sometimes."

"Is that why you're on lithium?"

"Yes. That and other reasons."

"What other reasons?"

"Mood disorder. And...sometimes I hear voices."

"Schizophrenia," I said. "Lithium is sometimes used to treat it, but it's not as useful as it is for bipolar."

"Are you hearing voices now?" River asked.

"No."

"What about when you turned and looked at Erin? When you said 'What if you're right, Erin? What if you're fucking right?'"

"I...don't know."

"All right." River turned to me. "I think we've gotten all we can out of him."

I sighed. "Logan, can you tell us anything else about your great-grandfather, Lucien Crown?"

"No. I didn't ever know him. He's dead."

"Dead is the word, all right," I said. "Big dead end."

"Not necessarily," River said. "I think this information will turn out to be very valuable."

After River glamoured Logan into forgetting our entire conversation and he'd gone into the ER to begin his shift, we drove home.

"Has anyone been able to break out of your glamour like that?" I asked.

River shook his head. "But like I said, I'm not all that experienced at glamouring. I know how to do it, but we seriously don't use it unless we have to. Our abilities are innate, but the skill must be learned. They grow as we age, which is why Bill was able to do what he did in the courtroom."

"And then Dante..."

"Yeah. That's pretty unheard of."

"Anyway, what do you think Logan said that could be useful?"

"It's not what he said so much as how he responded. He's resistant to glamouring."

I gasped softly. "Will he report this to someone?"

"He might, but no one will believe him. More important, though, is how he smelled."

I scrunched my nose in disgust. "He smelled like cheap men's cologne to me."

River chuckled. "Yeah, I got that too. But I'm talking about the scent you *can't* smell. The scent that comes from his blood, just like yours does. He's definitely descended from a vampire. His scent tells the tale. Or rather, it *wants* to."

"What do you mean?"

"His scent is masked."

"You mean like mine is?"

"No. Yours is naturally masked by a potion. His is... Something has been layered over his scent, and it's not good."

"Okay..."

"He has the scent. That irresistible scent that you and Jay have, but it's been tainted. He almost smells like... This is going to sound gross—it *is* gross—but he almost smells like raw sewage."

FIFTEEN

DANTE

*F*uck *you! I did not bring you back!*

I sat rigid on the couch, clamping my hands over my ears in an attempt to drown *her* out. Foolish, I knew. *She* wasn't something external that stimulated my auditory nerves. *She* was in my head, my mind.

Get. The. Fuck. Out.

I stood and paced around the small living room, my gaze constantly drawn to the *Texts* on the coffee table.

"Easy, Dante. You are stronger than whatever is trying to take power over you."

My father.

I turned. His ghost was standing in the doorway.

The door opened with a *whoosh*, and River raced in—straight through my father.

"Shit!" He turned. "Sorry, Uncle Jules. That was...heavy."

"That's a word from my day." My father chuckled.

"No. I didn't mean heavy as in serious. I meant it *felt* heavy. Like I was going through something. Not something solid, but something that was definitely there."

"I *am* definitely here. I'm a concentrated source of energy. That's what you felt."

Erin rushed into my arms. Time to gather my strength. Erin needed me to be strong. I could not show weakness around her. She'd witnessed me in *her* clutches twice before. I was determined that would never happen again.

"What is it, baby?"

"Logan. He's apparently..." She sighed. "I'll let River explain it."

I led Erin to the couch and sat down next to her.

River sat down in a chair adjacent to us. "Logan is not a vampire, not that we ever seriously thought he was. But he *is* descended from one. He has the scent."

"Like Erin and Jay?"

"Sort of. But it's been tainted. I'm not sure how or why. Something has been layered over his natural odor. It's..." River wrinkled his nose. "He smells like shit. Literally."

A human that smelled like shit. Sounded familiar to me. The goons who tortured me while I was in captivity. They'd started out smelling normal, but their scents had become increasingly putrid the more they tortured me. The more evil they became.

Had one smelled like a human descended from a vampire? Like Jay? Like Erin?

No one smelled like Erin. Her scent was special. But was it special only to me? Other vampires were attracted to it, clearly, but did it smell different, even more pleasurable, to me? With a blood bond?

But Jay... His scent was irresistible. Had Logan...?

No. Couldn't have been. I'd remember the scent.

Wouldn't I?

God. No, I probably wouldn't. Even now, I could only remember bits and pieces of what I'd been through. The more I remembered, the more I let *her* into my mind.

If I wanted to keep *her* at bay, I had to make peace with not remembering.

"I lived for nearly seventy years," my father said, "and I don't ever remember a human smelling bad."

"This was a first for me too, Uncle Jules," River said.

"Only two have ever smelled bad to me," I said solemnly. "The two who tortured me while I was captive."

Erin held on to me tightly. "Dante..."

"It's okay, baby. It's over."

In my head, it was far from over, but I didn't want her to worry.

"We have a lot we still need to discuss," my father said.

His words were meant solely for me. In fact, I wasn't sure if Erin and River had even heard them, for neither of them reacted.

"All right," my father said. "Did you learn anything else?"

"Yeah," River said. "If it means anything. He was quite resistant to glamouring, but he claims to have had a great-grandfather named Lucien Crown. He never met him and thinks he's dead, as he'd be over a hundred by now. His parents and all his grandparents are dead."

"My father is over a hundred. If Lucien Crown is a vampire, he could still be alive. Of course, we don't know if *our* Lucien Crown is a vampire."

"Isn't it probable that he is, though?" Erin said. "He claims to have a translation of the entire *Vampyre Texts*, and he ran a site called Nocturnal Truth."

"It would be probable if there were as many vampires as there are humans in the world," my father said. "However, there are only a fraction."

"Here are the facts," River said. "Logan Crown is descended from a vampire, and he has a putrid odor that most humans descended from vamps don't have. That is what we know. Everything else is supposition because of the way he reacted to the glamour."

"We also know," Erin said, "that he's on lithium for bipolar disorder, manic rage, and schizophrenia."

I nearly shot off the couch. "What?"

"It's true," she said. "The lithium is in his medical records, and he admitted to suffering from manic rage and 'hearing voices.'"

"We only know he's on the medication," River said. "We don't know why. We can't take anything he said as fact. He seemed to pull out of my glamour for a few seconds. It was really strange. But then he went right back in, or at least he wanted us to think he did."

"Could be the schizophrenia," my father said. "I've heard of such things, though I've never witnessed anything like it myself."

"He had to be glamoured," Erin said. "He wouldn't have come with us otherwise."

"Unless he had an ulterior motive," River said. "He wanted us to *think* we were getting information out of him."

"But he—" Erin stopped midsentence. "I see. Of course. The whole thing has been nuts. He came back, couldn't remember anything other than maybe he performed some surgery. Then today he remembers a baby, which just happens to tie in with the dream I had. Even though he couldn't have known about the dream, it does seem very convenient."

"Exactly," River said. "He could be playing us."

"But if he's not a vampire, wouldn't he be susceptible to a glamour no matter what?" I asked.

"Not necessarily," my father said. "A minute percentage of humans can't be glamoured. But I never came across one in my life."

"I haven't either," River agreed. "But Logan is an enigma in more than one way."

"He's a good doctor, if that means anything," Erin said.

"It means a lot, actually," River said. "It means he's smart and he cares about his work. It doesn't mean he's not capable of manipulating or being manipulated."

"Which one?" I asked.

"Could be either," River said. "But one or the other is happening, I feel sure of it. What Logan said to Erin and me today was either what *he* wanted us to hear, or what *someone else* wanted us to hear."

Your cousin is a good detective. He's intelligent and shrewd. But he's no match for me.

I slapped the side of my head.

"Dante!" Erin gasped. "What's wrong?"

"Nothing."

"That wasn't nothing."

"Drive her out, son," my father said. "You can do it."

I could. I knew that. I'd done it earlier and slept like a rock for a few precious hours.

River stiffened in his chair. "What's going on, cuz?"

"You're on the right track," I said.

"Good. Good to know."

Unless she was lying to me.

Didn't matter. Everything River said made perfect sense. He separated facts from supposition, truth from perception.

Don't fuck with me. River is on the right track. We are all on the right track. I see what is true and what is not.

So you do, Dante. Then you must see this, the most important truth of all. I'm here in your mind because you want me here.

SIXTEEN

Erin

Something wasn't right. Dante looked fine, but fine people didn't slap themselves on the head. "Could you guys excuse us?" I said to River and Julian. "I need to take care of him."

"I'm okay, baby," he said. "We need to finish this conversation. Figure out what we're going to do about Logan. About his supposed great-grandfather. The book. The blood bond. Most importantly, Lucy and the others."

Guilt again. With everything going on, I hadn't put Lucy at the front of my mind, where she deserved to be.

"He's right," River said. "I compartmentalize when I'm working, but Lucy is never out of my mind. I miss her."

"We all do," I said. "We have to find her."

"We will," Julian said, and then turned to River. "I think Erin's right, though. We should leave. Dante needs some rest. And you and I need to talk."

"About what?" Dante demanded. "Anything you have to

say to River you can say to me."

"I just want some more information about his conversation with Logan. Nothing that can't wait. You rest. Let Erin take care of you."

"But—"

Julian vanished, making me shiver. Would I ever get used to that?

"I'm beat," River said, feigning a yawn.

"Good fake, Riv." Dante shook his head.

"Whatever. I'm leaving. Jay's back at my apartment, and he'll want a full report. Uncle Jules and I can give it to him. I'll check in with you guys later." He left.

"Hey, babe." I stroked Dante's rough cheek. "What can I do for you?"

He stood and pulled me to my feet. "This." He crushed his lips to mine.

I opened to the kiss in an instant—not for me, but for him.

I always needed him, and now was no different. But right now, he needed *me*. I felt it in my muscles, in my bones, in the very core of what made me *me*.

Our tongues tangled and dueled for timeless moments, until I pulled away to gasp in a breath.

"Baby. Need you."

"I need you too."

He lifted me effortlessly into his arms and marched up the stairs to the bedroom.

I wanted to tell him how strong he was, how virile, how he could fight anything tormenting him and win.

But words would make no difference at this point.

Words were only words.

When he laid me on the bed, I quickly found the rungs of

the headboard and grasped them.

"Rope?" he asked.

"You don't need rope. Your strength and determination will keep me bound. Take me, Dante. Take me hard and fast. Demand what you want from me, and I'll give it to you. I'll give it all to you."

With a rapidity I'd never seen, he pulled off my shoes and socks, and then my jeans and thong.

"You're moving so fast," I murmured.

"Not fast enough," he said gruffly. He ripped my blouse down the middle. Right down the middle, and then tore the sleeves right off me. Then he removed my bra, which, thankfully, had a front clasp. Didn't stop him from ripping the straps, though.

My grip never left the headboard.

I lay naked, he still fully clothed, standing over me, the fiery rim around his dark irises in full force.

"I hear your blood hissing through your vessels, Erin. I hear your capillaries bursting. Your body is glowing a soft pink. Your blood makes you so beautiful, do you know that?"

Mere months ago, I'd never have expected to hear such words from a lover. Now? They made my blood boil, added to the light crimson of my skin, the harsh throbbing between my legs.

He closed his eyes and inhaled, and I knew well the fragrance he smelled. My arousal, but to him it was combined with all the other scents that attracted him to me.

"Erin, baby, I want you safe more than anything, but if that potion had cut off your scent from me... I would have handled it. I love you, and it wouldn't matter. But I'm so grateful I can still smell your unique aroma. That scent that drives me insane, makes me know without a doubt that we're meant to be."

Still he hovered above me. He opened his eyes, and the love in his gaze nearly melted me into soft butter.

"So beautiful. So perfect. So pink and gorgeous and delicious." He sat on the bed and spread my legs. "Plump and ready. Dazzling. Just dazzling. So full of blood. So ready for me."

I writhed, still holding on to the rungs of the headboard. My fingers itched to pull his head into my pussy, make him eat me.

My arms stayed put. Indeed, I almost believed I couldn't move.

His dark eyes were smoking, the amber ring around them moving like soft flames. His hair hung in disarray around his broad shoulders. How I ached to run my fingers through its silkiness.

I stayed put.

Two buttons of his fatigue-green shirt were undone, and tiny chest hairs peeked out. How I longed to tear the shirt down the middle, let the buttons scatter, just so I could feast with my eyes and lips upon his hard chest.

His erection bulged outward, still snug in his jeans. I wanted to touch it, rub it through the fabric, make him slowly crazy. Then pull it out and deepthroat him until I gagged.

I stayed put.

I stayed put while he melted me with his gaze, while the blood in my veins turned to boiling honey as I got hot, hotter, and then hotter still.

I opened my mouth to beg, but he placed his finger over his lips.

I didn't speak.

HELEN HARDT

I stayed put.

"I'll give you what you want, love. What we both want. But at this very moment, I want to take in your gorgeous body, your beautiful face, your shapely legs, your luscious pussy. You are a delicacy, Erin. A fucking feast." He inhaled. "God, I love you."

I opened my mouth again to return his sentiment, but he shushed me once more.

He slowly began to unbutton his shirt.

I grasped the rungs harder, my knuckles tightening. *Please, Dante, please. Inside me. Please.*

With one swipe, his shirt was on the floor, the buttons flying.

Yes! He'd heard me. Or felt me. Or something.

He kicked off his boots, toed off his socks, and then—

I gulped.

He was huge.

He was always huge. But tonight...

Oh. My. God.

"You're mine, Erin. Mine. All fucking mine."

In an instant he was on top of me, shoving himself into me, thrusting, thrusting, thrusting.

The orgasm hit me from nowhere. In a flash I was floating, truly floating above my bed, flowing like my blood flowed through my veins.

My whole body vibrated with intense prickles and tingles, and my pussy—*God, my pussy*—it clamped around that huge dick, and I relished the intrusive burn.

My eyes were closed and still we floated.

He plunged into me, deeper and deeper each time, and his cock grew larger, ever larger, giving me the ultimate pleasure.

Floating.

God. Fucking floating.

Until—

My eyes popped open. "Aaahhh!" I fell onto the bed, bouncing lightly.

Dante was hovering above me. Fucking hovering above me. In. Thin. Air.

"Dante!" I shrieked.

He tumbled down onto the bed. I rolled out of the way just in time to avoid him.

"What was that?" I sat up.

"I...don't know."

"You just...*levitated* us, for God's sake. You've *got* to know."

"Erin, I don't. I don't."

His cock was still hard.

He hadn't finished.

I reached toward him, but as soon as I touched him, he flinched.

I gasped.

He widened his eyes. "It's not you. It's... It's that darkness. It's here. With us." He stood, scrambling into his jeans and shirt. "Get dressed, Erin. We're leaving."

"This is our home. We're not going anywhere. *It* can leave."

"Baby, I get where you're coming from, but this isn't something to fuck around with. My father doesn't know what it is. Bea doesn't know what it is. All we know is that it *is*. Come on."

The urgency in his voice made me obey. I dressed quickly in the first clothes I could find and let him drag me out of the bedroom as soon as I was decent.

We nearly tumbled down the stairs.

"Is it here now?" Panic bubbled up around me.

HELEN HARDT

He stopped, cocked his head. "No. It didn't follow us down here."

I shivered, rubbing my arms. "That doesn't make any sense. Why would it stay in the bedroom?"

"I don't know. Damn it, Erin, none of this makes sense."

"Dante"—I reached for him—"we were *floating* up there. You realize that, right?"

He nodded.

"What was it?"

"Do I look like I fucking know?" He shoved his fingers through his hair, his hand shaking slightly.

"Easy," I said. "Has anything like this ever happened to you before?"

"Hell, no."

"Is it something vampires can—"

"Jesus, Erin. You *know* what vampires can do. Our senses are slightly better than yours. And almost all of us can learn to glamour. That's it. We don't have any other special powers. We don't burst into flames in sunlight. Garlic doesn't keep us away." He paced around the living room.

He was understandably upset. But— "Don't take this out on me, Dante."

"I'm not. I'm just fucking frustrated."

I tried soothing him once again with my touch, but he paced away from me. "What can I do to help you?" I asked.

"Baby, baby. I wish you could help. I so wish you could."

I gasped when Julian appeared before me.

"Do you know what's going on, Dad? Why I was able to levitate?"

"I don't know what you're talking about," Julian said. "But right now, we've got a bigger problem."

SEVENTEEN

DANTE

"Y our sister is missing."

The words echoed in my head, as if they had come from somewhere other than my father. Indeed they had. My father wasn't actually here. He wasn't actually saying words. I was interpreting his energy in the way it made sense to me.

For the first time, I truly understood what my father was now.

Your sister is missing.

"Dante?" Erin hedged.

"I heard him."

"Aren't you going—"

I closed my eyes. I was numb. I should be concerned for Em. She was my sister. My pregnant sister.

But with everything else...

I opened my eyes. "When was she last seen?"

"She had an appointment yesterday at Jack Hebert's," my father said. "He says she left and she was fine, but she didn't show up for work last night. Instead, she came here."

Erin lifted her brow. "She did?"

I nodded. "Dad intervened."

"Oh. Why, Julian? Why didn't you want her to come here?"

"I just needed to talk to her," my father said. "Then she went home. At least that's where she said she was going. No one has seen her since."

The untruths were getting to me. Correction. They'd already gotten to me. I needed to have a talk with Em. She couldn't hide the paternity of her baby forever.

But she was gone. Em was gone. Reality hit me in the gut.

"Have you been to her place?" I asked my father.

He nodded. "As soon as I heard, I searched her apartment. No clues. Her bed was unmade, but that doesn't mean anything. Em never made her bed."

I smiled slightly. Em had been a slob as a kid. Apparently she still was.

"What's Emilia's blood type?" Erin asked.

"According to Jack, it's B negative."

"Right. You told me that, how you couldn't possibly have B positive. All the other missing women have B positive blood, including Lucy. So why..." She rubbed her forehead. "There has to be some connection. But what?"

"That's not the most puzzling part of this," my father said.

"He's right," I said. "Em has the ability to glamour. A vampire can't be glamoured by another vampire. She must have been taken forcefully...or drugged. And if she was drugged..." My mind whirled. I couldn't let myself think of it. Couldn't...

"That wouldn't be good for the baby," Erin finished for me. "Oh, Dante. I'm so sorry."

"We'll just have to find her," I said. "That's all there is to it."

"We'll find her, son."

"I need to talk to Jack," I said.

"Your grandfather has already spoken to him."

"Bill knows?" I rubbed at my brow.

"She's his granddaughter. I had to tell him. Anyway, according to Bill, she left Jack's office after her appointment. She's feeling a lot better. Jack apparently gave her a tincture made of those herbs from your dream, Erin. They worked a miracle."

Erin's eyes widened. "Or...they did something else to her."

"Like what?"

"I don't know. My training is in western medicine. But..."

"What?"

"Bea gave me the remedy in my dream, but at first... At first she wasn't Bea. She was a doctor from the ER. Dr. Zabrina Bonneville."

"The one you were helping with research?" I asked.

"The same. She's a brilliant physician, but there's something about her. I had a patient who thought she looked exactly like another doctor who'd be in her sixties or seventies by now. Dr. Zarah Le Sang. Remember, Dante? Dr. Blood?"

I nodded.

"Plus, there's almost nothing about either of them online. Isn't that odd?"

"You think this doctor might have something to do with the disappearances?" my father asked.

"It's a long shot. She wasn't on duty the night the first two disappeared, and Cynthia North was returned unharmed. The one from the free clinic, Bella Lundy, was as well."

"But the others weren't," I said.

"No." She bit her lip. "Someone...someone at the hospital was feeding on me. We know now that it wasn't Logan. He's not a vampire. And it hasn't happened since—" She paced into the kitchen and back. "I'm going crazy. Just fucking crazy."

"Do you think this doctor might be a vampire, Erin?"

"I don't know. I just don't. Mrs. Moore, my patient who died, thought she could be the twin of Dr. Le Sang, except they had different colors of hair. I didn't think anything about it at the time, but now, I'm wondering."

"Vampires live slightly longer than humans, but we're not immortal," I said. "And we age."

"Hair can be dyed, Dante," Erin said. "A brunette could now be blond. If she's old, she could dye her gray hair."

"Her face would still show signs of age. How old does Dr. Bonneville look?"

"I don't know. Forties maybe. I know it doesn't make any sense. But here's more. Dr. Le Sang was a hematologist, a blood doctor, and her name was Dr. Blood. Cynthia North told me that when Dr. Bonneville visited her after she was returned, she'd said she was a hematologist. Blood doctors. Blood equals vampires."

"You might be stretching, Erin," my father said.

I shook my head vehemently. "No. She's right. Something doesn't add up here. You said a dream can be a premonition. What was she having you research, Erin?"

"Blood types with certain physical characteristics. I couldn't find anything."

"Where is this doctor now?"

"On vacation in Barbados with her husband."

"Do you know that for a fact?"

She shook her head. "It's what she told me. At the time, I had no reason to believe she was lying."

"She hasn't been at the hospital." My mind raced. "And no

one else has fed from you since she left."

Erin nodded.

"It's worth checking out," I said. "But first we need to find Em. I wish Bill weren't involved in this."

"He loves Emilia," my father said. "He wants to find her as much as we do."

"What if finding her means translating the *Texts*? Then what? Will he still be as anxious to find her?"

My father looked grim, even for a ghost. "I don't know, Dante. I just don't know."

I paced around the room, my heart pounding. "The website we needed is gone. We have no one to translate the *Texts*. My sister is now missing, along with Lucy and the others. And something is going on with me. How do we know where to start?"

"Dante, we start with Emilia, Lucy, and the others," Erin said. "They are the most important."

"Yes, yes." I raked my fingers through my hair. "You're right, of course. People trump the blood bond. Trump whatever's going on with me."

"It's all important, son, but I agree with Erin as well. River will file a police report about your sister, but we're not leaving this to the police."

"We sure aren't." I stomped my foot. "We have to find them." Nausea swept through me. My sister. Lucy. The others. All, save Em, with B positive blood.

Em. My baby sister. My pregnant baby sister, whose baby was also linked to Erin and her brother.

Too much to think about. Too fucking much.

But I had to. I had to think about it. Had to find them.

Because if I didn't, I feared Erin would be next.

Just the thought ignited a profound rage deep in my bones. My fucking bare bones.

I inhaled. Her scent was thick in the room, thick as it always was, and this time her adrenaline added a top note to the fragrance. Erin was worried too.

The dirt floor was rough on the soles of my feet.

"Fight. Show me what you have. Fight to the death."

I was strong. Yes. I knew that. Gabriel vampires were large and strong. But I didn't know how to fight.

"Fight or die in the arena."

Go for the nose. You'll take out his sense of smell and sight.

My grandfather's words.

I'd never had to use them. Would I use them now?

A door on the other side popped open, and a figure fell in. He was masked.

I touched my cheek.

So was I.

When had that happened?

When had I gotten here?

How?

"Fight! Fight! Show me who is stronger!"

Her voice was an echo. Where was she? This large room was dark, and although my vampire vision allowed me to see clearly, I didn't see her anywhere.

I inched toward the stranger in the room. He was taller than I, but I was broader. I bared my fangs.

He bared his.

He was vampire

"Fight!" she *said again.*

He looked upward.

And I crashed into him, bringing him down.

Yes, I was stronger. He was no match for me. But once I had him on the ground, I had no idea what to do.

He didn't fight back. Not at first.

"Who are you?" I asked.

He answered with a low growl.

I had nothing against whomever this was. Had she thrown one of the goons who tortured me into that room, I'd have pulverized him in an instant.

But this brother vampire? I had no motivation. No drive. No need to fight.

"Fight!" Her voice again. "Fight to the death!"

In a flash, the other vampire had overpowered me and pinned me to the ground.

Thud. Thud. Thud.

Fist to my cheek. My chin. My forehead.

My nose.

God, my nose.

Blood spurted out of it as the crushing of cartilage forced a searing pain across my skull.

Thud. *To my eye socket.*

Thud. *To my Adam's apple.*

Breathe. Couldn't breathe.

Couldn't...

Couldn't...

Then nothing.

EIGHTEEN

Erin

I rushed into Dante's arms.

He kissed the top of my head. "We'll find them, baby."

I pulled away slightly. His eyes were on fire, his irises blazing. He was angry. And afraid. But more than that, he was determined.

"We have no idea if the same people that took the others took Emilia," I said. "For that matter, we don't have any idea if the other disappearances are even related."

"Riv says they most likely are, and he's a pro." He cupped my cheek. "We'll find them. I won't rest until we do."

"You have to rest, son," Julian said. "And you have to train."

"Damn it, Dad, how can you talk of training when Em is missing?"

"That's exactly why I *can* talk of it. I need you at your best. I need you with every possible defense you have. You've grown strong, Dante. You've gained a lot of control, but there's something inside you that we don't yet understand."

"But there isn't time—"

"We will make the time. You must be at your best for what must be done."

"I'm fine. And when I find out who took my sister, I'll have no problem pulverizing them into a fine powder."

I pulled away. Rage shone in Dante's eyes. Pure, raw rage.

I'd seen him angry before. I'd seen him angry and aroused. I'd seen him possessive and protective. I'd even seen him unhinged.

But this?

This was new.

This was frightening.

He was willing to do whatever it took to go forward, undaunted, leaving nothing but dust in his path, and damn the casualties.

He swiped the back of his neck. "What is it, Dad?"

"The darkness," Julian said. "It's back."

"It can get the fuck out," Dante growled through clenched teeth.

I grabbed Dante's hand. "Let's go."

"We won't be chased out of our home," he said with a snarl.

"He's right, Erin. Stay put." Julian vanished.

"Julian! You can't tell us to stay here with some dark evil and then leave!"

"I'm still here." His voice echoed through the room. "I'm using my energy to find the source of the darkness. I'm—"

"Julian?" I said timidly.

No response.

"Do *you* feel it, Dante?"

"I only feel fucking angry that my sister's gone, your best friend is gone, and I can't keep some dark energy out of this house. I can't fucking protect you." His teeth descended, long and sharp.

"Maybe your father is mistaken. But please, in case he isn't, let's just leave, okay? We can go to River's."

His eyes softened a bit. "All right, baby. I want to talk to him about Em and the others anyway." He grabbed my hand, and we left. Then he turned. "Wait here." He dodged back inside and returned seconds later with his father's urn.

"I checked every database the department has access to," River said. "No Zabrina Bonneville or Zarah Le Sang anywhere in Louisiana."

I swallowed past the lump in my throat.

"You okay?" Dante asked.

I nodded. "I feel I should be surprised. But I'm not."

"That still doesn't mean she has anything to do with the disappearing women, Sis," Jay said.

"I know."

"I already told her that vampires age," Dante said, "so the two can't be the same person."

"Maybe mother and daughter?" Jay said.

"We still don't even know they're vampires," River said. "Just because her name means blood—"

"For God's sake, it's more than that." I tugged at the band holding my ponytail. Suddenly it was tight and giving me a headache.

"What, then?" Jay said. "What more is there?"

"Someone has been feeding on me, and it hasn't happened since Bonneville went on vacation."

"Still all circumstantial," River said.

"I know that, damn it!" I curled my hands into fists. "It's just..."

"Just what, baby?"

"It's a fucking feeling." I rolled my eyes. "I know how ridiculous that sounds. But I feel it in the depth of my bones. Find Dr. Bonneville, and we'll find those women. We'll find Lucy and Emilia."

NINETEEN

DANTE

"All right, Sis," Jay said. "Calm down. We're listening. But you've got to understand. Dr. Bonneville wasn't even on duty when two of the women were taken."

"I know it sounds crazy." Erin sighed. "I know it does."

"No one thinks you're crazy, baby," Dante said. "Hell, we're all a little bit crazy right about now. The four of us will figure it out. Plus we have my dad."

"Your sister's name is Emilia?" Jay asked.

"Yeah," I said, trying not to grit my teeth. "You know her?"

"The name rings a bell," he said, "but I can't quite place it."

The itch in my gums began. He didn't even remember my sister? If he weren't Erin's brother...

I met River's gaze. He shook his head slightly.

I stayed silent. I didn't know the whole story. But what I did know so far, I didn't like.

Not one bit.

"I'm sorry she's gone," Jay continued. "First Lucy, and now your sister. There sure seems to be a connection."

"I agree, partner," River said. "But it's still all circumstantial at this point."

"Riv, you're a great cop," Jay said, "but you're not using your instinct. Sometimes you have to go with your gut."

"I never imagined you were such a 'follow the rules to a T' kind of guy," I said.

"I'm not."

"But you are. You admitted you don't glamour on the job, even though you know it would make your job a lot easier."

"I succumbed twice," he said. "Not counting getting Jay and me this leave, which didn't do any good anyway, since Bill overpowered it."

"We'll get our jobs back, River," Jay said. "I'm not worried about it. And for what it's worth, I think it's cool that you don't glamour on the job. For the most part, anyway."

"If we don't have our ethics and morals, what do we have?" River asked. "Vampires would be feeding on humans, possibly draining them. We've learned to assimilate. We've learned to control our desire for human blood. That's how we've gotten along since the dawn of civilization, at least as far as our history is documented."

"I think that's a good thing, River," Erin said.

"You'd understand, Dante, if you had been—"

This time my teeth descended. "I *do* fucking understand. It wasn't my fault that I wasn't here, damn it."

"I know that, cuz. Unfortunate choice of words. I'm sorry." He shook his head. "I worry so much about Lucy, about Em. About finding them and the other innocent women, that sometimes I forget to think about..." He sighed.

His father.

Braedon was out there somewhere. Having seen the

condition my father's body had been in, I didn't harbor much hope for his twin brother.

"Uncle Brae is strong," I said. "He can take care of himself."

River nodded. "Right. Like Uncle Jules did."

"My father died on purpose. If he hadn't, he would have come out of this alive."

"You saw his body, Dante."

"I saw his body. I also know what was done to me. I came out of this, and my father would have too. I feel certain."

"You're right about that, son."

I looked to the left, where the voice had come from. "Dad."

"Sorry to interrupt, but Dante, I need to speak to you. Privately."

"You can say anything in front of all of us," I said.

"I feel very strongly about this. Please, Dante. Give me a few minutes. We can step outside."

I opened my mouth to protest once more, when a knock sounded on the door.

River opened it.

My grandfather stood on the other side.

"Bill," River said, holding the door open.

"I figured you'd all be here at some point," Bill said. "I've been waiting outside for a while. It took me this long to get the nerve to come to the door."

"What do you want?" I asked.

"I want to help. I want to help find Emilia and my great-grandchild."

"Are you willing to tell us what you know about the *Texts*?" I asked coldly.

"No, Dante. Emilia's disappearance has nothing to do with the *Texts*."

"What if it does?" River asked. "What if we can prove it? Would you tell us then?"

"You can prove nothing," Bill said.

"Don't be so sure of yourself," River said. "But even if it doesn't, the *Texts* might explain what's happening to Dante. Don't you want him to have use of this newfound power? He might be able to help find Emilia."

"We have no way of knowing if it will help," Bill said.

"Of course it will help, Dad," my father said. "If he can harness this ultra-glamouring ability, we could find out whatever we need to know."

"No, we couldn't. Not if the person who has Emilia is another vampire."

I huffed. He wasn't going to budge on the book. "We don't need your help, then."

"Not so fast, Dante," my father said. "He loves your sister as much as we do."

I had a hard time believing that one. But I couldn't deny the look of sadness on Bill's face.

"I've lost two sons." He held up a hand. "I know you're here, Julian, but you're dead. For all I know, Braedon is dead."

"I've told you, Dad, Brae is alive."

"Yes. The twin thing. I get it. But you could just as easily be wrong." He held up his hand again. "I got my grandson back, and even though our relationship isn't the best right now, I'm grateful. But I've taken enough losses for the last decade. I will not lose Emilia and her baby too."

"None of us is going to lose her," I said adamantly. "We *will* find her. If you want to help, tell us what you know about the *Texts*. If you don't want to do that, get the hell out of here."

"Dante." My father's voice was stern. "You and I. We need to talk. Now."

"Julian, you're not getting rid of me," Bill said. "Whatever you have to say to Dante can be said right here."

"For once I agree with Bill," I said, clutching Erin's hand.

"No."

It wasn't a yell. It wasn't even a command. It simply *was*.

And I knew I had to do what my father asked. This was important.

"All right. Where do you want to go?"

"We can step outside." My father vanished.

"Excuse me," I said, letting go of Erin's hand. "I'm sorry, baby. I'll tell you everything later."

She smiled and nodded, squeezing my arm.

I walked out the door to River's apartment. My father was nowhere in sight.

"The car, Dante."

His voice. I walked quickly to Erin's car and got in.

"This isn't going to be easy to say."

Again, only his voice. He did not appear.

"All right. Just say it, then."

A gruff sound—as if he were clearing his throat.

Then, "I concentrated all my energy on the darkness that has targeted you. I was determined, this time, to find its source."

"And...?"

"As I said, this isn't easy to say."

"For God's sake, Dad. Just say it."

"I double- and triple-checked my findings. I even conferred with a few other ghosts on this plane, and they agree with me."

Silence.

More silence.

My gums began to itch, even though I knew my fangs would do no good against a ghost. Against my father. "Would you get to the fucking point?"

"I was able to pinpoint the source of the darkness. Bea was right. It's not a demon or a ghost. It's a dark energy."

And I knew.

Before he said anything more, I knew.

"You're correct," he said.

"You know what I'm thinking?"

"I can tell, just by your movements. Your canine nerve is responding. You're becoming angry, and there's no reason for it. No reason other than what you and I now know."

I bared my fangs, growling.

Growling at the darkness.

Growling at myself.

"Are you sure?" I snarled.

"Aren't you?" my father replied.

I gnashed my teeth at his voice.

The darkness was here. Now. In the car.

The darkness hadn't targeted me.

The darkness *was* me.

THE QUEEN

You're changing, Dante.

I've been waiting.

Waiting for the darkness to overtake you.

Yield to it. Surrender to it.

Become what you are meant to be, and all those questions you have will be answered.

It is your destiny.

Continue The Blood Bond Saga with Volume Four

Unmasked

Coming Soon

MESSAGE FROM HELEN HARDT

Dear Reader,

Thank you for reading *Undaunted*. If you want to find out about my current backlist and future releases, please like my Facebook page and join my mailing list. I often do giveaways. If you're a fan and would like to join my street team to help spread the word about my books. I regularly do awesome giveaways for my street team members.

If you enjoyed the story, please take the time to leave a review on a site like Amazon or Goodreads. I welcome all feedback.

I wish you all the best!
Helen

Facebook
Facebook.com/HelenHardt

Newsletter
HelenHardt.com/Sign-Up

Street Team
Facebook.com/Groups/HardtAndSoul/

ALSO BY HELEN HARDT

Blood Bond Saga:
Unchained: Volume One

Unhinged: Volume Two

Undaunted: Volume Three

Unmasked: Volume Four
(Coming Soon)

Undefeated: Volume Five
(Coming Soon)

The Steel Brothers Saga:
Craving
Obsession
Possession
Melt
Burn
Surrender
Shattered
Twisted
Unraveled
Breathless (Coming Soon)
Ravenous (Coming Soon)
Insatiable (Coming Soon)

Misadventures Series:
Misadventures of a Good Wife
Misadventures with a Rock Star

ACKNOWLEDGMENTS

Dante makes a huge discovery in *Undaunted*, one that will set the tone of the remaining books. Exploring his darker side offers me incredible challenges as an author, and I can't wait to dive in further. I've also had a lot of fun writing our resident voodoo priestess, Bea. Researching the infinite wisdom of William Shakespeare and Henry David Thoreau and then making it fit the Blood Bond storyline has been exciting and fun!

Special thanks to David Grishman, former CEO of Waterhouse Press, for your belief in my work and advocacy on my behalf. It was a pleasure working with you, and I wish you all the best in your future endeavors.

Special thanks also go to David's mother, Haidée La Pointe, who graciously showed me around her home town of New Orleans. I had so much fun, and without your guidance, I wouldn't know about Pimm's Cups or the layout of St. Louis Cemetery. *Undaunted* definitely benefited from my time with you. I hope to see you on my next visit!

Thank you so much to my high school classmate, Brian Archer, MD, for all the information on how to treat Lucy's stab wound in the emergency room. As always, I do take creative license here and there, and any errors are mine alone. Gahanna Lincoln 1982 forever!

Thank you to my editor, Celina Summers, my line editor, Scott Saunders, and my proofreaders, Amy Grishman, Chrissie

Saunders, Michele Hamner Moore, and Michele Lehman. You each added your own special touch to this story, and I'm forever grateful.

Thanks as always to the team at Waterhouse Press— Meredith, Jon, Robyn, Haley, Jennifer, Jeanne, Kurt, Amber, Yvonne, Jesse, and Dave. Your belief in me and my work keeps me going. You are the best publisher!

Special shout out to *New York Times* bestselling author J.S. Scott and *USA Today* bestselling author Angel Payne for the glorious cover quotes. You are two of my favorite ladies, and I'm happy to return the favor any time!

To the women—and a few men!—of my street team, Hardt and Soul– you rock! The love and support you give me lifts me to new heights. Thank you for spreading the word about the Blood Bond Saga and for your wonderful reviews and general good vibes.

Thank you to my family and friends and to my two local RWA chapters, Colorado Romance Writers and Heart of Denver Romance Writers.

Most of all, thank you to all my readers. Without you, none of this would be possible. Things are heating up for our vampire and his woman, and I hope you all enjoy what's coming!

ABOUT THE AUTHOR

#1 *New York Times*, #1 *USA Today*, and #1 *Wall Street Journal* bestselling author Helen Hardt's passion for the written word began with the books her mother read to her at bedtime. She wrote her first story at age six and hasn't stopped since. In addition to being an award-winning author of contemporary and historical romance and erotica, she's a mother, an attorney, a black belt in Taekwondo, a grammar geek, an appreciator of fine red wine, and a lover of Ben and Jerry's ice cream. She writes from her home in Colorado, where she lives with her family. Helen loves to hear from readers.

Visit her at HelenHardt.com